For Mildred —
better late than never —
with affectionate greetings
from Arthur

February 17, 1953

THE SILVER PLUME

There are some defeats more triumphant than victories.

MONTAIGNE

We needs must love the highest when we see it,
Not Lancelot, nor another.

TENNYSON

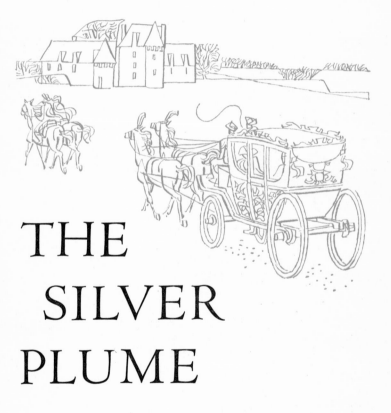

THE
SILVER
PLUME

 BY ARTHUR MEEKER

NEW YORK · ALFRED A. KNOPF · 1952

L. C. Catalog Card Number: 52-6406

THIS IS A BORZOI BOOK,
PUBLISHED BY ALFRED A. KNOPF, INC.

Published simultaneously in Canada by
McClelland & Stewart Limited.

To FANNY BUTCHER, *who opened the door for me*
to the world of writers, and was waiting
to be my best friend there when I walked through,
with deep affection and gratitude
for all the years between that day and this

This is a true story

Contents

Prologue

Leyden, August, 1645

As it happened, the bell had not yet stopped ringing by the time Charles arrived. Fearing to be late, he had run all the way from the Breedestraat to the brick gabled schoolhouse, taking the short cut through a maze of narrow lanes instead of the comfortable longer route past Sint Pieter's Church, as he generally did; then scrambling upstairs a dozen paces behind the last of the scholars. He could hear above him a heavy shuffling of feet as the boys filed into the classroom and settled themselves on their benches.

The door, alas! was already shut. On the threshold he paused for a moment to catch his breath before opening it again just as wide as was necessary—no more—and sliding through the crack and into his seat as unobtrusively as possible. Charles's heart was pounding and his breath still came in short, sharp gasps. He kept repeating to himself in a furious whisper: "The devils! *The devils!* Oh, if *only* I could . . . !" while anger rose in a wave from his belly through his chest to his brain, where it set the nerves in his temples to throbbing and appeared likely, as always, to blow off the top of his head.

It took him several minutes to recover a semblance of composure. Fortunately he occupied the end seat on a bench towards the back of the hall. The professor was rather short-sighted; the class in Bible history was the first to be held after the mid-day meal; and it was clear, from his empurpled and tightly stretched countenance, that Master Blommers had dined even better than usual.

3

Besides it was, even for the first week in August, a very warm day. Sunlight poured in the tall, uncurtained windows to produce on the whitewashed walls an almost intolerable glare. Although these windows were open, no air seemed to come through them. Even the handsome linden, which stood just outside and was wont to keep rustling its foliage with a kind of delicate impatience, looked as motionless as a tree made of pasteboard. Charles, as a rule, spent a good deal of time staring at that linden. He knew it intimately, as one does come to know inanimate objects one sees every day, and could easily have sketched it from memory to the last green-feathered twig gracefully outlined against the pale dazzle of the summer sky.

But today he had much too much on his mind to throw it more than a casual glance. While Master Blommers, after his habitual preliminary hemming and hawking, began calling the roll, Charles looked anxiously at the vacant seat at the other end of his own row, which was now the only one left unoccupied in the great hall of the Leyden Gymnasium. Master Blommers proceeded, puffing stertorously, in strict alphabetical fashion: "Backer, Jan . . . Bosch, Albert . . . Druyster, Petrus . . . Geldorp, Willem . . ."

When he had got as far as the P's and pronounced "Potenijk, Charles," Charles jumped to his feet with a valiant "Here, sir!", paying no heed to the spiteful giggles from the bench behind him, the last in the hall, where the bigger boys sat. (Those would be Hendrick Ruysch and Egbert van Schooten and their group of toadies, from whom he had just escaped. Ah, but he had a score to settle with *them,* later on!)

"Renetz, Jacob," the next name on the list, elicited no response. Master Blommers said it three times in a very loud voice, as if loath to believe that such a model pupil could be derelict in his duty. Then he coughed, peered owlishly over his spectacles, hitched up his snuff-stained broad linen collar, and continued with "Santvoort, Dirck"—it was, after all, really too hot to bother!

Charles's thoughts were in a tumult. It was as much as he could do to sit still, and certainly, though he kept his eyes fixed firmly on Master Blommers, it was to be doubted whether he heard a word the good professor was saying about the origins and moral significance of the Book of Exodus. . . . *Where could Jacob be?*

Charles had not been unduly concerned when, after dinner at Mijnheer Potenijk's, he had been unable to find his chum, with whom he usually shared the walk back to school —as he shared his bed, and board, and perhaps the majority of his thoughts. He'd simply surmised that Jacob had gone on ahead on business of his own and would wait for him somewhere along the way, as in such cases he invariably did. Even when the hope proved false, Charles had not minded too much, although he could have done with Jacob's help. For it was just as he was crossing the Vischbrug that he had been overtaken by Egbert and Hendrick, who, seeing him alone, had at once burst into raucous squalls: "Bastard! Foundling! Tinker's brat! What do you think you're doing at a school for gentlemen's sons? Yah! If you care what's good for you, get out and go follow the gypsies—*they* know how to handle base-born rogues like you!"

As he remembered their taunting words, Charles clenched his hands in renewed fury; his eyes smarted with sudden tears. God knew, he ought to have got used to it by now! He'd been at school for almost four years; ever since it had been bruited about that Mijnheer Potenijk, the respected cloth merchant of the Haarlemmerstraat, with whom he boarded, was not his father—that though he had taken his patron's name he had no right to it—that no one knew what his name really was—the rougher boys had plagued him continually.

Some, it was true, were sorry they'd done so. Charles was small for fourteen—Jacob, a year younger, was half a head taller—but he had nearly always managed to give a good account of himself when he took on his tormentors. One by one, though—not in pairs! Wiry as his small frame was, and valorous as was his spirit, he could hardly hope to thrash Egbert and Hendrick, who were fifteen past, together. He'd contrived to slip away from them now only by agreeing to meet them in the Mall as soon as the lecture was over. That he would have been perfectly willing to do, with Jacob at his side; for Jacob was one of the best fighters in school. Not that he got excited—not he! As calm and unhurried as Bet, Mijnheer Potenijk's sturdy cart-horse, he merely rolled up his sleeves, set his square chin, gazed straight ahead with his placid blue eyes—which were just the colour of the sky behind the linden outside the window—and went to work. . .

Thanks to such magnificent assistance, Charles had oftener than not emerged from his trials victorious. Yet now, just when he was needed most, Jacob had failed him. Where, oh, *where* . . . ?

Master Blommers droned on about Moses and Aaron; the minutes passed with a horrible, unnatural swiftness— who'd have supposed that a lecture on Bible history could ever seem short?—and Charles became nervously aware, from divers stirrings and mutterings behind him, that Hendrick and Egbert and their followers were laying plans for his undoing. He would have scorned to look round; he held his head, in fact, higher than ever, his gaze never swerving from Master Blommers' egg-shaped face, as if utterly engrossed in his teacher's prosy exposition of the Seven Plagues of Egypt. (What was the Plague of Locusts—nay, even the Plague of Boils—to the agonies he was suffering now? But courage—courage—don't forget the Spartan boy with the fox that gnawed his vitals—like him, he must give no sign!)

Five minutes before the bell for dismissal was scheduled to ring the door opened once more and Jacob came in. Instead of scuttling to his seat, as any of the forty-odd other boys would have done—including, Charles realized regretfully, himself—he marched, phlegmatic and nonchalant, across the hall to his appointed place, sat down, crossed his legs, glanced inquiringly along the length of the row to where his friend was sitting, and gave Charles a slow and speculative wink.

On the stairs going down they found each other. Charles began at once with his story: "Jacob, where have you been? I've been almost out of my mind with worry—wait till I tell you! Egbert and Hendrick—"

But Jacob, for once, seemed unwilling to listen.

"Never mind about them! I've got something much more important to tell *you*, young man."

"Oh, but, Jacob, I promised to meet them in the Mall after school. It was the only way I could get them to let me go. I couldn't find you anywhere—there wasn't anything else to do. *Please*, Jacob! You know what they want. . . ."

Jacob stopped short on the landing, while a stream of

boys poured past him, and for the first time really looked at his chum.

"I know what they want, all right," he said. "But we just can't be bothered with 'em today. I told you, *something has happened*. I've got to speak to you alone."

"But what will they think if I don't—"

"I don't care *that* what they think!"

Jacob, who always spoke slowly, even had a way of snapping his short, thick fingers with deliberation that made the commonplace gesture uncommonly significant. "We can deal with those rascals tomorrow. Oh, to be sure, I'll help you—when *haven't* I done that?"

"You're the best friend I've got in the world," said Charles simply.

"Well, then," said Jacob, his loud boy's voice sounding rather gruff with embarrassment, "trust me a bit more, why don't you? Now listen! Here's my plan for the afternoon. (We can easily give Hendrick and Egbert the slip in the street—don't worry about them!) I found out at dinner time that Mijnheer Potenijk was sending Jan with the wagon to Katwijk to fetch some manure for the garden—seaweed and that sort of stuff—so I begged a ride for us both. Mijnheer doesn't know anything about it, but he wouldn't care if he did know. I fixed it with Jan—'twas easy enough—I gave him half a florin to buy tobacco. Lucky my quarterly allowance 'd just been paid. We're to meet him at three, or as soon thereafter as possible, in the square by Sint Pieter's Church. Don't you see? 'Twill be perfect for us. We'll have all the way over to talk, and all the way back—and as long as it takes him to load up besides. Hurry up! There's no time to lose."

"Seaweed stinks," was all Charles said, wrinkling his nose fastidiously.

But he followed Jacob briskly none the less out into the hot bright sunshine, where the little town of Leyden basked with its cobbled streets and green, tree-fringed canals, its gabled brick houses, and its air of ancient, meditative peace. Three o'clock was just striking from the tower of Sint Pieter's, to be echoed, a minute later, by the tower of Sint Pankras'; then from all over the city there arose a tinkling clamour of other bells in other steeples, chiming in melodious rivalry like so many giant music-boxes. Jacob was right; they *would* have to hurry.

The class, chattering as shrilly as a flock of sparrows, dispersed without much delay. Glancing nervously about him, Charles could discover no trace of his enemies; doubtless they'd already departed for the rendezvous, which lay some distance out of town—so that was all right for the time being anyhow. (No escaping a nagging suspicion, though, that sooner or later fate would catch up with one there!)

Meanwhile the two boys increased their pace as they passed the frowning old prison of the Gravensteen and turned into the square dominated by Sint Pieter's, vast and comfortable, an old stone dragon dozing in the clear afternoon light. Jan, too, was dozing, his unlighted pipe stuck fast in the corner of his mouth, on the driver's bench of the wagon, which he had drawn up in the shade of the church. Even Bet, Mijnheer's dappled grey mare, though her long whitish tail kept up a ceaseless swishing to ward off flies, held her head low and relaxed, as if she might be more than half asleep herself.

After a brief consultation Charles was elected to wake the

slumberer. This he did rather neatly by patting old Bet, whom he was fond of, and talking to her.

Jan straightened up with a start; said "Eh!" and "Hey!" besides other things less polite; then lighted his pipe and told the boys to hop in. He picked up the reins, chirruped to Bet—who gave a final flick with her tail—and they were off towards the western gate and the highroad that led to the sea.

The pavement was rough and the big springless cart rattled and bumped a good deal. Its sides were so high that the boys, crouched on a pile of empty sacks on the boards at the bottom, were unable to look out. With nothing to shield them from the blazing sun, the heat was very nearly unbearable, too. However, here at least was privacy. Once outside the town Bet settled to a steady jog-trot across flat green fields dotted with cows and an occasional windmill—one knew they were there even though one could not see them —while Jan, certain that she could be trusted to find her own way, relapsed into a kind of sitting-up sleep. If he had wanted to, he could not possibly have heard the conversation going on behind him; the noise of the wheels took care of that.

Charles and Jacob looked at each other.

"Now, then!" said the former.

"Well, then!" said the latter—and grinned.

Jacob, who was never excited, appeared to hesitate for a moment.

"I don't suppose," he finally began, "that you've the slightest idea what's been going on lately at the Potenijks'?"

He turned the phrase as a question, so Charles, looking puzzled, replied: "Nothing special that I can think of. What do you mean, Jacob? We've said our prayers and eaten our meals and gone to school and helped in the shop, just as we always do. It's true, we've had a bit more time to ourselves, maybe. Mijnheer has let us off three—no, four—afternoons in a row, hasn't he? But that's just because business is slack in the summer, I guess."

"Ah!" Jacob assumed an air of conscious wisdom. "Do you think so? *I've* found out something different. Old Potenijk's not the fellow to let us apprentices be idle—not even you and me, who are meant to work in our spare time only as long as we're still in school. I tell you, he's sent us off to get rid of us, because he doesn't want us hanging round the place. He's had a caller every afternoon this week."

"What of that? Hasn't he dozens? What else would he keep a shop for?"

"But this was a special caller—Frenchman named La Cosse. Does that mean anything to you?"

Charles shook his head.

"Never heard of him."

"Then of course you can't imagine what he was after?"

"No—how could I? What did he want?"

Sure of his effect, Jacob replied succinctly: "You."

Charles stared.

"*Me?* What could he possibly want of me?"

"Can't say, my boy. He had letters with him from Paris —that much I know, though I didn't see 'em. He told Mijnheer they gave him legal authority to take possession of your person. He said he meant you no harm—that the people he represented had only your welfare at heart. It'd be greatly to your advantage to go with him, he said; he'd see to it you had a career in the army, or anything else you liked

—if only Mijnheer would sign the papers for your release."

"And what," asked Charles, big-eyed, "did Mijnheer say to that?"

"He refused point-blank. He said he'd had his instructions—he'd promised a friend of his to take care of you; to feed, clothe, and educate you; to let no harm befall you—but never, on any account, to hand you over to anybody else. 'It'd be as much as my life is worth not to live up to that promise,' he told La Cosse. 'Besides, why should I break my word to an honest gentleman, who's paid me well for everything I've done?'"

Charles was considering deeply.

"How do you know all this? It sounds to me like a story—something you've made up out of your head." (Even as he spoke, however, he realized that Jacob—no fool—had far too little imagination to be able to invent anything at all.)

"I know, all right." Jacob was fortunately too much absorbed in what he was telling to take offence. "Where do you think I was the other day, when you went swimming in the Rhine with Albert and Willem? Mevrouw Potenijk sent me into the shop for an ell of bleached linen to make a new cap—I almost ran into the French Monsieur! I didn't like to burst in upon them, so I hid in the back room a minute; and as soon as I saw what was up you can bet I was in no hurry to leave!"

"Well?" Charles demanded.

"Well—that's all, really. I mean, all that happened the first day. La Cosse went on arguing, but Mijnheer wouldn't budge. You know what he's like when he's made up his mind. I waited till he'd shown the fellow out; then I went back into the passage, opened the door, and came in once more, making noise enough so old Potenijk would hear me. I truly don't think he had any suspicion I was there before. But then . . . Monsieur La Cosse came back the next afternoon."

"Did you see him again?"

"Not that time. Grietje told me about it afterwards. He brought another man with him—Monsieur d'Estrades, the French Commissioner to the Stadholder of Holland. He's a count, too, I think—anyhow, Grietje said he was wearing a big feathered hat and was dressed in velvet and lace. They stayed 'most an hour. Grietje was sent for to fetch in some wine; she heard some of what they said. It was still all about you. Monsieur d'Estrades tried to persuade Mijnheer to agree to what La Cosse wanted. He talked and talked—got awfully angry and red in the face! He kept pounding the floor, Grietje said, with a kind of gold stick he was carrying, and shouting that his master would hear of this—he'd make a full report to His Most Christian Majesty—and *then* they'd see what would come of it! But Mijnheer got just as angry himself, and shouted back that he didn't care a damn what His Most Christian Majesty thought: they were, thank God! on free Dutch soil, where a man's word was as good as his bond, and no power on earth or in Heaven could compel him to break it. So, after a while, the Commissioner and La Cosse went away—there wasn't anything else for them to do.

"The day after that, La Cosse came alone. This time he didn't go into the shop or ask to see Mijnheer at all. He walked about in front of the house and stared up at the windows. (Where were you? Oh, I know: it was the afternoon Mijnheer sent you to see if those new Italian silks had come by the Flanders post.) I was playing ball in the street. After a while he spoke to me—asked me what my name was and where I lived. I told him I was Jacob Renetz, son of the town clerk of Rotterdam—that my father was dead and my mother had put me to school in Leyden and 'prenticed me to Mijnheer Potenijk, the cloth merchant. Then of course he asked if I knew you. I said I did. And he said he'd give me something nice if I'd help him coax you to go away with him. 'I've already spoken to your master,' he said, 'but I can't seem to make him understand I mean Monsieur Charles no mischief. I represent persons in France who have always taken a deep interest in his welfare and who have sent me to Holland now to find out what I could do to help him. They intend to assure his future and see that he learns a better trade than a linen draper's. I give you my word of honour, I've papers on me to prove my right to my mission. Now I'll tell you how it is, my lad: you get young Charles to come along with me peaceably and you're welcome to join us. I'll engage my patrons will make it well worth your while. What say you to three thousand crowns in your pocket and a glorious future in the armies of His Majesty Louis XIV?'"

Jacob stopped, out of breath; and Charles—almost equally so, though he'd spoken scarce a word—cried out: "Yes—and then? *And then?*"

"Then," Jacob went on impressively, "I answered no, just as Mijnheer did. If he thought it wrong, it must be so—three thousand crowns or no three thousand crowns! Besides I smelt a rat—so'd you have, Charles—La Cosse is a horrid man."

"How do you mean, 'horrid'? What does he look like?"

"Oh, well," said Jacob, not too helpfully, "he looks like a

Frenchman, don't you know—they're all alike, in my opinion. I dare say the Commissioner's not a bit better, even if he
has a plumed hat and a collar of Flanders lace. This chap's
got shifty eyes and a pointed nose and he's so covered with
scent he stinks like a polecat—that's all I remember. I didn't
get to talk to him much longer anyhow, 'cause just then the
door opened and Mijnheer ran out on the steps, shaking his
fist and bawling that if La Cosse didn't take himself off, and
that in less than no time, he'd have the law on him! Then he
pulled me into the house and slammed the door in the Monsieur's face. And all that happened yesterday."

"Yesterday! Why in God's name didn't you tell me before?"

"I promised Mijnheer I wouldn't. I'm telling you now
only because something else happened today after dinner to
make me change my mind. Believe it or not, you'd hardly
got out of the house when a big gilded coach turned into the
Haarlemmerstraat and drove up to the door. Mijnheer hadn't
gone back to the shop; he was sitting with his wife in the
living-room window. There wasn't time to do anything—not
even to get rid of me—before there came a knock; in a minute Grietje came in and said Monsieur Rondeau would like
to speak to Mijnheer Potenijk. Of course Mijnheer sent me
out directly, but I ducked into the passage and came back as
soon as I thought it was safe. The door was shut; I could
hear through it pretty well, though. The new man didn't
scold like La Cosse, but his voice was very clear—and you
know I understand French even if I can speak it just a little.
. . . Charles, *he* wants you, too! He asked straight off if La
Cosse had been there and seemed pleased when Mijnheer
told him he'd sent him about his business. 'Well done, sir!'

he said. 'My employers will see that you are suitably re-
warded. You will lose nothing, I warrant you, through your
honesty and faithfulness to your trust.' 'I don't give the boy
up, sir,' says Mijnheer, as testy as you please, 'to you, or La
Cosse, or the Prince of Orange himself. Get that through
your head! I swore to a certain party I'd keep him safe, and
that I mean to do until that party reclaims him. Now be off
with you! I've no more time to waste.' 'Ah,' says Monsieur
Rondeau; 'but this time, sir, I think you'll discover the case
is somewhat different. I represent the family, you see. I have
been sent to find you by no less a person than . . .'

"Just then, worse luck! old Mother Potenijk flung open
the door, caught me listening at it, and gave me a clout on
the ear—so off I ran to school, and here we are! Now what
do you make of it all?"

If Jacob had expected his friend to show wild excitement
over the news, he must have been disappointed. Charles's
face had turned pale during the recital and his grey-green
eyes were wide with suppressed emotion; but he said nothing
at all for a moment. Even when he found words he seemed
to be speaking more to himself than to Jacob.

"So they've come for me at last!"

The voice was almost a whisper.

Jacob felt slightly annoyed.

"Who's 'they'?"

"My people. My own family. I always knew they would."

"But who *are* your people?"

"That's what I can't tell you. I have as little idea as you,
Jacob."

"What *do* you know about yourself?"

"I've told you most of what there is to tell. I've been in

Leyden now almost as long as you have. You saw the man who brought me here to Mijnheer Potenijk's. He's a captain in the army, a French volunteer in the service of the Stadholder. His name is Monsieur de la Sauvetat. That's all I know about him. I'd never seen him before the day he came to get me—at least I don't think so. I've never seen him since. He never writes to me either. He does send money, though, quite regularly, to Mijnheer, for Mijnheer told me so."

"And before that?"

"Before that I was in Waterland. I've told you about that, too. I lived with the village schoolmaster, Simon Cernolle, and his wife; they brought me up with their own children. I called Mevrouw Cernolle 'mother' and Pieter and Antje my brother and sister, because they bade me do it. I knew they weren't my relatives really, but I had no others. They were poor people and not very kind. I hated their dark little house; it had an earthen floor and we were so near the Haarlemmer Meer that sometimes in winter the water would rise so high it flooded the place. No; it wasn't a good life."

"How long were you there?"

Charles narrowed his eyes.

"I'm not sure. I wish I were. If I knew that, it might help me get other things straight in my mind."

"You weren't born there, then?"

"No! Certainly not! Before I lived in Waterland I had another home—I think in another country. It wasn't a flat land like Holland. There were hills and woods, a broad, winding river. . . . I seem to remember driving once in a coach with a great many horses. We turned a corner suddenly and saw a castle with ramparts and towers rising straight from the river. Somebody said—perhaps it was my nurse—: 'Why, it's the Château de Préfontaines!' There were always people round me then. I'm almost positive they were French. I know, when first I came to Waterland, I used to speak it quite a lot. But Master Cernolle beat me when I did and wouldn't give me anything to eat unless I asked for it in Dutch. . . . Oh, it's all so far away and long ago! Often I've thought it must be a dream. Real life is Leyden, and the Gymnasium, and the house in the Haarlemmerstraat—and you, and the Potenijks, and Grietje, and Jan. I haven't been unhappy here. Still I've always hoped that some day . . . This *can't* be where I belong. My God, Jacob, do I even *look* like a Dutchman?"

"No," replied Jacob promptly. "You don't, and that's a fact."

Indeed, the contrast between the two boys, of approximately the same age and dressed precisely alike in coarse grey shirts and black cloth breeches—the latter made very full and fastened just below the knee—could hardly have been more striking. Jacob, with his fair, square good looks, his level blue eyes, his fresh rosy complexion, might have posed for a portrait of a typical young Hollander. He had, besides, his share of racial stolidity; a comfortable air of meaning to look before he leapt, of being willing to leap only in the last extremity—and, even then, of being quite sure where he was going to land. Charles, on the other hand, short, lean, nervous, with his curly black locks bisected by an arresting streak of silver, and his small brown face, which seemed merely a frame for the strange sea-coloured eyes—black-fringed, enormous, set always, as it were, on far horizons—was a creature from a different planet. They shared a look now, though, of momentary exaltation; then Charles beat a tattoo with his fist on his friend's solid chest, crying out in sudden impatience: "Confound it! We're wasting time! Why the devil didn't you tell me at once? We ought to have gone straight back to the Potenijks'—you know we ought! Perhaps when we get home tonight it'll be too late: Mijnheer may have sent the new man packing just as he did that villain La Cosse. Oh, Jacob, how could you plan it this way?"

"Don't worry," advised Jacob. "Monsieur Rondeau will still be there."

"How can you be sure?"

"I tell you, I *know*. He's not a bit like the first perfumed popinjay: this fellow's come to stay till he gets what he wants. I could tell it straight off from the way he spoke. It's just as well we're not around for an hour or two, while he and Mijnheer talk the matter out. Oh, no, there's nothing to worry about! Only . . . if you can, in the meantime, try not to think about it too much."

"Why, what else can I possibly think of?"

"I know," said Jacob, flushing uncomfortably. "What I mean is, don't let your hopes get set too high. The whole thing may have some quite ordinary explanation."

"What do you call 'ordinary'?"

Jacob looked still more unhappy and placed his hand, with an awkward protective gesture, on Charles's shoulder.

"I've thrashed every boy in school who's said it, or even dared to hint at such a thing, and I'm ready to thrash 'em again—you know that. But between ourselves—isn't it likely you're just La Sauvetat's bastard? . . . Hey, there! Don't choke me! I only said 'likely'!" For Charles had pushed his chum to the bottom of the cart, seated himself on top of his stomach, and started to pummel him vigorously. Surprise had made Jacob an easy victim.

"You take that back, you scurvy, lying Dutchman, or I'll . . . I'll . . ."

"All right! All right!" Jacob was laughing almost too hard to speak. "You're the only son of the King of France—or the Emperor of Germany, for aught I know. Yes, I mean it—I swear it! Only let me get up now, for we're almost in Katwijk."

That they might have told some time before by the sudden freshening of the atmosphere. Peering over the side of the cart, the boys could see that the flat green fields, the cows and the windmills, had been left behind. Bet was picking her way now along a sandy track that wound amongst dunes towards the coast, where the sluggish Rhine lost itself in a row of reedy marshes. Then came the dike that protected the land from the sea; just below it Jan drew rein and turned to say he was going on to the village and would return for them in an hour.

Jacob and Charles jumped out and started climbing the dike. As Bet moved off Jan called over his shoulder: "Mind you don't keep me waiting!" "All right, we won't!" the boys shouted back dutifully. But they were beginning to forget about Jan even as they shouted: once they reached the top a new world lay revealed. Gone were the languors of Leyden in August: here there was nothing but sun, wind, and space, a feeling of limitless freedom. Directly beneath them were more sand dunes, tufted with long, coarse grass; beyond the dunes lay the wide brown expanse of the beach, littered with shells and seaweed. Beyond the beach the still wider ocean, the jade-green North Sea itself, heaved and roared, sending wave after wave in to curl and break on the shore.

For a minute the boys stood still where they were, drawing deep breaths of the clean, salty air. Then with one accord they scrambled down on to the sand and raced wildly for the water.

This was their greatest treat, and one they enjoyed only rarely. Although Leyden was scarce a league distant from the sea—when the wind was due west they could smell it and, in winter, the fields around the town were often white with gulls taking refuge from the weather—it might, for all they saw of it, Charles sometimes reflected dejectedly, have been ten times as far.

The wonderful, cold, swirling breezes acted like a tonic on their spirits. Forgetting everything else in the rapture of motion, they ran back and forth until they could not run any more. Then they wrestled like puppies in the warm, dry sand; built a fort lower down, where it was wet; chased the grey, scuttling crabs; gathered the strange small flowers that grow on dunes and some sea-shells (which invariably, one knew, by the time one reached home, would have managed to get themselves chipped); made a fire of driftwood in a sheltered corner and lay beside it, while they watched a brig sailing north—where was it bound for? Hamburg or Lübeck, or perhaps as far as Sweden?

Jacob quite lost his stodgy composure. As for Charles, he felt like another person. He seemed to have found his right element: why hadn't he wings to breast the wind like the sea gull out there? . . . No, not *that* one . . . the other yonder,

just disappearing round the point! It was always the farthest
thing he yearned for. . . .

The time passed too quickly. It seemed only a few minutes before they heard Jan's voice and saw his bullet-head
appearing over the dike. (As he was wearing wooden shoes,
he did not attempt to climb all the way up.) Charles realized then, with a start, that not once in an hour had he
thought of what Jacob had told him.

On the homeward journey, tired by their romp, the boys
would have liked to sleep in the bottom of the cart among
the sacks of fertilizer. But Jan, unexpectedly strict, would
not permit it: "What'd Master say if I brought ye home
smelling like a couple of herring?" There was nothing for it
but to resign themselves to sitting aloft on the driver's bench,
one on each side of the bulky, blue-smocked figure.

So placed, they were naturally unable to resume the interrupted conversation. Charles sat silent, thinking about the
two Frenchmen and wondering what their coming was
likely to mean in his life. At the moment he was more than
half inclined to take the whole thing as a stupid mistake or
a joke. Nevertheless, as they clattered past the brick houses
of Leyden—rosy red now in the declining rays of the sun—
he could not help asking himself whether the gilded coach
would still be in the Haarlemmerstraat. . . .

Yes! To be sure, there it was, taking up, with the six jet-
black horses that drew it, an unconscionable amount of room
in the narrow cobbled street before the Potenijks' house. A
crowd of curious neighbours surrounded it; several of the
apprentices, too, were hanging out of the shop window to
gape at the scarlet-liveried coachman, who held his nose

haughtily in the air and was obviously trying not to notice the commotion he had caused.

"Mijnheer can't be in the shop, then," whispered Jacob, as he observed the apprentices. "Never mind: we must just try to slip in without being seen."

The door to the house, immediately adjacent to the shop, was not latched. Inside the dark little hall seemed full of confusion. There was a babble of voices; strange servants ran to and fro with trays; Grietje shot out from the passage that led to the kitchen bearing a dust-covered bottle—there was a glazed look in her eyes—she did not even see them! The door to the parlour stood open: not the ordinary living-room, where the boys got their tasks and ate their meals and Mijnheer smoked his pipe after dinner, but the Grand Saloon, used only on feast-days, an oppressive apartment that boasted a floor of dark green herring-bone tile, a tall stone chimneypiece surmounted by a garniture of Delft, heavy carved furniture, and a plethora of ornaments of china, brass, and crystal, through which the boys were wont when needs must to steer a wary course.

Stout Mevrouw Potenijk, wearing her Sunday black silk and her best cap—all starched frills and mauve ribbons—could be glimpsed seated in an armchair by the chimney-piece, fanning herself and looking frightened. As the boys scampered past towards the stairs Mijnheer Potenijk stepped out into the hall without warning: he was as big and blond as his wife, and generally as impassive; but today he shared her air of perturbation. When he caught sight of Jacob and Charles he gave a smothered exclamation; then called the latter to him, in a tone that brooked no delay, and gave him a little push across the threshold of the Grand Saloon.

"Here," said Mijnheer Potenijk, sounding oddly hoarse and breathless, "he is!"

There were several men in the room, but Charles had eyes for only one of them, a dark fellow with a thin, intelligent face. This stranger, who was richly dressed in a fashion unknown to the burghers of Leyden, swept off his plumed beaver hat, dropped on one knee, and, much to Charles's confusion, seized his hand and kissed it.

"My Lord," he announced, in a clear, solemn voice, "I have come to take you home."

Charles brushed his curls out of his eyes, wishing he'd remembered to empty the sand from his shoes and that he had had time to run upstairs to don his jacket.

"I don't understand," he said slowly, using the tongue he had not essayed in years. "Who are you?"

"I am Rondeau, Sieur de Montville, my Lord's secretary. This is La Mestairie, Sieur de Préfontaines, my Lord's equerry. And these, so it please him, are my Lord's servants —valets and lackeys, grooms and postilions."

"But who, then," asked Charles, "am *I*?"

Rondeau knelt again and said, still more solemnly: "Tancrède, Duc and Vicomte de Rohan, Prince of Léon, Scotland, and Navarre, Comte de Rennes and Porhoüet, Baron de Lanvaux, Peer of France!"

Part One

Paris, August, 1645—February, 1646

I

"Gravelines,
"This Fourteenth of August, 1645

"My dear Jacob:
. "I beg you to forgive my long silence, and to believe me
when I say that today is the first time since leaving Leyden
I have been able to take up my pen to inform you that, so far,
all has gone exceeding well with us on our journey. The
weather continues fine and warm. We have been travelling
fast, yet not so fast as I fain would go, and that for the
strangest of reasons. Did you know—but I am sure you
didn't: I had no idea of it!—that France and Spain are at war
with each other? Hence all Flanders, which belongs to
Spain (I did not even know that!), has been turned into a
battleground, on which the forces of His Most Christian and
His Most Catholic Majesties advance or retreat according
as luck favours or deserts them.

"As Frenchmen we have had to take care to remain within
reach of our own lines. 'Tis on that account we avoided
Dunkirk, which is still in the hands of the Spanish general
Piccolomini (only he's really Italian, Rondeau tells me—
how can that be?), and are spending the night instead at
Gravelines, held by our men since last summer's campaign.
The latter is a fine town all surrounded by walls on the river
Aa, not far from the sea. We have been well received by the
commander of the place and lodged with due honours in the
citadel, whence we set forth on the morrow for Calais.

"Now you will say, this is all very well—but what about *me*? There was no chance of a talk in private before I left Leyden: things seemed to happen so fast that I hardly knew myself where I was or what to think. Indeed, even now I'm in a state of bewilderment. Rondeau says it is quite natural, and that I must not mind, for I'll grow used to everything in time. From the moment he went to the town magistrates and showed them his papers, and the procuration he brought from Paris, there was no doubt of the rights of the case— even Mijnheer Potenijk realized he would have to let me go.

"During these last few days, shut up in the coach for hours on end with Rondeau and La Mestairie, I've asked them a monstrous lot of questions. They are splendid fellows—particularly the former, who has been as kind to me as if I were his son—and have both been in my family's service for years, so naturally they have a great deal to tell me. I think at last I've got the story straight.

"You have heard, I dare say, of my father—Henri II, Duc de Rohan. That's a great name even in Holland, for most of your countrymen belong to the Reformed Church and Rohan was famous for years as leader of the Protestants in France. 'Twas thanks to his courage and military genius that the party held out as long as it did: Rondeau says he was the soul of it—not a man in his army but would gladly have given his life for his chief. These wars of religion were long and bloody. On one side was the King, Louis XIII, with his minister Cardinal Richelieu and all the best generals; on the other, only my father, and a handful of faithful followers. Yet they never could catch Papa! Even when at last he was forced to lay down his arms and make peace, it was a peace with honour: his debts were paid and he was allowed to leave the country in full possession of his rights and fortune.

"That was sixteen years ago. From France, says Rondeau, he embarked for Venice to enter the service of the Doges, accompanied by my mother and my sister Marguerite. (My mother's name is Marguerite, too; she's a daughter of the Duc de Sully, the famous Sully who was Prime Minister in the reign of Henri IV. I've read about Grandpapa in history books—only of course I did not know then he *was* my grandfather!) After a while Papa fell to thinking it would be well for him to buy the isle of Cyprus from the Sultan of Turkey. I'm not sure where Cyprus is—are you?—and I did not like to ask, for Rondeau seemed to think I ought to know. Anyhow, Papa felt it was his duty to provide a refuge in times of persecution for those of his religion; for who knew how long they would continue safe in France, with their terrible enemy Richelieu at the head of the government? As it was, they had had to abandon their fortresses and let them be dismantled: Montauban, La Rochelle, and the rest were all lost. (I have read about that, also.)

"In order to raise two hundred thousand crowns to buy the island, he had to dispose of some of his properties at home. The Rohans, you know, are one of the oldest and most illustrious families in France. There's been more than one alliance between them and the ruling houses of Europe; in their own province of Brittany they have castles and estates so vast and numerous that Rondeau admits even *he* is not sure he could name them all. But Papa had promised the King he would stay out of the kingdom, and of course he could not break his promise. There was nothing for it save to send my mother. He hated to have her go, but he trusted her as himself: she must be a wonderful woman. She agreed at once to undertake the mission and left Venice with my sister and Papa's best friend, the Duc de Candale, who was to protect them in Papa's stead.

"'Twas a long and dangerous journey in the dead of winter, and grievously hard on my mother, who was heavy with child. Indeed, she'd scarce got to Paris when she was brought to bed of a son—on the eighteenth of December, 1630—to think, Jacob, that at last I know when my birthday comes, like other boys! She was not living at Papa's house, but at the house of a friend: no-one was supposed to know she was even in Paris. She and Monsieur de Candale considered the matter carefully and decided it would be fatal if the King and the Cardinal came to learn that the Duc de Rohan had a male heir in France, so they put me out to nurse. The project for Cyprus fell through, and my mother was anxious to return to Venice; but by now the court had found out where she was and refused her a passport to leave.

"A few years later the battle of Corbie was fought, when the Spaniards beat the French so badly it was feared Paris would be taken. All who could, fled to the country; my mother sent me to Normandy, to the Château de Préfontaines, which belongs to the father of La Mestairie. (You can see, Jacob, what a great family the Rohans must be, when even their servants are nobles.) While there I was stolen by soldiers—doubtless spies in the pay of the Cardinal. He was a bad, cruel man, La Mestairie says, who kept the kingdom for twenty years in his thrall. Nobody knew what to do! They did not dare tell my parents the truth, so they wrote to say I had died of a fever. Not long after that, Papa died, too. He was killed in the battle of Rheinfelden; by that time he'd half made up his quarrel with the King and was serving him in Switzerland—they still so much mistrusted his influence that they were loath to let him come home.

"Poor Papa! He never knew what had happened to me; he thought the duchy would be extinct. My mother and sister went on living in Paris. Seven years passed. The old King died, and the Cardinal, too. Rondeau says things are quite different now in France. The new King's just a little boy, and his mother, the Regent, is gentle and kind. Her minister Mazarin is gentle, too; nobody is afraid of *him*. So the nobles can do as they please again. Meanwhile my mother had found out—I don't know how: Rondeau doesn't know either—that I was alive and living in Holland. Can you imagine how happy she was?

"Now I feel it is all I can do to wait till I get to Paris to embrace the family from whom I've been separated so long. Just think, Jacob! I've a mother and sister I've never even seen! My one regret is that I shan't find my father there as well. Rondeau declares I am very like him: *he* had a lock of white hair like mine—is that not strange? 'Tis a family trait; they call it the 'topknot' of the Rohans.

"Since coming to Flanders I have quite made up my mind to be a soldier like my Papa. I have not yet seen the French general, Monsieur, the Duc d'Orléans, the young King's uncle, because he has been away with the army since the taking of Bourbourg. But Rondeau has presented me to his aides, the Maréchal de Gassion and the Maréchal de Rantzau, both of whom have received me courteously. In truth, so have all the French officers I've met: they are marvelous fine gentlemen, with their plumed hats and high leather boots. Above all, I find their manners most pleasing

—gay and carefree and amiable, not in the least like the lumpish folk of Leyden. (Forgive me, Jacob—you know I don't mean *you*.)

"I am sure there can be nothing more glorious than a military career. If only I were a man already, so that I could show my family I am worthy of the name I bear!

"Now I must close, as Rondeau has just come into my chamber to see why my candle's still burning; he says it is high time to quench it and get to bed, as we are to start at dawn. I am, thank God, well and happy at this present, as I hope that these lines may find you. I send my humble duty to Mijnheer and Mevrouw Potenijk, and to you, dear Jacob, a pledge of undying friendship—I will never forget you.

> "Your affectionate friend,
> "The Duc de Rohan.

(Really Charles, you know! I suppose you should call me 'Tancrède' now. I say it to myself every day and still can't get used to it.)

"P.S. I open this to add that I asked Rondeau about La Cosse and why he wanted to get hold of me. Rondeau said he had no idea who he was, but that certainly he was up to some mischief. We have put the affair in the hands of the Leyden magistrates; they've pledged us their word they will search for him until they find him and have him arrested. Then we'll be able to learn where he comes from and all about him. But Rondeau assures me that in any case there's no reason to worry: Monsieur de Rantzau is giving us an escort as far as Calais, where my cousin the Comte de Charost is governor; he'll see we get safely to Paris. Oh, Jacob, isn't it all like a fairy-tale? Often I feel I am dreaming, and will wake to find myself in our big bed in the attic at the house in the Haarlemmerstraat, with your yellow head on the pillow next to mine. At that, I've wished a dozen times a day you were with me. I do miss you sadly, for Rondeau and La Mestairie, kind as they've been, are so much older. Never mind, my dear—I'll send for you soon: would you like to be my squire instead of a linen draper?

"P.P.S. Of course, you'd have to learn to ride a horse, to handle sword and musket, and to talk French; but I think it would be worth it, don't you?

"P.P.P.S. What have Hendrick and Egbert to say now?"

"Calais,
"This Seventeenth of August, 1645

"My dear Jacob:
"I take up my pen once more to continue the report of our journey to Paris. The trip from Gravelines to Calais was short and uneventful. We left early in order to avoid the great heat of mid-day. It is warmer than ever; on account of the dust in the roads Rondeau and La Mestairie think it best to keep the coach curtains tight shut. This would trouble me more, were the country we passed through worthy of note; but it seems that Holland and Flanders are one! There's nothing to see but flat fields and canals as far as the eye can reach.

"Calais itself, where we arrived the day before yesterday, is as fair a town as we have yet found on our travels, and bigger than most; it lies on the ocean and has a great harbour full of ships, for there is much traffic between here and England. The English coast is scarce five leagues away, but up to now, though the sun shines without ceasing, there has been a light mist over the water that prevents us from seeing it.

"We are lodged in the castle in a commodious suite of rooms as the guests of my cousin, the Comte de Charost, who is governor of the city as well as captain of the King's bodyguard. (I don't see how he can hold both posts at once, do you? But that is the sort of thing I can't ask about. One of the chief difficulties in my new life, I foresee already, is going to be learning how to find out what I want *without* asking.) As soon as we gave our names at the gate we were received most politely and ushered to a high stone banqueting hall, where, at a long table, the Count was sitting at dinner with his friends. There were twenty or thirty of these at least, laughing and talking and making such a racket that I despaired of being able to attract their attention. You know I speak French fairly well, but when everyone jabbers at once 'tis hard to make out what they mean. Fortunately Monsieur de Charost chanced to glance up and caught sight of me standing in the doorway. He jumped up forthwith and embraced me, crying: 'Why, this must be the little Dutchman of whom we've heard so much!'

"I was so taken aback at first I scarce knew what to do. My host bade me sit next him, plied me with meat and wine as much as I could hold, and presented the company to me.

"Since then I have taken all my meals with them. My cousin 'holds a table,' as the French say: that is, he eats in public twice a day, and any gentlemen of quality who are passing through Calais are welcome to a place at his board. You can imagine, with a war on in Flanders, that there are many of them. Indeed, we've hardly seen the same faces more than once, yet the number never seems to diminish. (No matter who comes, though, I still keep my place at the Count's right.) Most of these gentlemen knew my father, the late Duke; nearly all have proffered their services and declared they are anxious to help me in any way they can. Not a few are Protestants—or belong to 'the religion,' as 'tis the fashion to put it in France—: these, it goes without saying, are my devoted partisans. As for Monsieur de Charost, he is hospitality itself; I have never met a finer nobleman.

"When I first saw him I was almost afraid of him: he's a man about forty, and monstrous tall—so, he says, are all the men on his side of the family, the Béthunes: his father and my grandfather Sully were brothers. Moreover, he has piercing eyes, a nose like the prow of a ship, and a big, booming voice that can be heard above all the din of the banquet hall. I soon found, however, that he was as kind as Rondeau and vastly more entertaining. The very first afternoon he took me over the castle, showed me the fortifications and the great cannon commanding the port, as well as his own private collection of arms—swords and pistols, muskets and harquebuses. Never have I seen such a splendid array! I could have spent hours admiring them. My cousin remarked 'twas a pity I could not be his guest a while longer, for then he would be pleased to instruct me in their use.

"As it is, he has been much concerned about my appearance. There was no time in Holland to think about clothes; we are not stopping long enough anywhere to have things made; but the Count says I cannot possibly descend at the Hôtel de Rohan clad in my coarse linen smock and wide Dutch breeches. His own doublets, of course, were much too ample for the purpose; but they have managed, I know not how, borrowing here and borrowing there, with his tailor to make alterations, to turn me into a courtier fit for the Palais Royal. Jacob, I wish you could see me! When first I beheld my train of valets in Leyden I wondered what the dickens I'd find for them to do—but now I know full well! This morning it took them nigh an hour to dress me. What with ribbons and laces, perfumed ringlets, a plumed beaver hat, and a sword in its scabbard, I did not know myself. What pleases me most are my high boots of glossy Italian leather; when I walk about they make a fine clumping sound.

"Thus attired, I went to my cousin's cabinet to attend his *lever*. This is the hour after breakfast when his valets shave and dress him, while he examines his letters, issues orders for the day, and gives audience to those who desire to consult him on private matters. Directly I scratched on the door (did you know it wasn't polite to *knock?*) I was admitted; an armchair was brought for 'Monsieur le Duc'; and as soon as he could Monsieur de Charost dismissed everyone else from the room, so that, as he said, we might chat at our ease undisturbed.

"As you can imagine, our conversation turned chiefly on the affairs of the Rohan family. I am naturally anxious to learn as much as I can before my arrival in Paris. Today, alas! my dear Jacob, I heard something from him that sheds a new light on my situation, and not a pleasant one. It appears that my mother, the Duchess Dowager, is awaiting my coming with the utmost impatience and the liveliest feelings of joy. Not so my sister Marguerite—or 'Margot,' as my cousin calls her. With sadness I find that there has lately occurred a serious rift in our family. Just two months ago my sister married Henri de Chabot, Sieur de Saint Aulaye, a young man as well born as herself (in fact, he's our cousin), but lacking both fortune and prestige. The Count, who's forthright of speech, asserts that Chabot's a pauper; worse still, he has never fought a duel and his military career is, so far, a blank. In short, up to now, his chief celebrity at court has lain in his skill as a dancer: la Chabotte, a kind of courante very popular with the Queen's Maids-of-Honour, was invented by him!

"These drawbacks my good mother might eventually have overlooked, had there not been a more serious one: Chabot is a Catholic! As staunch a supporter of 'the religion' as my late father himself, she did all she could to prevent the match. But, after all, Margot is eight-and-twenty, a little too old, as Monsieur de Charost says, to be placed under lock and key. The ceremony was performed in the country without my mother's knowledge or consent. Since then my sister has renounced the church of her fathers and has given her husband a written promise that, if they have children, they will be raised in the Roman faith. As if that were not enough, she has contrived, through her intrigues at court, to have the title of Duc de Rohan bestowed on her bridegroom by letters patent issued in the King's name by the Queen Regent: henceforth, he's to be known, forsooth! as the Duc de Rohan-Chabot.

"All this happened but a few weeks ago. You can, therefore, easily picture the rage and dismay of my sister when she learned that the brother she supposed for seven years was dead, had miraculously returned to life. If I am accepted as Duc de Rohan—as Charost says I undoubtedly will be—'twill be the end of her pretentions, and Chabot's.

The great estates, the titles and honours, must all be given back.

"Since my cousin imparted this sorry news I have, I confess, worried a great deal about the future. Of course, it is easy for me to guess now who sent La Cosse to Leyden, and why. (I have confided my suspicions to Charost; he is sure I am right.) My sole consolation is that, as far as we can see, my brother-in-law has few partisans at court. The messengers he dispatched hither—as soon as he heard I was on my way to Paris—to present his compliments and enlist allies for his cause, have found no-one willing to receive them. On the other hand, as I told you, I have been overwhelmed by offers of service: when I quit Calais, on the last stage of my journey, I shall be accompanied by some sixty cavaliers—volunteers returning from Flanders—who have sworn to see no harm befalls me. We are waiting now only for my personal escort, sent by my mother—that is Monsieur de la Piaillière, captain of the guards of the Maréchal de la Meilleraye, who is Grand Master of the Artillery at Paris, hence the official guardian of the city. He is expected tonight; if he comes, we shall be off tomorrow.

"It grieves me to see that Rondeau and La Mestairie—who naturally must have known this all along: why in God's name didn't they tell me?—are confoundedly suspicious. They are forever conferring in corners with Monsieur de Charost; prating of spies and secret documents, daggers and poison vials, and such nonsense. Indeed, 'tis as much as I can manage now to get them to let me out of their sight!

"For myself I have no fear. Why should I? My cause is just. What I hope is that, once I get to Paris, I shall be able to solve this perplexing problem. Surely all that will be necessary is for me to seek Madame de Chabot and sue for her friendship! She has a woman's heart: how can she deny me a sister's affection? Must there not be some way of contenting everybody? The Rohans have so many titles and castles that, if I wished, I could easily create her husband Baron of This, Count of That, Marquis of Something-or-other, rich beyond his most ambitious dreams—and still keep the dukedom as my own rightful property.

"Dear Jacob, pray that I may be successful in my mission; for, if I fail, my happiness will be incomplete at best. I trust you are well and have not forgotten me. I send my duty to Mijnheer and Mevrouw Potenijk, and to you, as always, the most sincere assurances of my perfect esteem. (That is French courtier language for 'best love,' my dear!)

"Your affectionate friend,
"The Duc de Rohan."

"Saint Denis,
"This Twenty-First of August, 1645

"My dear Jacob:
"This is the last letter you will receive from me before our arrival in Paris. Indeed, we are almost there now; the abbey of Saint Denis, where I am writing these lines, is but a league's distance from the north gates of the city.

"We have been here since mid-day, having slept last night at Creil, and might well have finished our journey ere now. Truth to tell, had I been consulted, we should have done so: 'tis maddening to be so near the goal, yet unable to reach it! The delay has been caused by a number of gentlemen, who with the best of intentions have ridden out here to welcome us. They have been coming on horseback and in coaches all afternoon; a new party have just made their entrance and are calling for wine in the hall next to which I am sitting. (They want me to join them, but I am afraid to drink anything: my poor head's all-a-buzz already with names and titles—how shall I ever learn to distinguish one from another?)

"Most of them are my kinsmen; I had not realized before I had so many cousins! Chief among these are Hercule de Rohan, Duc de Montbazon, governor of Paris, and his son, the Prince de Guémenée. The latter is nothing to look at: a squat little man, with squinting eyes and a sharp nose, who seems to make jokes all the time and then to laugh at them longer and harder than anyone else. But Monsieur le Gouverneur is vastly impressive. He is the tallest man I have ever seen—even taller than my cousin Charost—and old as he is (I took him for near eighty and Rondeau says I guessed right), he stands as straight as a guardsman. Handsome he's not; his long face is so bony and narrow that it gives him somewhat the look of a horse; but his fine grey beard adds dignity, and his voice is as deep and solemn as the great bell in Sint Pieter's at Leyden. When he clasped me in his arms and exclaimed: 'The boy has his mother's eyes, but he's a true Rohan all the same—welcome, sir, to the city where you were born!' I felt, as never before, that I had come into my heritage—that everything was as it was meant to be.

"On one subject my kinsmen are agreed: my sister's marriage is generally blamed, and no-one I've spoken to has a good word to say for Chabot. The whole troop intends to escort me from Saint Denis to the Hôtel de Rohan in the

Place Royale, where my mother awaits me. I am to ride in
Monsieur de Montbazon's carriage as far as the gates; there
he has promised me I may alight and mount Timoléon, the
magnificent chestnut battle charger that was my father's
favourite, so that I may enter Paris as a soldier's son should
do.

"As you know, I have never ridden horseback before.
Fortunately Monsieur de Charost, foreseeing just such a
contingency, gave me instructions as to how to comport
myself, and allowed me to practise mounting and dismount-
ing from his own great horse till I felt I had the knack of
it. Let us hope I don't bring disgrace on the proud name of
Rohan!

"I must be brief, for dusk has fallen and I think the procession will soon be ready to start. They are gathering in
the square outside the abbey: what a crowd of coaches and
coachmen and prancing steeds! Now the postilions are light-
ing their torches—I can hear the hiss of the flames and smell
the smoke from here—and Rondeau has come in to tell me
the governor is waiting. Oh, Jacob, if only you were with
me! To think that in less than an hour I'll be embracing my
mother!

"Farewell! and pray don't forget
"Your affectionate friend,
"The Duc de Rohan."

II 🌿

Monsieur de Montbazon's six prancing bay stallions had cherry-red ostrich plumes on their heads and his coach was even bigger than the Rohans'. The back bench had been made unusually high—owing no doubt to the governor's exceptional stature—so that Tancrède, try as he would, was unable to touch the ground with his feet. He sat, therefore, half suspended, wedged tightly between his two august relatives, and striving, not altogether successfully, to fix his mind on the future. This was, he told himself, the most important night of his life. . . . If only the gentlemen wouldn't push so! Cousin de Montbazon had such very long legs that his knees began to spread as the journey progressed, especially after—as soon happened—the motion of the carriage sent him to sleep. Cousin de Guémenée was much shorter, so that his legs were not a problem; but he was so stout that he took up much more than his share of the bench.

How dark it was in the swaying coach, and how dark in the lonely country outside! There was nothing to see save trees and fields, with here and there a faint light to show where the infrequent farm-houses were. It was a warm, breathless night; the air felt heavy with unshed moisture; a veil drew itself gradually over the sulky moon, while the stars disappeared one by one. As they passed the hill of Montmartre, with its windmills gaunt and menacing against the night sky, a few light raindrops started to patter down on the carriage roof.

All of a sudden the road grew narrower and smellier, the

houses that bordered it closer together, and they were in the Faubourg. At the Porte Saint Denis the procession came to a halt. Cousin de Montbazon, waking with a start and a smothered exclamation, issued an order in his immense, sonorous voice; a groom led up Timoléon, saddled and bridled. Then Tancrède, feeling very small indeed, stepped out of the carriage, gave his hand to La Mestairie—as Charost had instructed him to do—and, not too awkwardly, scrambled up on his mount. (Thank fortune, though, it was too dark for anyone to see his face clearly!)

Timoléon was a tremendous animal, standing well over seventeen hands at the shoulder; but luckily Tancrède's few equestrian experiments had been made on the Flanders mare Bet, who was even larger. The great horse seemed to understand what was required of him. He had shaken his head alarmingly once or twice when the groom brought him forth, but now, as Cousin de Montbazon gave the signal to proceed, he moved forward at a stately trot through the gates into Paris.

Tancrède's first feeling was disappointment. He had supposed that Paris must be different from anything else he had seen, and much more splendid; but the winding lanes and tall, thin, crooked houses looked just as dark and just as dirty as those outside the walls. (France was not nearly so clean as Holland, though out of loyalty to his new country he had not told Jacob so.) There were more of both, that was all; and certainly more people in the streets, who eyed the clattering, jingling cavalcade with frank curiosity. Tancrède sat very straight in the saddle, trying not to show he knew he was the centre of attention. ("There he is! There goes the little Duke!")

Rondeau, riding beside him on a grey Barbary pony with a very long mane and tail, was busy pointing out landmarks to his charge. This street they were in was the rue des Deux Portes, so called because it connected the gates of Saint Denis and Saint Martin. The church yonder to the right was Saint Nicolas; that clump of dark old buildings next to it, the abbey of Saint Martin des Champs. Next came the walled enclosure of the Temple, a city within a city, bristling with towers and battlements; then the modest convent of the Filles du Calvaire. (Tancrède nodded, but he could not really look at anything.) Finally they turned into a much broader street, where the houses were larger and handsomer . . . the rue Saint Louis, said Rondeau.

Here at a word from Cousin de Montbazon the horses started to canter. With a whoop the postilions dashed out in front, their torches trailing tails of fire like comets behind them; the buglers of Monsieur le Gouverneur shrilled triumphantly. Tancrède had all he could manage now to keep his seat on Timoléon and to hold his reins as Charost had taught him to do. After a few breathless minutes they rode into an arcaded square—one had just time to notice that the houses were built all alike of pink brick and white stone with very high pitched roofs, and that there was a statue of a man on horseback in the middle—crossed it diagonally at a full gallop, while the buglers sounded a final flourish, and drew up in front of the corner house, one of the finest in the square.

"And this, my Lord," said Rondeau, somewhat unnecessarily, "is the Hôtel de Rohan!"

Tancrède had already started to slide out of his saddle before he remembered that he must wait to let the equerry help him. (One was always being brought up short in this country by the numbers of things a French noble could not do for himself.) By this time Cousin de Montbazon's coach had arrived. The old man descended from it slowly and majestically; he was involved in an argument with his son. "Zounds, sir!" Tancrède heard him say. "What's worth doing at all is worth doing right. Come up with us now; you need stay but a moment."

Cousin de Guémenée shook his head with a smile—not a very agreeable one. "No, sir, I beg you'll excuse me. Madame de Rohan, I fear, is having one of her little evenings. My wife and I'll be glad to take care of the company for you. Besides, as you know, *she* never wanted me to . . ."

It was impossible to hear the end of the sentence, for Cousin de Montbazon gave an exclamation of disgust and bawled out quite rudely: "Get along with you, then! I've no time to waste on lily-livered cowards!" Then he turned to Tancrède, held out his hand, and said, in a very different voice—kind and encouraging—: "Come, lad! Your mother's impatient to see you, I know."

At this point the party broke in two: Rondeau and La Mestairie following the big, old Duke and the little, young one into the Hôtel de Rohan, while the rest of the troop swept off in the wake of Cousin de Guémenée to the Hôtel de Guémenée, which it appeared was next door.

Inside his own house for the first time in his life, Tancrède was greeted by the stout Swiss porter in scarlet-and-gold and two rows of liveried lackeys, bowing to the floor. As they mounted the spiral stair with its graceful wrought-iron railing he gained a fleeting impression of marble halls and rich tapestries, tall gilt mirrors, and scores of candles reflected in them. . . . At the top of the stairs two more lackeys were waiting to fling open the doors on a great room hung with crimson damask, where supper was being served.

On the threshold Tancrède halted, somehow unable to proceed. His heart was beating fast and he kept repeating to himself: "This is it! This is it!" He could see a long table lighted by many more candles; hear a clash of plates and cutlery, a clinking of goblets, a babble of voices laughing and talking . . . all men's. (But then *where* . . . ?)

Cousin de Montbazon, seeing his hesitation, stalked ahead, paying no heed to the hubbub within—which, to be sure, ceased at once on his entrance

"Madam," the bell-like tones proclaimed, "I have brought you your son!"

When Tancrède looked round, a few minutes later, to thank his benefactor, he found that the old man had mysteriously disappeared.

For the time being he was swallowed up by the crowd of courtiers. There were smiling faces everywhere, hands extended in greeting, exclamations of surprise in high, light French voices: "My Lord, we never guessed you'd get here so quickly!"

Tancrède had eyes for his mother alone. At first—how strange that was!—he had not even seen her. But now she detached herself from the group of guests and came swiftly forward, all rustling and tinkling, to take him in her arms. He smelled the scent of jasmine in her hair, felt her tears warm on his cheek, heard her voice—low and tremulous—crying out: "Tancrède! My son! Can it really be . . . ? Yes, of course, it is! Oh, my dear, how I've waited for this!"

After a moment she held him off from her, so that, as she

said, she could look at him; and then, of course, he could look at her, too.

Tancrède hardly knew what he had expected. It was very odd: in his conversations with Rondeau and La Mestairie, and even with Cousin de Charost, he had never asked them point-blank to describe his mother. If he had been obliged to put his vague vision into words, it would probably have approximated a more elegant edition of Mevrouw Potenijk —a matron in a cap, tall, dignified, and old—for the Dowager Duchess was nearly fifty. Could this little, slender, restless creature, with her pointed face and enormous, black-fringed grey eyes (so like his own) be anyone's mother? Although she wore a widow's tight triangular cap on her crown, from which lustreless sable ringlets fell to her shoulder, and was dressed in black also—a black twinkling with brilliants that caught the candlelight to reflect it like myriad stars—she did not look in the least as if she were in mourning.

Tancrède felt he ought to say something. It seemed impossible to speak until he had swallowed the lump in his throat, which horribly wouldn't go down. Perhaps his mother was embarrassed, too, even though she kept kissing him, and saying in that queer husky voice how glad she was to see him, her painted eyes wide with excitement, her smiles a little too brilliant and constant. ("No, not *Moeder,* darling; you must call me Maman!")

Quite naturally it was she who first recovered her composure, remembering that it was her duty to present her guests to her son. This she did formally: Tancrède had still not got used to being bowed to and having his hand perpetually kissed: since he had left Leyden, of all the nobles he had met only Cousin de Montbazon was his equal in rank.

There were not, he found, so many people in the room as he had thought—Maman's table was set for ten only. These young men—for the eldest looked scarce five-and-twenty—bore a strong resemblance to the French officers in Flanders. They also looked like one another: how would one ever be able to tell who was who? Two only made a definite, if not an especially pleasing, impression. The Comte de Miossens, with his snub profile and shrewd sherry-brown eyes, was, said Maman, a Gascon—which accounted for his rough, slipshod accent. (Every time he opened his mouth the others all laughed, even before they heard what he was going to say.) But did it account as well for the impertinence of the appraising stare he turned on the new Duc de Rohan? . . . As for the Marquis de Vardes, a handsome, strapping youth with curls as long as Maman's, what time he was not poised, like Narcissus, to admire his own image in one of the numerous mirrors that hung in the Crimson Cabinet, seemed to be spent surveying the latest arrival with veiled dislike through his long, silky eyelashes.

The others, Tancrède discovered, were almost oppressively polite. They asked him how he did, what he thought of (A) Paris, (B) the Queen Regent, (C) Cardinal Mazarin; when he expected to be presented at court; and if he felt the campaign in Flanders was likely to be over soon—to none of which questions, except the first, was he able to give satisfactory answers.

Maman, roving restlessly about the room, suddenly exclaimed: "My dear, forgive me! Where are my manners? You must be starved! Or have you supped already in Saint Denis?"

Tancrède shook his head; he had forgotten about food.

Apparently the meal had been nearly finished, for the platters of entrées and roasts that covered the table were nearly empty; even the towering iced puddings and pyramids of fruit had a devastated look. But Maman clapped her hands smartly to summon the servants and bade them bring in a fresh supply—everything started all over again. She also made her son sit next to her in the chair that had previously been occupied by Monsieur de Vardes, who gave the interloper a quick dagger-glance as he moved one seat farther on.

Tancrède did his best to eat to please his mother. It wasn't the ten pairs of watching eyes—eight of them friendly—that spoilt his appetite. No, nor even the fact that his burgher palate was not trained to appreciate such sophisticated delicacies as broiled ortolans or *cochon à la daube*. (Often on the trip he'd have given worlds for a good plain stew, or for a mug of ale instead of the vintage wines he was plied with daily.) But how could one think of supper at a time like this? . . . Here he was at home at last—if so splendid a palace, all marble and gilt, rare tapestries and richly carved woods, could be so considered! He *had* a home like other boys—and a family! For there was the mother he'd dreamed about, that sparkling, exquisite little lady, gazing at him with pride and yes, of course, love—right beside him, striving to foresee and grant his every wish. ("Darling, wouldn't you like a little more pheasant *pâté*? And you haven't even touched the mushrooms in Burgundy!")

How wonderful it was! How happy he must be! That is, of course, he would start being happy as soon as he had got used to everything. It was only natural for him and Maman to feel shy with each other at first. That wouldn't last. As soon as these swaggering, conversational young men had gone they would be alone together. And then things would surely come right between them.

Maman meanwhile, in the intervals between pressing dainties upon him and lamenting his lack of appetite, made inquiries about the journey. She asked almost as many questions as her young men, talking very fast and not always waiting for an answer. . . . Had he been sorry to leave his friends in Leyden? Was the carriage quite comfortable? ("I was so sorry, my dear, not to send you the best one—it had gone to have the cushions recovered and the wretched workmen didn't get it back in time—I do hope you didn't mind too much!") Had Rondeau and La Mestairie looked after him properly? How had he found our good Charost in Calais?

Maman, in fact, talked so much that Tancrède found he had to say little in return. Miossens' and Vardes' occasional attempts to engage her interest could not distract her more than momentarily. Yet even when supper was over neither they nor their companions showed signs of taking themselves off. They were very much at ease, Tancrède could not help thinking, these perfumed dandies, lolling back in their chairs with their doublets partly unbuttoned, and smoking their pipes quite as if a lady were not in the room. Some of them called for glasses of hippocras or rossolis (whatever they might be!) with an offhand air, as they might have done in their own homes. Others fell to playing cards without asking their hostess's permission. Vardes and Miossens started a game of tric-trac in the corner.

Impervious to their strange want of manners, Maman moved from group to group, chaffing her guests, receiving their sallies and compliments with sidelong glances and her invariable husky laugh. She did not leave Tancrède—who, not knowing what else to do, sat where he was at the supper-table—for long at a time; the best of her looks and smiles, he could not but see, were still his. (Did Monsieur de Vardes see this, too? And was that why he went on looking cross in his corner?)

Tancrède tried his manful best to keep erect and interested, but presently, in spite of his efforts, his head began to droop—it had, after all, been a very long day. Maman perceived it at once and berated herself again for forgetfulness.

"My dear little boy, you must be exhausted—you shall go to bed directly! We've so much to say to each other, haven't we, darling? But it will keep till morning. I bid you goodnight; sleep well, and as late as you can. Tomorrow is Sunday. But thank God! you've been brought up in the true church and don't have to rise for early mass."

Before he could tell what was happening Tancrède found himself being given a final scented kiss, then handed over to Rondeau—who had been waiting outside for orders all this time (one hoped he and La Mestairie had had their supper, too)—and swept away up another flight of marble steps to the state apartment prepared for Monsieur le Duc de Rohan.

As the doors to the Crimson Cabinet closed behind him he could hear the babble of masculine voices break forth once more.

III 🌿

HE WOKE EARLY to the sound of pealing bells. They were ringing all over the city, some faint and far away, some so urgently near that it seemed as if they must be just outside the windows. In Leyden he had been used to the chimes of Sint Pankras' and Sint Pieter's playing their precise and delicate airs, but this was quite different—an importunate and deafening clamour that went on for many minutes, as though the ringers were determined to rouse everybody in Paris.

Tancrède knew the bells were no concern of his, so he lay where he was in his great bed and stared up at the scarlet canopy above him, dotted with the gold-embroidered lozenges of the Rohan coat-of-arms, which, since the curtains were drawn, was all he could see. His eyes under their long black lashes looked grave and heavy, not because he was still sleepy, but from all the sleep he'd slept. He'd been too tired the night before to worry or wonder as Thomas, the valet, undressed him; he'd tumbled into bed and fallen almost at once into a deep, refreshing slumber. But now he began consciously to try to sort out his jumble of impressions, to review in detail the extraordinary things that had happened to him.

He thought about the confused and tumultuous family reception in Saint Denis, and the long drive to the city with tall, kind Cousin de Montbazon and short, fussy Cousin de Guémenée; then about his first breathless ride on Timoléon through the streets of Paris, his arrival at the pink-

and-white house in the Place Royale, Maman's puzzling supper-party in the Crimson Cabinet, and his meeting with Maman's young men.

About Maman herself he thought less. It was odd—without being able to help it, his mind seemed to shy away from directly considering her. He found himself remembering instead detached traits of her person and manners: her sparkling eyes, her husky laugh, the pretty way her hair grew in short curls on her very white forehead, that trick of playing with her fan all the time she was talking—of making it flutter and thrill like a captive butterfly. What she was really like, he somehow shrank from venturing to guess—still less, what their relations as mother and son were likely to be.

Should he get up? The light filtering through the scarlet curtains was growing perceptibly stronger; he could hear some sparrows chirping on the ledge outside the windows. On the other hand, Thomas, who slept in an adjoining antechamber, was still snoring lustily. Tancrède knew he was supposed to call him when he wanted to rise. But *must* he? Might he not have at least one taste of liberty on his first day at home? After all, why not . . . ?

The temptation was too strong to be resisted. Cautiously he pushed back the curtains and laid his feet on the bare parquet. It creaked a little, but not enough to wake Thomas. Then, still scarcely daring to breathe, he stepped down from the raised platform on which the bed stood, in an alcove shut off by a railing (Tancrède wondered what the railing was for), and tiptoed across the room to the big oaken chest near the door, where his clothes were kept.

Since arriving in France Tancrède had never dressed himself without Thomas' help. But he had not observed the latter's procedure in vain: less than twenty minutes later he stood in front of the tall mirror over the mantel, gazing with awe at the small but elegant figure reflected therein, complete to the last fold of lace and knot of silken ribbon. Only the care of his hair eluded him; brush and comb were on the toilet-table in the antechamber; it seemed wisest merely to smooth the dark tangle with his fingers as best he could— when his hat was on it didn't show too much.

The same prudence restrained him from exploring his new quarters. There were, he knew, several more rooms— he had passed through them last night—beyond the antechamber towards the front of the house. The bedroom, with its carved and gilded ceiling, its heavy oak furniture, the tapestries of hunting scenes on the walls (had it once been Papa's?), was at the back. After a moment's indecision Tancrède opened one of the windows—which was really a door—and stepped out on the balcony.

It was, he saw at once, going to be another very warm day; the courtyard below was flooded with sunshine. On the right stood a lower building, obviously the stables; on the left another tall pavilion, built of the same pink brick and white stone, appeared also to be part of the Hôtel de Rohan. Towards the rear the prospect was closed by a high wall, against which stood rows of orange trees in tubs; over the top of this wall could be glimpsed the trees in somebody's garden. There was no-one about; the early morning hush was broken only by the sparrows, which had scattered at Tancrède's approach and were now hopping about on the cobblestones, quarrelling energetically. . . . Yet stay! Just as he had decided there was nothing worth looking at and it might be better to try to steal past Thomas, in the hope of getting to the front room, where he'd at least have a view of the square, a little girl in a hooded brown taffeta cloak came hurrying into the court through a door Tancrède could not see because it was directly beneath him, and started across it in the direction of the tall pavilion.

Involuntarily he took a quick step forward and leaned over the rail of the balcony, the better to see her. The slight noise caused her to look up just as he looked down; their glances met. . . . "Oh!" said the little girl; and then stood still.

She was a pretty child, with soft, bright dark eyes and rosy cheeks; about twelve or thirteen, Tancrède decided. Neither frightened nor even particularly shy, she still did not offer to say anything more after her exclamation of surprise; he realized he would have to speak, if he wanted to detain her. And he did want to: she was the first person of his own age he had seen since parting from Jacob in Leyden.

After a short pause he called out—softly, for fear of waking Thomas: "Who are you?"

"I'm Sidonie," replied the little girl, as if that were identification enough.

"Sidonie *who?*"

"Sidonie de Montville. My father is Monsieur Rondeau, secretary to the Duchesse de Rohan. Do you know him?"

"Why, yes—yes, I do; very well." Tancrède was overcome at finding that his friend, who had never mentioned them, had a family. "Then you must live here, too, at the Hôtel de Rohan?"

The little girl nodded. "We do. That is, not in this house; our lodging is in the garden, on the other side of the east pavilion." And she pointed towards the pink-and-white building on the left.

"Oh," said Tancrède. "Who else lives there with you?"

"Nobody else; just Papa and I. My mother is dead and I haven't any brothers or sisters. I have a dog, though, named Pyrame, and a cat named Thisbé, and three birds—two linnets and a white sparrow."

"Oh," said Tancrède once more. He did not know quite how to proceed, but fortunately, once the ice had been broken between them, young Mademoiselle de Montville seemed not at all bashful. She glanced at him now with friendly curiosity and then remarked: "Now you know about me: who are *you*?"

Tancrède considered seriously. "A week ago I couldn't have told you. Now I'm the Duc de Rohan. At least I suppose I must be, for everybody says so."

Sidonie did not look so much abashed as he had feared she might.

"To tell the truth, sir, I thought so all along," she said. "That's why you have such a funny accent; I knew straight off you were a foreigner."

Tancrède flushed.

"I'm *not* a foreigner—I'm just as French as you are! Only I lived so long in Holland, where I had to speak Dutch all the time. But now that I've come home again it'll be different: it's *got* to be!"

Sidonie's soft, bright eyes looked softer than ever with sympathy.

"I know. I'm sure it will be, sir—I mean, my Lord. (That's what Papa says I'm to call you.) He told me all about you last night; he says it's wonderful how much you've learned already."

"I like your father. He's been very kind to me. I'd like to see him again. Where is he now?"

"At home in bed, I suppose. Poor Papa! He was so tired after his long journey I didn't call him this morning when I got up to go to mass at Saint Paul."

"Is that where you've been?"

"Yes, sir—I mean, my Lord."

"But didn't I hear bells just a few minutes ago?"

"Oh, those were for the six o'clock mass," explained Sidonie. "I always go to the one at five o'clock in summer; it's so much nicer when the weather's fine."

"I didn't hear the bells for that," said Tancrède reflectively.

"I expect you were asleep then, like Papa. You must have been tired, too."

"I was. But I'm not any longer. I'd like to go for a walk right now. Where are you going, Mademoiselle?"

"Home to Papa, to see he gets his breakfast."

"I wish I could go with you."

"Well, why don't you? I know!" cried Sidonie suddenly, clapping her hands. "Come and have breakfast with us, and then I can show you Pyrame and Thisbé and the birds, and we can play in the garden afterwards; there's heaps of room."

Tancrède's face brightened, but only for a moment.

"I'd like nothing better, but I don't see how I can, very well. My valet's asleep in the room next to mine. I can't get out without walking through it, and if I do that, I'm sure to wake him. And if he wakes, he'll say it isn't proper—he'll go fetch my breakfast himself. I'm always having things fetched for me."

Sidonie observed that she did not see what good there was in being a duke if one couldn't do as one pleased, to which Tancrède rejoined rather gloomily that, as far as he could tell, dukes *never* did as they pleased—for a week or more he'd not been his own master.

"Never mind, then," said Sidonie. "Come to see us later, if you can. I'm sure your mother will let you; she's very fond of Papa."

"I do hope so," said Tancrède. "There's really no-one for me to talk to here."

"Very well; I'll expect you this afternoon. Good-bye, my Lord; I've got to go now!"

Mademoiselle de Montville dropped a funny, abrupt small curtsy and tripped off just as Tancrède heard a step behind him and Thomas' elderly, querulous voice exclaiming: "My Lord, my Lord, where are you? There's a light collation waiting in the Green Cabinet and a message has come from Madame la Duchesse: Madame la Duchesse presents her compliments to Monsieur le Duc and requests the honour of his company at church—you're to be ready to drive to Charenton in half an hour."

As Tancrède took his way downstairs, very conscious of his glossy elegance—for Thomas, of course, had dressed him and groomed him all over again—and somewhat preoccupied by his efforts not to trip over his sword, he met his mother just emerging from her own apartments. Maman this morning looked completely different from the restless siren of the night before. She was still dressed in black, but had exchanged her sparkling gown for sombre mourning draperies and a long veil; she had assumed, also, a mien in keeping with her appearance and swept down to the door, with her maids a respectful pace behind her, every inch the dignified widow of the leader of the Huguenots.

In the carriage she relaxed long enough to bid Tancrède

good morning and ask how he had passed the night, but her mood remained distant and abstracted; and when she presently clapped a mask over her face she seemed, as it were, extinguished: there was nothing for it save to retire into one's own thoughts and extract what pleasure one could out of the long drive to Charenton.

Tancrède had not known before that Protestants could not worship as they pleased in Paris. To tell the truth, he had never thought much about religion. In Leyden nearly everybody had belonged to the Reformed Church, but the Catholics, too, had a church of their own and both parties lived in harmony together. In France, it appeared, the case was otherwise. He did not like to ask why, nor even where Charenton was; but it soon became clear that it was some distance outside of the city. They passed through the Porte Saint Antoine, guarded by an immense turreted castle Maman told him was the Bastille; then along a thoroughfare bordered by houses with gardens. The farther they went the larger the gardens grew, and the more widely spaced the houses; finally the latter ceased altogether as the carriage plunged into a deep green wood—the Bois de Vincennes, Maman said briefly.

Now Tancrède began to notice that they were by no means alone. The road was full of coaches like theirs and troops of men on horseback; here and there they overtook a band of pilgrims on foot, chanting psalms lustily as they marched along in the dappled light and shade of the great forest. The crowds grew denser and denser: as they left the Bois de Vincennes and approached the outskirts of Charenton the traffic was so heavy—complicated now by rows of whining beggars on the sidelines—that they could proceed through choking dust at a snail's pace only.

Maman, irritated, called to the coachman to hurry; they were late, she declared; the second bell was just about to ring. And indeed, as they crossed the village street lined with inns to the big square building of the Temple, standing with its dependencies in an enclosure on the river's edge, the great, solemn notes tolled out slowly—not in the least like the nervous hubbub of the chimes of Paris.

Tancrède alighted first and turned to offer his hand to his mother. That, he felt, must be right, and her answering smile reassured him; but he was unprepared for the commotion their entrance caused. On the threshold Maman removed her mask, flung back her veil, and advanced with a queenly tread on her son's arm. It seemed to the latter that every face was turned in their direction; he could hear a low murmur: "That's he! That's the young Duke!" Maman was visibly swelling with pride, and the boy did his dutiful best to swell, too. But he was still not used to being stared at; the realization that all during the service people would continue to steal looks at him and discuss his case in whispers made him rather uncomfortable.

He tried not to think too much about it, to fix his mind instead on the Temple itself, which was not at all like any church he had seen. The enormous room with its vaulted ceiling covered with frescoes of scenes from the Bible looked more like a lecture hall: there was no altar; a raised platform in the centre provided space for the pulpit and for two chairs —one for the minister, Monsieur Drélincourt; the other occupied by a pompous gentleman in an official-looking black robe who, Maman volunteered, was the Marquis d'Arzilliers, Deputy General of the Reformed Churches of France.

It was not so hot as it had been outside, but the air was appallingly stuffy—it smelled, thought Tancrède, as though it had been breathed so many times over that all the good had gone out of it. A small captive finch flew about under the roof, cheeping continuously as it made desperate attempts to escape from its prison. Tancrède endeavoured not to let it distract him from the Scriptural readings, the chanted prayers and hymns. Two marriage ceremonies provided a welcome diversion, but during the lengthy interval when communion was being administered his thoughts began to wander again as helplessly as the finch. And the sermon seemed endless. . . .

If it had not been for the hour-glass resting on the pulpit-rail—which, after all, was irrefutable testimony—one would have sworn that Monsieur Drélincourt preached for at least twice the appointed time. He was an ugly little man anyhow, with a bad defect in his speech and an uncouth accent that recalled the Gascon Comte de Miossens'. However, had he been eloquent as an angel, it was doubtful whether his remarks this morning would have been listened to with more than perfunctory respect. As the rasping voice droned on Tancrède became increasingly aware that his own unrest was as nothing compared to the state of seething excitement that afflicted every man, woman, and child in the Temple of Charenton.

The final benediction had scarcely been pronounced before the congregation rose with one accord and streamed out on to the steps, gobbling like turkeys.

Maman took her time about leaving; she was determined, it seemed, to savour to the full the intoxicating sense of her new importance. Only the crowd's respect for the Rohans' exalted rank prevented mother and son from being over-whelmed by their admirers. La Mestairie and Thomas and the Duchess's lackeys succeeded in marking off a kind of square in the court, in the middle of which, with their backs against the church, Maman and Tancrède took up their stand, as at a wedding reception, to receive the acclamations of the assembled Protestants of Paris.

It was a little frightening at first, but once he had got used to having his hand kissed, and to seeing even quite elderly men kneel before him, Tancrède had to admit the experience was exhilarating. He soon gave up trying to remember names: Maman rattled them off as fast as she could, pausing only to underscore those she deemed of particular significance. Thus Tancrède met his uncle, the Comte d'Orval, Equerry to Her Majesty the Queen Regent, a long, lean gentleman with a nervous stutter, and his wife—born a La Force—a sallow lady with a pale, dissatisfied eye; the stoutly jovial Maréchal de Châtillon and his dove-like consort; and many another. Gradually as these worthies defiled before him he began to see that to them he was a person of great actual, and still greater potential, importance. He heard the old Maréchal de la Force—Aunt d'Orval's father—who was so tottery that it took two pages to support him, say to Maman in his quavering voice: "My dear Marguerite, this is indeed a glorious day for us all. Praise the Lord, I have lived to see *his* son at Charenton!"

Something in the old soldier's simple fervour struck an answering chord of emotion in Tancrède's heart. He realized, as never before, the true meaning of what was happening to him—that the whole thing was much more than the fantastic carnival masquerade it sometimes seemed to be. To these people he was a living symbol of faith, a promise of future achievement. Vaguely, without being able to put it into words, he felt he was on his honour now not to fail them—never, whatever befell, to betray their trust in their dead leader's son and the great name of Rohan.

It was surprising when they got back to Paris to find that Monsieur de Miossens and Monsieur de Vardes had come to dinner. (Had they no families of their own to be with on the sabbath?) Tancrède was still more astonished to see that their guests had not waited for them, but were already at table: was that the French fashion? The two young men jumped up with profuse apologies, which Maman brushed aside with a careless laugh; apparently their behaviour seemed natural to her.

Maman, in fact, was in excellent spirits. All the way home she had chatted cheerfully, no doubt in relief that the morning's ordeal was over. (Tancrède quite saw now that it had been an ordeal.) And with her young friends she embarked at once on a lively conversation.

At first Tancrède did not pay much heed to it: they were saying things he couldn't understand about people he didn't know. He was slightly oppressed by the complicated ritual of mealtime at the Hôtel de Rohan: it would have been pleasanter to eat without the intimidating presence of Lejeune, the butler, who stood at Maman's right hand, with an air of immense dignity, to present each plate for her inspection and to direct the movements of the corps of silent lackeys. The courses, too, were a series of exotic mysteries. . . .

Eventually his attention was arrested by Maman's account of the triumph at Charenton, which, it appeared, had far surpassed her expectations. "I was sure of Orval, of course, and old La Force, and one or two others—but really, my dears, we had the whole Temple at our feet! There's no doubt in my mind now what course to pursue."

"When do you intend to go to the Palais?" inquired Mios-sens, spearing with his fork an especially succulent morsel of the ragoût of heron—one, it was obvious from Vardes' expression of pique, that the latter had likewise had his eye upon.

"Very soon, I should think. My list of petitioners is almost complete. There are just a few names I should still like to add: Guémenée signed yesterday, but so far his wife hasn't been willing to help us. Tiresome creature! I suppose she considers herself better than the rest because she was born a Rohan and married one, too. However, she's sure to come round now—Anne always has to be on the winning side!"

Seeing Tancrède's look of bewilderment, Maman added that she had been busy the last few weeks—ever since the great news from Holland had reached her—in having a document drawn up to be delivered to the law courts of the Palais before the Chambre de l'Edit, the assembly whose special mission it was to judge the affairs of the Huguenots. This document, she asserted, had been signed by most of the members of Papa's family as well as her own: the Montbazons, the Chevreuses, the Béthunes, the Selles . . . one could not begin to remember them all. Now it would be necessary only to wait until she was able to present her son to his relatives at their houses and secure their personal suffrage in addition to their legal support. "And there won't be the least bit of trouble about that, after the splendid impression you made today. Then we'll be off to the Palais to fire our opening gun!"

Tancrède still looked bewildered.

"I don't understand, Maman. Why do we have to go to court?"

"My dear, these things are beyond my comprehension, too! Martin, my intendant, tells me it's best to proceed precisely in accordance with the letter of the law. Whatever happens then, we'll be perfectly safe."

"But what *can* happen? If I'm Papa's son and heir . . ."

"Ah, but we must get the judges to say so in black and white! I'm stating that you were stolen from me and kept hidden unlawfully for seven years, and asking them to recognize you and confirm you in your rights and privileges. At the same time we're going to request authority to appoint a warden to regulate your financial affairs. Our lawyers have thought of everything. I don't believe there's the slightest loop-hole that Margot . . ."

Maman bit her lip and subsided into silence.

"That's just it!" cried Tancrède. "What of my sister in all this? Am I not to see her at all? Is there *no* way . . . ?"

Miossens, who, having disposed of the ragoût of heron, was now attacking with equal enthusiasm a venison pasty, remarked brightly that the less said about Madame de Chabot the better. That undutiful slut would soon come to her senses and be forced to sue the Duchess for forgiveness.

Maman's eyes flashed dangerously; she seemed suddenly as angry as she had been pleased before.

"Never mention her name again in my presence! I tell you, she's dead to me—*dead!* I recognize her no longer."

The uncontrolled violence in her voice was frightening. Tancrède had never heard her speak thus. He did not know what to say next, though he felt there was a great deal in the situation that remained unclear. Fortunately at this point Monsieur de Vardes, who had been listening without saying a word, surveying them all, half contemptuous, half amused, through his silken lashes, roused himself to explain, in a patronizing drawl, that the Chabots also were going to law.

"You don't suppose—do you?—they're willing to give up a fortune like that without a struggle. Like as not, my young friend, your first sight of Mistress Margot will be on the opposite side of the great hall of the Parliament of Paris. Madam, I feel sure your lawyers must already have informed you, but 'tis certain Madame de Chabot's been taking measures of her own. I had it yesterday direct from her cousin Sully, who, as you are aware, has been on her side from the first. She and her husband have got up a rival petition with no less than eighty signatures. Sully says the list is headed by Chabot's great friend, Monsieur le Duc d'Enghien. As heir to the title of First Prince of the Blood his name will carry much weight. And then, too, I need not remind you he's high in favour just now with the Queen and Mazarin, since his victory this month over the Germans at Nördlingen. Monsieur le Duc's an enemy to reckon with—bold as an eagle and crafty as a fox. Doubtless 'twill be the battle of the century."

"And we're going to win it!" exclaimed Maman, still with that disturbing thrill of anger in her voice.

"But," objected Tancrède, "I still don't see . . . Why need there be a battle? If I'm the Duc de Rohan . . ."

"Ah, my dear young man,"—Vardes dropped his words out languidly one by one, as if the effort to form them were almost too great—"the Chabots, you see, won't admit it. They don't think you are—or they pretend they don't, which comes to the same in the end. Dear madam, pray forgive me—this plum tart is so delicious I really must have another slice!"

After dinner Maman announced she had business to attend to and dismissed her son with a brightly mechanical smile and a kiss. (It seemed strange that their guests did not take the hint: both young men remained lounging in their chairs, as if they had the entire afternoon at their disposal.)

Tancrède did not know what to do. The conversation at table had planted a number of new and troubling thoughts in his brain, but at the moment he did not feel like letting them grow as they undoubtedly would, if left to themselves. Then he remembered Sidonie's invitation: since there was no-one to stop him, he descended to the ground floor, walked out into the court below his bedroom, and crossed it in the direction of the east pavilion.

On the farther side of that there was a large garden, laid out with neat gravelled paths and flower beds bordered by clipped shrubs, with a fountain in the centre. Beyond the garden stood a high hedge of evergreens that had a gate in it. Tancrède passed through the gate and entered a grassy enclosure, shut off at the other end by a row of small two-storeyed pavilions. Here, dressed in her best Sunday white silk with pink bows, and promenading sedately with a fluffy black dog on a leash, he found Mademoiselle de Montville.

She smiled when she saw him, looking pleased but not surprised.

"So you've come, my Lord! I am very glad to see you."

Tancrède soon discovered that he was glad, too. He had never known a girl before except Antje Cernolle, the schoolmaster's daughter, who had been too young and too stupid to count, really; he had feared at first he might feel shy with one. But Sidonie herself was not in the least shy; she chatted and laughed directly and seemed to take their companionship so agreeably for granted that it was almost as good as having Jacob back again.

With pride she displayed her modest domain—the suite of elegant cubbyholes on the entresol of the middle pavilion that constituted Monsieur Rondeau's *chambres de parade*, and the iron balcony with its flowers in pots and miniature hanging garden of greenery. She also introduced her visitor to her pets: the singing birds in their cage; Pyrame, who barked a welcome at his mistress's bidding and presented his paw most politely; and Thisbé, curled in a Persian-blue ball in her wicker basket. (The kitten purred satisfactorily when stroked, but otherwise refused to be roused from her after-dinner nap.)

"Papa's napping, too," said Sidonie. "That's why I don't think we'd better stay here; I'm afraid we might wake him. I'd thought we might play in the big garden, but Madame de Guémenée is receiving this afternoon and someone might come and tell us to stop—she lives just next door. I know what, though—let's take a walk!"

"Oh, I'd like that," said Tancrède. "I haven't seen anything of Paris yet. It was dark when I came, and this morning when we drove to Charenton we seemed to leave the city almost at once. But can we get out without going all the way back where I came from?"

"Wait here a moment; I'll show you how."

Sidonie tripped into the house; when she returned she was wearing the pretty fawn-brown taffeta cloak Tancrède had first seen her in. She then opened a door in the garden wall the boy had not noticed and led the way through it into a succession of narrow, ill-smelling alleys, which turned and twisted until it seemed that they must be completely lost.

Sidonie, however, continued to advance as if she knew precisely what she was about; and sure enough, the last of the turns brought them out without warning into a broad, bustling street, the rue Saint Antoine.

Crossing this thoroughfare, the children entered another much smaller street that took them straight to the Quai Saint Paul and the river. Tancrède had never seen the Seine before. He was rather disappointed in its size, but it was interesting to watch the traffic on its sluggish green surface: cargo boats moving up and down, ferries plying between the two banks and the islands in mid-stream. After this amusement palled Sidonie proposed a stroll in the Arsenal gardens.

The Arsenal itself was not open to the public. "That's where they make guns and bullets and armour, and everything else the King's soldiers need. The Grand Master of the Artillery lives there—he's the Maréchal de la Meilleraye, you know."

Tancrède surveyed with curiosity the monumental gate on the quai, flanked by a pair of rather grim looking cannon.

"Yes, I know. I've met his captain of the guard—a fellow named La Piaillière. Maman sent him to Calais to help escort me to Paris. If I could find him, we'd get him to show us around. Shall I ask one of the guards where he is?"

Sidonie demurred. "Oh, no, don't let's! I'd rather not see things that are made for killing people. Besides, we haven't any right . . ."

Tancrède lifted his chin. "No right? I'd like to know why not! My Grandpapa Sully was once Grand Master of the Artillery himself. Rondeau told me so."

Sidonie was impressed. "Is that what you'd like to be some day, my Lord?"

Tancrède shook his head stoutly. "No, Mademoiselle! I'm going to be a soldier like my father."

Inside the gate they came to the Mall, a very long promenade marked off by three rows of elms and divided from the river by a wooden palisade. For the first time since coming to Paris Tancrède saw a real grove of trees. Up till then it had seemed a city of stone—even the Place Royale had nothing but dusty gravel in the centre. Here in the pleasant grassy shade the Parisians took their Sunday ease: soldiers and merchants, workmen and lackeys, mothers with children and troops of young girls. Tancrède and Sidonie found much to divert them. There was a queer dark man wearing earrings with a pair of performing apes, who danced a courante on their hindlegs while their master played a lively tune on his pipe. There was also a pedlar bearing a cage of bright-coloured birds on his shoulder. Tancrède longed to buy one for his new friend, but found to his dismay that he had left his purse at home. Sidonie, who had a few pence in her pocket, insisted, much to his embarrassment, on treating him to some dragées and a spice-cake purchased from a wandering sweetmeat-vendor.

But of course the principal attraction in the Mall were the men playing mall itself. The game was new to both children: they joined the crowd round two rather rough-looking boys Tancrède thought might be sailors and watched them batting their wooden balls through the wicket with long, flexible-handled mallets. After a while, noting his interest, the players suggested he join them.

"Don't do it," whispered Sidonie. "My Lord, I beg you not to—I don't like their looks!"

Tancrède hesitated. He did not much like their looks either. On the other hand, if he refused, they would take him for a coward—and that would be worse than making a fool of himself.

"I've never played before," he said diffidently.

"Never mind, young master—we'll soon show you—why, there's nothing to it at all!"

Tancrède was not sure about that; the mallet was a good deal heavier than he had supposed. However, he felt things had already gone too far—he could not back out now with honour. And, after all, it was not so hard as he had feared. He managed to send his ball several times through the wicket, much to his own surprise and the applause of the sympathetic bystanders. ("The young un's got pluck!" he heard one man say to his wife.)

In the long run, though, even beginner's luck could not save him. The sailors—if sailors they were—chalked up impressive scores after his; and when the game was over, instead of saying good-bye, they held out their hands for a forfeit.

"What will you pay us, young master?" asked one; while the other—the larger and more ill-looking of the pair—gave an impudent wink. "You can't expect a lesson for nothing, you know. Come, sir—hand over a pistole at least!"

Tancrède flushed crimson and broke into a sweat of fear. How awful to be caught like this without any money! He did not know whether Sidonie had more in her pocket or not, nor even how much a pistole was worth (it sounded like a lot); but in any case this was *his* problem—he could not ask a girl to help him. He had really nothing of value except the jewelled watch Thomas had pinned on him that morning, which he suspected—though no-one had said so—must have belonged to his father. That he could not part with. . . . Sidonie was twisting her fingers together in an agony of nervousness—he *must* say something!

"I—I'm sorry," he stammered, his French beginning to desert him in the emergency. "I've nothing to give you. But if you come—Hôtel de Rohan—"

The boys roared with laughter.

"Never mind the cash—we'll take our pay another way—if your young lady here is willing to oblige. Come, sweetheart: can you spare us a kiss apiece?"

Tancrède clenched his fists and turned as pale as he had been red before. This was worse than he had feared. It did not matter what became of him, but to think that gentle Sidonie should come to harm in his care was horrible beyond words. Yet what could he do to prevent it? They were two to his one, and quite twice his size. Well, never mind. . .

Suddenly Sidonie gave a piercing shriek.

"Monsieur de Ruvigny! Monsieur de Ruvigny!"

A tall red-haired fellow in a soldier's leather doublet strode through the crowd and took charge of affairs with cool competence—or, rather, merely showed himself capable of doing so, for on his appearance the sailors slunk off without waiting to be dealt with. Sidonie, who had kept up admirably during the crisis, flung herself into her rescuer's arms and burst into tears; while the red-haired man saluted Tancrède over her heaving shoulder with a wide, pleasant grin: "The last time I saw you, my Lord, was seven years ago, but I'd know the topknot of the Rohans anywhere. Monsieur le Duc, your servant, sir!"

IV

THE NEXT MORNING soon after breakfast Tancrède received a message from his mother asking him to attend her *lever*. He had not known that ladies had *levers*, but he soon found out his mistake after scratching for admittance on the door to her private cabinet. Madame de Rohan, wearing a lemon-yellow silk dressing-gown, all an artful confusion of ribbons and laces, was seated in front of a mirror at a table near the window, having her hair brushed by old Ursule, one of her waiting women. (The other, young Jeanneton, was busy in a corner sewing feathers on her mistress's hat.)

In the crude, unflattering light of a grey August day Maman looked older than her son had yet seen her: there were sharply sagging little lines at either corner of her mouth and her curls displayed an inky blackness. (Tancrède realized, with a small shock, that they must be dyed. Poor Maman! Perhaps her hair was quite white underneath.) She seemed, however, in a high good humour, laughing and chatting with Monsieur de Vardes, who sat on a tabouret next the dressing-table and showed himself livelier than usual. Was that because Miossens was not there?

At all events the Marquis succeeded in capturing a greater share of the Duchess's regards than were vouchsafed her maids, or the string of retainers who appeared one by one to get their orders for the day. With incredible rapidity Maman dealt with the cook and the butler, the equerries and the Swiss porter; even Monsieur Rondeau, submitting his list of her afternoon's appointments, and the intendant, Monsieur Martin—a grave, elderly personage with a beaked

nose and round, unwinking eyes like a disapproving owl—
who had still more important business to discuss, were disposed of in a minute or two.

Maman seemed to know precisely what she wanted and
to make her decisions with unvarying assurance. But was
she really listening at all? Tancrède could not help feeling,
too, that she had scarcely more time for him than for the
servants. True, she smiled brilliantly when she saw him,
gave him an affectionate kiss, and inquired with concern
how he had passed the night; but when he replied, with
Dutch literalness, that he had not slept so soundly as the
night before, she smiled again, murmured: "That's splendid, darling!" as she waved him to an armchair (a duke
couldn't sit on a tabouret), and returned at once to her scru-
tiny of her mirror—she was busy dabbing things from little
boxes on her face—and to her chaffing dialogue with Vardes.

After domestic affairs had been settled other people began to arrive. In quick succession Madame de Rohan inter-
viewed her bootmaker, her coachmaker, her florist, a book-
seller who came to solicit the honour of her patronage for a
new collection of gallant poetry, and two of the authors to
be represented therein. These last, breathless with embarrassment, gabbled some sample quatrains for the Duchess's
approval. She smiled at them just as she had at Tancrède,
said: "That's splendid!" in the same tone of amiable abstraction, and dismissed them both before they had a chance to
bore her.

It was not until a lackey announced that Monsieur le
Marquis de Ruvigny was below and craved a word with
Madame la Duchesse that Maman came suddenly to full
attention. She raised her eyebrows and laughed.

"Shall I see him?" she said to Vardes, who scowled as he replied, untruly, that it made no difference to him. "You know, madam, I constrain you in nothing."

"Very well, then," said Maman; "show him up, Gilbert."

As his saviour of the day before made a smiling, self-assured entrance Tancrède looked at him with interest. He had been eager to make inquiries about Monsieur de Ruvigny, but had not known how to begin. Moreover, he could not very well have said anything without confessing his own escapade in the Arsenal gardens, which he and Sidonie had agreed had much better be kept to themselves. What, therefore, was now his confusion to see his new acquaintance clap him on the back and hear him shout, in a loud, cheerful voice: "And how's our young hero this morning? I give you my word, madam, he's his father over again. I swear, if I'd not happened on the scene when I did, he'd have started two duels at once for a fair lady's sake!"

There was no help for it, the story must out; and it lost nothing in Monsieur de Ruvigny's spirited narration.

Tancrède glanced nervously at his mother; fortunately she seemed to be amused. Since Ruvigny's coming her manner was quite altered. Strangely enough, she'd given him her hand almost as though she were not sure whether she wanted to or not; but after that she paid little heed to anyone else. Monsieur de Vardes made one or two vain attempts to regain her ear; then he rose, with the male equivalent to a flounce, and took ungracious leave of his hostess.

Maman was unruffled by her gallant's bad temper. No sooner had he left the room than she sent both her maids away. Tancrède got up, rather expecting to be sent away, too; but his mother looked at him as if she'd only just realized he was there, and said: "Ah, my dear, I want you and Monsieur de Ruvigny to be friends!"

"We're that already, aren't we, Monsieur le Duc?" said Ruvigny; and Tancrède, blushing, replied that he hoped so.

From the ensuing conversation he learned that the soldier was just home from the German campaign—where was France *not* fighting this summer?—during which he had commanded a cavalry regiment under the Duc d'Enghien. He gave them a vivid account of the battle of Nördlingen in Bavaria—of the crushing success of the French troops and the appalling slaughter that had bought it. "No, thank the Lord! I wasn't wounded—or not badly enough to matter: who'd count a sabre scratch or two? The fighting's still not quite over, you know. I'd meant to stay with the army a bit longer, but as soon as I heard the news about you and your son, madam, I knew where my first duty lay. So near the end it wasn't hard to get leave. I struck out alone for Paris as soon as I could—and here I am, ready to offer myself to Monsieur le Duc. Dear madam, it's like old times to be with the Rohans again! Lord! but it takes me back . . . I don't suppose you are aware of it, young man, but I knew and loved your father dearly years before you were born. In fact, all I've learned of the art of war I owe to him. That's why I felt, when he laid down his arms and went into exile, there was nothing for me to do but follow him to Venice. And ever since then I've been more or less in the family's service. Their fortunes are as dear to me as my own. Sometimes I've wondered why I didn't simply don their livery and be done with it! To tell the truth, 'tisn't my fault that we're not even more closely connected. If it hadn't been for these plaguy continual summer campaigns, I might have persuaded Mademoiselle de Rohan to marry me—and then all these troubles could have been avoided: we'd not be in the fix we are today."

Maman pinched her lips together, looking all of a sudden alarmingly severe.

"None of that, Ruvigny! Remember, I've strictly forbidden—"

Ruvigny laughed unresentfully.

"My fortune may be no better than Chabot's, but at least I belong to the right church. However, 'tis no matter; what's done can't be undone. The question now is—"

"A propos of your marrying,"—Maman seemed determined to interrupt again—"it's high time you were thinking of settling down, my friend. How old are you? Past your fortieth birthday, I fancy. I've a great mind to take a hand in finding you a suitable bride this winter. I've given the subject some thought already. There's, for instance, the daughter of Tallemant, the banker. The child's not at all bad looking—I've seen her at Charenton—and they say her old father's so rich he stuffs his mattresses with mortgages! Surely you might do worse . . ."

But Ruvigny only laughed harder.

"No, madam, no! I beg you'll desist. Nothing, believe me, is further from my mind than matrimony. Since Margot wouldn't have me, I vow I'll die a bachelor. I'm here, dear lady, simply to make myself useful. How can I best serve Monsieur le Duc? Would he like lessons in fencing and riding, I wonder? They might not come amiss to a budding courtier. My time, I assure you, is entirely his. You know, my Lord,"—turning to Tancrède once more—"I've a particular interest in your welfare, for 'twas I gave the Duchess the clue that led to your discovery."

Here was news indeed! Tancrède's eyes asked his mother for confirmation; she nodded assent, but said briskly: "I suppose, my dear, we must be grateful. But after all, in the circumstances, it was the least he could do for us."

Since she did not offer to enlarge on this cryptic explanation, he was left to wonder, as often before, why grown-up people said so many things they only half meant—or, worse, that seemed to mean one thing and really meant another. . . . Were Maman and Monsieur de Ruvigny enemies or friends? It was impossible to tell. She treated the soldier with an odd mixture of familiarity and mock-severity: they seemed to know each other very well, but not to trust each other altogether. When they talked it was as if they were crossing swords lightly in a kind of experimental duel.

Tancrède had plenty of time to meditate on what puzzled him, for his elders now embarked on a discussion of Madame de Rohan's preparations for the lawsuit, which was not only long but hard to understand—and the parts he could understand sounded dreadfully dull. What brought it to an end at last was Maman's glancing at the clock, jumping up from the dressing table in a swirl of laces and sighing silk, and exclaiming that she would have to fly—they were due at the Hôtel de Sully in a quarter of an hour.

It was only then Tancrède learned that he and his mother were engaged to dine with his grandmother, the Dowager Madame de Sully, who lived most of the year at her castle of Villebon near Chartres, but had driven into town especially to see her grandson.

"I can't think how I could have been so careless of the time. You know what my mother is like if one's even ten seconds late for a meal—I dare say she'll hardly speak to us!

Ruvigny, don't leave me, there's a good man! Maman has always been fond of you; she won't be half so formidable if you come, too."

Happily the Hôtel de Sully was just around the corner in the rue Saint Antoine. Before they knew it the carriage was entering a fine stone courtyard and drawing up before the sculptured façade of the biggest and grandest house Tancrède had yet seen. The boy had scarcely time to worry about what was coming, or even to wonder how it was that he had a grandmother of whom he had never heard. (Because Grandpapa Sully was dead, he had naturally supposed Grand-maman must be dead also.)

A pair of flunkeys received the party at the door and escorted them up a waste of stone stairs. As they mounted Maman explained to her son that the place belonged to her nephew, the young Duc de Sully, who was, alas! "on the other side. We don't speak any more. I hate coming here! I must say, if Grand-maman had the slightest consideration for my feelings, she'd not subject us to such an ordeal. But old people are so set in their ways: she's stopped at the Hôtel de Sully all her life and I suppose, at eighty-four, she doesn't see any reason to change."

Tancrède had never seen anyone in the least like his grandmother. They found her in a small dark cabinet, hung with fading tapestries, at what seemed to be the top of the house, seated in a high-backed, throne-like chair, and dressed in black satin trimmed with fine Flanders lace and an open ruff, such as ladies had worn at the court of Henri IV and Marie de Médicis; her snowy hair was brushed up under a sort of triangular frilled bonnet. Rachel de Cochefilet, Duchesse douairière de Sully, did not, even from a child's point of view, betray her full age. The tall, spare figure was only slightly stooped; the chiselled profile had lost none of its fine-drawn distinction; her keen blue eyes, wise with experience though they were, were not an old lady's eyes. She seemed, however, to have faded somewhat, like the tapestries, till she resembled less a living woman than the portrait drawing of that woman, framed on the wall behind her stately head. And her voice when she spoke, though deep and firm, with none of the cracks and quavers associated with extreme old age, sounded remote as an oracle's.

She surveyed her daughter bleakly and remarked at once, without preamble: "The filet will be ruined."

Maman, strangely subdued, murmured that she was exceedingly sorry and then moved forward gracefully to present Tancrède and Monsieur de Ruvigny.

Grand-maman gave an unexpected high cackle of laughter as she extended her thin old hand for the latter to kiss and muttered something under her breath that sounded like "So the dog's returned to his vomit!" (But of course it could not have been really; that would be too rude; besides, what did it mean?) Tancrède also kissed her hand, trying his best to imitate the nonchalant ease of the officer's sweeping bow, and not to show how frightened he was. The dowager peered at him sharply, then shook her head and sighed: "The child's a thorough Dutchman, Marguerite!"

"He's been in Paris only two days, Maman. Naturally, it takes a little time . . ."

"Well, well," said Grand-maman, smiling—which was by no means so reassuring as she perhaps meant it to be, for her teeth (she still had all of them) were long, blue-white, and distinctly carnivorous—"I dare say he'll improve. Be a good boy, my dear; do as your elders bid; and no doubt you'll turn out to be a credit to us in the end. Now shall we go into dinner?"

In the dining saloon, which was as dark and diminutive as the cabinet where they had been received, they were joined by still another relative one had not known about: Philippe de Béthune, Comte de Selles, who was Grand-maman's brother-in-law and therefore, Tancrède supposed, his own great-uncle. Uncle de Selles was likewise an octogenarian, an odd, dwarfish figure with pipestem legs, heavy-lidded eyes that appeared to see more than they were intended to, and a disconcerting habit of tapping the floor with an ebony stick to emphasize his remarks.

As they prepared to sit down to table Grand-maman struck Ruvigny a smart blow on the shoulder with her folded fan and said: "Ha, my friend! Will you give the benediction?"

Rather to Tancrède's surprise, the Marquis obliged at once with a long, pious prayer, which apparently he had had ready at the tip of his tongue. Madame de Sully then motioned her grandson to the seat on her right, with Uncle de Selles on his other side.

A meal with this pair of antique autocrats was a trying affair. Not only had Tancrède his usual difficulties with the food and the cutlery, but it seemed that whenever he'd finally succeeded in preparing a morsel and conveying it to his mouth, either one or the other of his redoubtable neighbours would dart a question at him concerning his tastes and pursuits—and he'd have to stop eating to answer.

There was no respite until, as one had known it would,

the talk turned to the impending lawsuit and its protagonist was allowed, for the time being, to lapse into blessed obscurity. It was clear that both Grand-maman and Uncle de Selles shared Maman's opinion of Sister Margot's behaviour and were looking forward with lively anticipation to her defeat at the hands of Parliament. At the same time neither of them expressed any anger with Chabot, the cause of it all.

"Can't say I blame the young fellow," remarked Uncle de Selles, in his squeaky, little, old voice. "You couldn't expect any man worth his salt to turn down such a golden opportunity. Damme, I'd have done the same thing myself if I'd stood in his shoes!" And he pounded his stick once more as he exploded into a volley of senile chuckles.

"Besides," added the ancestress thoughtfully, "I never believed he had much to do with it anyhow. The whole business, I'll wager, was managed by Margot with Enghien to help her. She was a headstrong creature from the first. Ah, Marguerite, if only you'd taken my advice when she was younger and whipped some sense of obedience into her! I've always maintained, there's no better way to train up a child in the way it should go: thrash 'em soundly night and morning, purge 'em once a week on general principles—and you'll have a dutiful son or daughter."

Maman agreed, a trifle absent-mindedly. She had, Tancrède noticed, been in a state of voluntary partial eclipse ever since her arrival at the Hôtel de Sully, contenting herself at table with a simple stool instead of the armchair her rank entitled her to, and seeming anxious to avoid any topic that might provoke a controversy. Eventually it developed that a measure at least of her docility was due to her preoccupation with other matters: when dinner was over she made their excuses winningly and as soon as they were safe in the carriage once more she turned to her companions to announce with satisfaction: "There! *That's* done! Now for it, my son —we've got to begin our real work for the day."

That afternoon remained in Tancrède's memory as undoubtedly the most gruelling of his Paris experiences. Through the brooding, moist August heat they made what appeared to be a complete circle of the city, stopping at the house of each of the relatives who had consented to sign the petition. According to Maman, this was a ceremony by no means to be dispensed with: the tribe had a right to meet their new chief. "For that's what it amounts to, my dear— young as you are, the reigning Duc de Rohan is head of the family. Don't forget to make your best bow and kiss all the ladies' hands. And show your teeth as much as you can; that always makes a good impression. I've noticed you don't very often smile, but when you do the effect is exquisite. Now here we are at the Hôtel de Montbazon. You remember— the old man who fetched you in from Saint Denis. He's an excellent soul, but as narrow-minded as they make 'em, which is odd when you consider the kind of woman he married. His wife is a savage! The less said about her morals the better, and as for her looks—though some people pretend to admire them—all I can say is, if I had a bosom like that, I'd make at least an attempt to hide . . . dear Marie, how are you? I've never seen you so handsome! What a ravishing new gown! Maître Thomas, I suppose? I vow I'm desperately jealous—he never showed *me* that delicious swooning blue taffeta!"

Long before Maman had got to the end of her list Tancrède grew tired and bewildered by the numbers of names and faces he had to relate to one another and try to keep straight in his mind. Sustained by his mother's relentless intention, he moved from paneled chamber to paneled chamber, paying his respects to an endless succession of languid ladies on golden beds. . . . One could but marvel why their hostesses without exception appeared to have retired fully dressed in the middle of the day, and then asked all the gentlemen they knew to come to see them.

Nothing in his life in Holland had prepared him for the complicated ritual of the *ruelles* and the Précieuses enthroned in them. (He found out soon enough, though, what the bedroom railings, which had puzzled him at the Hôtel de Rohan, were for: they served to separate the sheep from the goats; it was a mark of special favour to be admitted to the cramped spaces beyond the barrier.)

Manfully young Monsieur de Rohan performed his duty, bending over lily-white hand after lily-white hand, murmuring the polite phrases he had been coached to deliver, and smiling continually till he felt his smiles had utterly lost their meaning and he feared his face might crack from the strain. Presently the pageant became a bright-coloured blur: afterwards it was hard for him to recall which of the painted and perfumed beauties was which: was the Princesse de Guémenée the one who had chestnut ringlets and a lisp, and the Duchesse de Montbazon the raven-haired Amazon with a mouth like a cherry-purple gash in her waxen face—or t'other way round?

The clan, as a whole, received him kindly, though Tancrède suspected he was as much an object of curiosity to them as of affection: so might they perhaps have greeted the appearance of some fascinating new addition to the royal menagerie at the Louvre. As time went on he became heartily sick of being patted and poked—of having the ladies scream with joy when Maman, as she invariably did, called attention to his silver lock, and the gentlemen exclaim triumphantly they'd like to know how Chabot expected to get around *that!* (There was another cause of misgiving: was it not more than possible that this mushroom enthusiasm had its source less in love for the newcomer than in hatred for a scheming adventurer who had wormed his way into the sacred circle of the Rohans? For these were not Huguenots, moved by the passionate piety of the persecuted—save for his own particular branch, Tancrède learned that the family was solidly Catholic.)

The one bright spot in an afternoon of fatigue and confusion was their brief halt at the Hôtel de Chevreuse. Here, for a wonder, the golden bed was empty; for Cousin Marie de Rohan, the Duchesse de Chevreuse, its rightful occupant, was, Maman explained, in exile in Flanders. The Duke, her husband, an affable old fellow, greeted his youthful kinsman and then mercifully let him alone. (He was deep in a game of piquet with his valet.) Moreover, his nephew, the Duc de Guise—who also appeared to be wifeless—asked Tancrède to go out to the stables, while their elders were gossiping, to look at a new shipment of horses from England. There they inspected as well a litter of beautiful silver-grey Italian whippets Guise said he had given his uncle.

"You can have one, if you like, as soon as they're old enough to be weaned," said the good-natured scion of the House of Lorraine, who seemed even more cordial than Monsieur de Chevreuse and equally indisposed to ask impertinent questions: the young dukes parted the best of friends.

It was late when they left the Hôtel de Chevreuse, but Maman, weary but indomitable, declared that there was one last name on her list they dared not overlook: Tancrède's Aunt Anne, Mademoiselle de Rohan, Papa's sole surviving sister, was the only member of the family who had refused to sign the petition.

"She's an old maid and a scholar, with her nose always buried in books—and fearfully set in her ways! I can't help hoping, though, my dear, that if you succeed in making a good impression . . ."

Tancrède was by this time so deflated that he felt gloomily certain he would be unable to make any impression at all.

Unlike every other lady he had been taken to call upon, Aunt de Rohan possessed neither a paneled chamber nor a golden bed with a railing. In fact, she did not even have a house of her own, but lodged in a small, crowded apartment in a narrow street near the river, surrounded by half-blind cats and stuffed birds and a dusty litter of books and manuscripts—some of which, Maman averred, while they were waiting for their hostess to come in, were in Latin and Hebrew. And Aunt de Rohan herself, despite her nephew's fears, turned out to be a gentle, near-sighted old woman with grey corkscrew curls and glasses so thick that her eyes behind them appeared to be made of glass also. She was, alas! very deaf and spoke in tones so low as to be all but inaudible, varied by an occasional loud, unmodulated phrase such as people who cannot hear their own voices often let fall.

Her manners were unexpectedly gracious: she saluted

her guests politely, plied them with sweetmeats, offered them wine (which was fetched by a tottering witch of a maid as deaf as her mistress), and seemed genuinely pleased to see them.

Tancrède, sitting a little apart in a daze of exhaustion, paid scant heed to the chat between her and his mother. It was only as the latter rose to go that one speech came through clearly, cutting across his tired mind like a lightning flash of alarm:

"Dear Marguerite," said Aunt de Rohan, kissing Maman affectionately on both cheeks, "I dare say it's true. Indeed, if you say so, I'm sure that it is. But I owe it to my honour and conscience to tell you that the whole story's quite new to me. *To be frank with you, child, I never heard of Tancrède before!*"

V

Tancrède was long to remember the date of the twenty-ninth of August, for that was the day on which he presented his mother's petition to Parliament. Very early in the morning the train of carriages set forth from the Place Royale: Cousin de Montbazon, with whom the boy rode, had succeeded in assembling most of the male members of both families, the Rohans and the Béthunes, so that they made really quite an impressive show clattering down to the river, across the Pont au Change with its double row of houses, along the rue de la Barillerie to the gloomy gate flanked by pepper-pot towers, and into the big courtyard of the Palais itself.

The courtyard was crowded; so was the grand staircase inside; but Monsieur de Montbazon was accompanied by so many advance guards and lackeys that people seemed to melt away at the approach of his party, who were thus enabled to reach the top of the stairs with the calm inevitability of cream rising to the surface of a bottle of milk. They made their way through the busy hive of the Galérie Marchande, where merchants had their booths and plied a thriving trade in silks and velvets, costly laces, precious stones, hats, masks, fans, gloves of scented leather, books, and pictures. It seemed strange to Tancrède that business should be tolerated on the very threshold of the august law-courts of the city, but Cousin de Montbazon told him that for centuries it had been so. The room was full of ladies who had come to look at what there was to buy, and of gentlemen who had, apparently, come to look at the ladies. Indeed, Cousin de Guémenée temporarily deserted his duty to exchange a few quick whispered words with a fascinating little person in bright green silk, who hid her eyes coquettishly behind her fan and burst into gales of nervous laughter at everything he said.

Behind the Galérie Marchande lay the dusty stone vastness of the Salle des Pas Perdus—Hall of Lost Steps— "What a funny name!" thought Tancrède—the assembly room where lawyers met their clients. Here the noise was even worse; it sounded like the roar of the sea; and the place was so jammed that it seemed as though it must be impossible to cleave a passage through it. But again, as on the stairs, as soon as the majestic old governor showed himself people fell back respectfully to create a little free space about him.

Two men wearing short black gowns and curious four-pointed black bonnets rushed up at once to Cousin de Montbazon and begged to be presented to the Duc de Rohan; these, it appeared, were the family's legal representatives. Monsieur Joubert was as short and round as Monsieur Pucelle was tall and lanky: both broke into simultaneous torrents of French, so rapid and voluble that Tancrède would have had great difficulty in following what they said, even if the terms they were using had been familiar to him.

There ensued a lengthy and almost totally incomprehensible conversation between the lawyers and the gentlemen, during which there was nothing to be done except stand still, with what patience one could muster, and try at least to *look* intelligent.

Finally Cousin de Montbazon brought the colloquy to an end by nodding his hoary head and exclaiming in his resonant voice: "Very well, then! If the Chambre de l'Edit is in session, let's delay matters no longer."

Plump little Joubert thrust a roll of parchment into Tancrède's hands; the procession reformed, headed by the two dukes, and proceeded through a door on the right into a still larger room, all red and gilt, hung with blue velvet embroidered with gold fleurs-de-lys—the Great Hall of the Parliament of Paris.

It was over in a moment. Tancrède had barely time to observe the intimidating row of grave councillors, bearded, bewigged, in their sable robes, before the registrar barked out a few words of inquiry; Joubert and Pucelle launched into renewed volubilities; then Tancrède was pushed forward and bidden to hand his roll of parchment to an usher, which he did; the Chambre de l'Edit bowed to the nobility, the nobility to the Chambre de l'Edit—and that was all there was to it.

What he never forgot was his encounter, on their way out of the hall, with Monsieur de Chabot and his friends, on their way in to present their rival petition. As it happened, the two groups met in the doorway and recoiled from one another, repelled by a mutual shock. Tancrède had never seen his brother-in-law before, but he needed no-one to tell him the name of the mincing young man with wide-open eyes fringed by long, curling black lashes, and an air of brittle elegance verging on fragility. (It was not hard to believe that this delicate creature was renowned rather for his prowess in the ballroom than on the battlefield.)

For an edgy moment the principals stared at each other

without uttering a word. Chabot raked his enemy up and
down with what was meant to be a withering glance. Tancrède did not flinch under it: he returned the look squarely,
with a kind of instinctive disdain, while inside him rose a
cold, still anger, entirely unlike the helpless rages he'd suffered when his schoolmates had teased him in Leyden.
Though it was easier to control its outward manifestations,
the new feeling stirred him as the old had never done. Now,
he told himself, he knew how much there was at stake; now
he felt as a man and a Rohan should. . . .

As he stood there, hands clenched, pulses pounding to an
unaccustomed rhythm, he became conscious that their re-
spective followers were beginning to ruffle up ominously:
there was a tremor of indignation, a muttering, a faint rattle
of swords in their scabbards. . . . But for the awe-inspiring
presence of Monsieur le Gouverneur some sort of trouble
might well have arisen between them. At this point, sensing
the danger, old Cousin de Montbazon rapped out a stern
word of command and swept off imperiously at the head of
his troop.

Later in the day the lawyers arrived at the Hôtel de
Rohan with the gratifying news that the Chabots' petition
had been flatly refused. Madame de Rohan's, on the other
hand, had been at least partly successful, for she had been
granted authority to appoint a warden for her son. As for
the main point at issue, Tancrède's right to his title, that
would have to be fought out in court as soon as Parliament
reassembled after its annual holiday, which began next
week and lasted till Martinmas. The great question now,
according to Messieurs Joubert and Pucelle, was, who was
to try it. The Rohans had asked to have the hearing in front

of the Chambre de l'Edit, as a Protestant body sure to be favourable to them. The Chabots, it appeared, were equally anxious to come before the Grand Chambre, the twenty-five councillors of the Superior Court, who would undoubtedly be far more susceptible to the influence of Monsieur le Duc d'Enghien and his clique. The sole means of settling this vexing dispute was to appeal to the Queen's council, and that, the bonneted ones declared, they intended to do very shortly.

Tancrède hardly knew what to think of it all till Maman, giving him his cue, professed herself delighted by the turn things had taken and dismissed the lawyers with extravagant thanks and a dazzlingly meaningless smile. However, she was distinctly less pleased the following morning when the warden, one Jacob Joly—who had been chosen some time before in consultation with Cousin de Montbazon—presented himself for his initial interview.

After due consideration Maman had decided to receive this latest recruit to their cause in the library, otherwise known as the Green Cabinet, a book-lined chamber adjoining her private apartments that displayed the glacial neatness of a room seldom used. (Her own rooms were invariably in a state of rather splendid disorder.) Tancrède, who had his breakfast here every morning, was partial to the Green Cabinet: he had often glanced longingly at the rows of leather volumes stamped in gold and wondered when he would find time to read them. There was also, over the mantel, a fine portrait of his father in armour, wearing the blue ribbon of a knight of the Order of the Holy Ghost, which he was wont to study at intervals, seeking, not very successfully, to trace some resemblance between his own immature features and the high forehead, prominent nose, and heavy-lidded dark eyes—so wise, so brooding—of the first Duc de Rohan.

Today the remains of the meal had been scarcely removed when Madame de Rohan, fully dressed at what was, for her, an unheard of hour, made a bustling entrance, followed by Rondeau and old Martin, the intendant, and set the stage for the scene to come. Five minutes later she was discovered, with her son beside her, seated at the desk, pen in hand, gravely considering a sheaf of papers the secretary had just handed her. When the lawyers were announced she looked up with a preoccupied smile that increased to benevolence as she gave them her hand and bade them be seated.

But it soon became evident, even to Tancrède, that Maître Joly was not to be subjugated or imposed upon by ordinary means. A fair young man, with hair so light as to look almost white, a plentiful sprinkling of freckles on his broad, blunt countenance, and stern blue eyes that glinted behind his glasses with a daunting intelligence that belied their shortsightedness, he showed himself immediately to be a person of parts—enterprising, sagacious, devoted to his duty. And, unfortunately for Madame de Rohan, his conception of that seemed to include a brisk inquiry into his client's personal financial affairs.

The great Rohan fortune, it went without saying, was untouched and inviolable until such time as the succession could be legally established. Nevertheless it developed, with unpleasant rapidity, that after the Duke's death Maman, up to her ears in debt, had agreed to cede her share of the estate to her daughter in return for the liquidation of her dotal and dower rights, which included a handsome income, divers goods and chattels, and an item of fifty thousand crowns in cash.

Very well: the Duchess had her income, and the goods —but what had become of the fifty thousand crowns?

Nobody in the Green Cabinet appeared to be able to explain. Maman talked a great deal, hazarded various unlikely suppositions, appealed to her servants for help. . . . "Martin, wasn't it *you* bade me buy those farms in Picardy last spring?" And, "Rondeau, my dear man, I'm almost positive that if you could just lay your hands on that other account book . . ."

At the end of a quarter of an hour's futile feinting and deploying of her scattered resources she was forced to retreat to a position where it was ignominiously clear that (A) the money was gone, every penny, yet (B) money would be needed, a great deal of it in fact, in order to wage the battle in court.

"In the circumstances, madam," Maître Joly summed up severely, "the only thing for you to do is to try, by appealing to Parliament, to revoke your donation to Madame de Chabot. That, I don't mind telling you, will be a difficult matter—a most difficult matter indeed. Anybody can give things away, but it takes something close to a miracle to recover them. I must say, it's a thousand pities you were ever persuaded—but that's neither here nor there now. As a further step we must request a grant from the estate of, say, twenty thousand crowns to defray my Lord's expenses until such time as the suit comes to trial. There ought not to be much trouble about it. I'll make application at once to the proper authorities . . . assuming, madam, of course, that you agree to the proposal?"

Maman assented graciously; she was agreeable to everything; let Maître Joly and the lawyers arrange it to suit themselves. They were men, and men, she implied, always knew best. Fragile and innocent—since her attempt to play the woman of affairs had so signally failed—she turned on belatedly her full battery of feminine charms, in an effort to convince by more obvious methods.

Maître Joly, however, remained proof against blandishments as he had been against play-acting: it was plain he thought her a sadly silly woman. Shortly afterwards he took his leave with a brusque "Madam, good day!" and "Your servant, my Lord!" and bowed himself out, bleakly intelligent to the last.

Thenceforth, although he and the lawyers met almost daily at the Hôtel de Rohan—making the most of the few precious weeks of Parliament's recess—neither mother nor son was taken into their confidence.

Meanwhile Tancrède settled down by degrees to his new life. He was so young and so anxious to please that it did not take him long to adapt himself to the conditions, nor did he question, save occasionally in his own thoughts, the necessity for them. No doubt all French boys of his station had to do the things he did. . . . It was a strange existence, at once crowded and empty, studded with social obligations, yet essentially lonesome.

His mornings were occupied by studies of quite a different sort from the grammar and calculus, Latin and Bible history, of his schooldays in Leyden. Although Maman and Cousin de Montbazon had decided that he was too young, and still too little proficient in French, to attend Monsieur Benjamin's celebrated academy, he was set none the less to acquiring the polish and graces expected of a young gentleman at the court of the Regent. He was given lessons in deportment and dancing; learned to play the lute after a fashion and—also after a fashion—to chat Italian, which, according to Maman, since the accession to power of Cardinal Mazarin had become a necessary accomplishment.

Ruvigny was his master in fencing and riding. Maître Joly himself undertook to instruct him in more serious subjects, of which the main requisites seemed to be smatterings of history and geography. After his tasks for the warden were done Tancrède often lingered on by himself in the library, where at last he felt free to browse as he liked. Papa's collection was catholic enough, comprising the best classic and modern authors. But what surprised and delighted the boy most was to find—why had no-one told him before?—that Papa was an author, too.

Fascinated, he poured over the pages of the recently published *Memoirs;* of *The Voyage of Monsieur le Duc de Rohan made in the year* 1600 *through Italy, Germany, the Low Countries, England and Scotland;* of *The Perfect Captain, or Abridgement of the Gallic Wars and Commentaries of Caesar, with some Remarks* . . . dry enough, many of them, in all conscience, but of consuming interest to the writer's son. And there was Papa himself, in the gold frame over the mantel, observing his heir with an expression that, as time went on, appeared to grow warmer and more sympathetic. There was even, in certain lights, the hint of a smile about the firm lips under the perfect bow of his waxed moustache . . . or, if that were perhaps too much to claim, one might still say that Papa looked as though he might be *thinking* of smiling!

From these solitary hours in the Green Cabinet, and his
detailed and ardent conning of its former owner's works,
Tancrède tried his best to reconstruct the personality of a
man he'd never known. Side by side with this attempt
there was kindled in his young heart the steady flame of a
double resolve: to be worthy of the father who'd bred him,
and of the religion that was the passion of that father's life.

Aside from his work his time was his own—often more of
it than he knew what to do with. His mother he saw com-
paratively little, except for half an hour each morning when
he attended her *lever*. Even then they were never alone.
Monsieur de Vardes was always there, too, and the servants,
besides a whole string of tradesmen and visitors. That was
a great disappointment: he had so looked forward to *having*
a mother, to being with someone he could love with his
whole self, and who would love him in the same way.

Not that Maman failed to show him affection. She kissed
him whenever they met, often several times; asked how he
did and if there were anything he wanted; made, not in-
frequently, almost feverish protestations of pride and devotion. It was just that there was not much room in her life
for any boy of fourteen, even her own. She was seldom at
home; and when she was there it seemed as if she were
always resting up after something, or getting ready to go out
to something else. Her schedule included a devastating
round of indispensable futilities: balls at the Palais Royal
and the Luxembourg, concerts at the Tuileries, plays and
ballet performances at the Petit Bourbon or the Hôtel de
Bourgogne. How could one expect—or even want—to be
included among the guests at such strictly adult festivities?

Madame de Rohan went driving also, these fine early

autumn afternoons, with her gallants under the browning leaves of the Cours la Reine. And in the evenings, if nothing was especially planned, she would entertain the young men at supper in the crimson-hung banquet saloon of the Hôtel de Rohan. As the weeks slipped by Tancrède grew used to these almost nightly receptions. He supposed that all great ladies in Paris must give them; it did not occur to him to wonder why Maman had no women friends.

As for the young men themselves, he grew used to them, too, and came to like them well enough. Only Monsieur de Vardes still held aloof and continued to regard him with what appeared to be plain dislike. This—since Vardes was palpably his mother's favourite—was hard to understand; but where friendship was so pointedly refused, Tancrède scorned to make advances. Maman herself often paid little attention to her guests. They came and went as they pleased; she was glad to see them arrive, but never strove to detain them. Yet one had an odd feeling that she needed an audience—that, if the vapid and noisy crew were not there, she would hardly know what to do. It was as if she could not exist without them . . . more troubling still, as if she used them as a defence between herself and the person who had the best right to be near her.

Once a week, regularly every Sunday, the Duchess and her son made the trip to Charenton; and there, just as regularly, they found themselves surrounded by a throng of fanatical partisans. It became ever clearer to Tancrède that he and his case were supremely important to the Huguenots, in whose memories the deeds of his father were still as fresh as though they'd taken place yesterday. The prospect that they might be led once more to victory by a Rohan duke filled them with new hope and a fierce ambition to recover their ancients rights and privileges.

Maman, inhaling the incense of their flattery, would swell with vicarious pride; her ambition, too, at these times was boundless—even though she pretended to hide it and made a show of laughing at the grim old warriors and their fervent zeal for the cause. . . . "Poor darlings! It's quite touching, really; they take it all so fearfully in earnest!" (For it was not smart at court to belong to the religion.) Yet it was precisely then that Tancrède felt closest to his mother; they were united by the singleness and passion of their purpose.

There were many hours, just the same, when he was left to amuse himself as best he was able. In the very beginning he felt singularly depressed by his loneliness, and the fact that, with a houseful of people, there was really nobody for him to talk to. The valets and lackeys all had their appointed tasks and little enough time to spare from them. Tancrède's tentative efforts to start a conversation with one or two of the many young men who waited upon him were met by uncomprehending stares and a monosyllabic servility that effectively crushed his desire to establish friendly relations. Servants, it seemed, *weren't* people.

Nor were others outside of the Rohans' tight little circle. That he ascertained, once for all, not a week after coming to Paris. He happened to be out driving by himself, and the carriage had come to a halt in a traffic jam on the Pont Neuf. Tancrède was staring, spellbound, at the lively crowd of pedlars and jugglers, mountebanks and pamphleteers, who were jostling one another and crying their wares with brassy persistence, when his eye was caught by a boy about his own age who looked so much like Jacob that at first he thought it must be he. . . . A moment later he saw his mistake; this one was smaller and younger, dressed in greasily filthy rags —a waif no doubt, or a strolling player's brat: there were many such on the Pont Neuf. Still the resemblance was startling, and in spite of his rags the boy looked so cheerful and jolly that Tancrède felt impelled to seek contact with him.

Leaning forward, he called through the window of the carriage to La Mestairie, who was riding postilion, to say so.

The equerry had cultivated the art of concealing his feelings too long and too sedulously to be caught off guard: the blank, good looking face remained blank, though his eyebrows shot up as he replied: "That dirty little fellow over there? Why, he's a beggar, my Lord!"

"I don't care if he is—I want to speak to him!"

"Impossible, my Lord!"

The carriage was already beginning to move again. Suddenly Tancrède was gripped by a feeling of indignation: was he, or was he not, the Duc de Rohan?

"La Mestairie," he cried sharply, "I command you to do as I say!"

And then, of course, La Mestairie did. But it was no good, after all. The boy obviously thought, when the grooms brought him over, that he was going to be flogged or thrown into prison, or worse—he could do nothing but blubber with fear. Even after Tancrède had reassured him he remained perfectly unintelligible in some guttural dialect of his own. There was nothing to do except tell La Mestairie to give him a gold piece, which he seized and bit before diving into the crowd without a word of thanks to his benefactor.

"Drive on," said Tancrède, crestfallen against the ducal cushions. So beggars weren't people either. . . .

It took him some weeks to find his way to old Ursule, his mother's waiting woman, a Bretonne born, who spoke French with an accent more marked than his own. Ursule was so old that it was impossible to guess when she had been born—older than Grand-maman even—; she appeared to have got to some timeless realm where age did not matter any more. A frail, tiny creature in cap and shawl, she passed her days in a cabinet—scarcely more than a cupboard —off Maman's dressing-room, bent over her sewing. Such small, fine stitches she took! And never once while she talked did she drop one, or raise her round, jet-bright black eyes from her work.

Like the majority of her race, the old woman had been nurtured on fairy-tales, fanciful legends of the dragons and witches and sorcerers that used to inhabit the dark Armorican forests. These she retold dramatically, without claiming to believe them. Hardly more credible to her audience of one were her accounts—purported to be true—of the deeds of the Seven Saints of Brittany; of strange superstitions connected with stone menhirs and dolmens, and the cult of the dead. (Did Ursule really think that Death himself was a spirit called Ankou, driver of a phantom coach that picked up souls by the wayside?)

But she knew still other stories, whose authenticity was unquestioned, about the heroic past of their province and the noble part played therein by the Rohans.

Tancrède wondered sometimes why none of his relatives seemed to live in Brittany any longer. Most of them had been born there, and all still possessed certain family estates; but as far as one could gather Cousin de Montbazon, Cousin de Guémenée, and the rest rarely stirred out of Paris—or if, by chance, it were necessary for them to leave town for a little, they simply retired to country houses in the immediate neighbourhood. . . . Maman, of course, did not count, as she was not a Rohan born.

Ursule—a snob, like all good old family servants—had a rather poor opinion of the Béthunes, who could not trace their pedigree back, like the Rohans, to an almost mythical antiquity. "They may be descended, as they claim, from the House of Flanders, or they may not: that, my dear, I don't presume to judge." She broke off a thread as she spoke with a vicious snap that somehow indicated her opinion of the aristocratic pretensions of the great Duc de Sully. She herself had been in the household since the days of Tancrède's paternal grandfather, René II, the last Viscount. In her youth she had been maid to his grandmother, that iron great lady, Catherine de Parthenay, and had endured with her the horrors of the siege of La Rochelle during the wars of religion. Breathlessly Tancrède hung upon her words as she described the ordeals and privations of that awful time: how they had waited and waited, through the long frozen winter, for the help from England that never came; and of how Madame de Rohan, old and ill as she was, had refused to give way and had set an example to the garrison, devouring fricassee of shoe leather and soup made of rats with the rest.

"Ah, my little Lord, Madame la Vicomtesse was a woman in a million! She'd have held out till she starved to death, if the men hadn't given up at last. Such ardour, such piety—

all for the sake of what she thought her duty to God! . . . No, my bonny, *I'm* not a Huguenot. None of the Bretons are. But it doesn't behoove us to question the creeds of our betters. I only know I was edified by her example, and shall be till my dying day."

Tancrède could not but think the maid's example even more extraordinary, since she had suffered what the others did, unsustained by their blazing faith in the justice of the Protestant cause. He did not say so, however, since it was obvious Ursule's code would not admit that plebeian stomachs had the same right to feel the pangs of hunger as those of the nobility.

Best of all he liked to hear of the beauties of the land he was to reign over. Lovingly the old woman dwelled, with the nostalgia of one long exiled from her birthplace, on every detail, painting a vivid picture of the fertile fields, the spreading oak forests of the Duchy of Rohan in the south, with its string of stately castles—Blain, Pontivy, Josselin—and the wild Pays de Léon far to the west, where giant breakers beat unceasingly upon a desolate and rockbound coast. (No wonder he loved the sea! It must have been in his blood since before he was born.) Ursule also quoted the family motto, *A Plus!* ("On to More!") and their famous war-cry, *Roy ne puis, duc ne daigne, Rohan suis!* ("King can't be, duke won't deign, Rohan's my name!"), which she told him was almost literally true: Madame la Vicomtesse had flung the words in admonishment at Tancrède's father and had done her best to keep him from accepting the title from the King. "She said 'twould bring him naught but ill luck—and strange to say, from then on till the day he was killed in battle against those ruffians in Switzerland, he had troubles a-plenty, though *his* courage never failed either. Ah, my Lord, you've a race to be proud of there!"

Tancrède agreed with her. His heart thrilled as he listened and realized more and more clearly what a glorious heritage he had. Might he be found worthy to succeed to it!

Another unfailing source of pleasure—when it was available—he presently discovered in the society of Rondeau and his daughter. The better one got to know him, the more apparent it was that the Sieur de Montville was a simple, kindly man, utterly loyal to the interests of his young master. (There was reason for this, to be sure, since, as he himself freely confessed, he owed all he was to the Rohans, having risen through years of faithful service from a humble *valet-de-chambre* to his present position of trust and landed proprietorship.) As for Sidonie, Tancrède soon felt he had found a sister in her. At times, it could not be denied, he still missed Jacob—there were things you couldn't say to any girl—but on the whole her companionship satisfied him. She was simple and kindly, too—and merry withal: after the first greeting, with its punctilious curtsy and "How do you do, my Lord?", they soon forgot differences in rank and chatted and romped as naturally as if they had known each other all their lives.

As a result of their first mishap the children had been warned not to venture out into the city alone, but Rondeau often took them on small excursions—to Notre Dame; to the Pont Neuf, to see the wonderful water-clock of La Samaritaine; to the King's menagerie at the Louvre; even as far afield as the Tuileries gardens, where he treated his charges to ices and cakes at Renard's, the fashionable restaurant.

On bad days they were forced to seek diversion at home, exploring the endless passages and chambers of the Hôtel de Rohan. Here they could speculate, equally endlessly, about the identity of the people in the rows of family portraits gazing woodenly down from the walls of the picture gallery, or admire the collections of arms in the guard room, and the cabinets full of ornaments in the various salons—treasures brought home from the Orient by sea-faring ancestors: ivory chessmen from India, rare Chinese idols of chrysophrase and jade, a marvelous little golden bird with ruby eyes that, when wound up, flapped its wings and sang like a nightingale.

Then Tancrède sometimes spoke to Sidonie of his hopes for the future, and of his fears—which recurred now and again, without warning or reason—that he might fail to live up to all that was expected of him. "For they do expect so much, you know; and I can see in a way they've a right to. How on earth can I ever make myself good enough for—all this?"

Times without number Sidonie assured him, in her soft little voice, that she was certain her friend would grow up to be the finest Rohan of the lot; and just as often Tancrède would realize, with a fresh start of pleasure, that there were some things you couldn't say to any boy.

On the whole, though, his best resource was Ruvigny. Every afternoon at two he took his place in the front window, watching eagerly for the first glimpse of that jaunty red head, the officer's cheerful, beaming smile. Monsieur de Ruvigny was not handsome, and his manners—quite the reverse of those of Maman's young men—were often as blunt as his rough-hewn, undistinguished features; but there was an exuberance about him, an air of delight in himself, in his friends, in life in general, that acted like a tonic on all who met him. His bright blue eyes—which looked as though they were laughing even when his mouth was sober —his hearty handclasp, the unforced joviality of his "Greetings, my Lord! And what have you learned about life in His Majesty's good city of Paris since last I saw you?" seemed to make it impossible to be downcast or doubtful.

Nor could there be any question of his devotion, or of his patience in teaching his pupil—though he admitted himself the boy was unusually apt. As soon as he saw that the Marquis really did not expect a great deal, and had treasures of indulgence stored up for beginners' mistakes, Tancrède got ahead very much faster than he had dreamed he could: he was, they found to their mutual pleasure, one of those fortunate beings who coördinate mind and muscle naturally and appear to learn without effort. Ruvigny even consoled him about his size—for Tancrède often worried over being of less than average stature, fearing that it might have an adverse effect on his future military prowess. "God bless you, no! Half the best fighters I know are little men. In fact, 'tis a drawback in the field to be oversized: you lose in quickness what you gain in bulk, and the bigger you are, the better target for the enemy. Besides, my Lord, who persuaded you that you'd finished growing? You may believe me or not, but when I was your age I came up no farther than your shoulder—yet look at me now!"

The argument was impressive: the Marquis was six feet tall, with a deep chest and broad shoulders, and the easy carriage of a man who'd known how to make the most of his natural advantages.

During the hours of instruction he kept strictly to business, but in the guard room, relaxing over a mug of ale after a bout with the foils or a brisk canter in the Cours Saint Antoine, Ruvigny revealed himself as likewise a teller of tales. He had had, up to now, a richly adventurous life. Tancrède discovered one day with awe that his hero had even killed a man—the celebrated bravo and bully Bois d'Ennemetz—in a duel in Venice. "Not that I'm proud of that, mind you. I was a young fool in those days. Your good father raked me over the coals for it then—and he was quite right. Ah, if only I'd set myself after his pattern, I'd have fewer regrets to plague me now!"

With keener enjoyment he liked to narrate the details of his many years with the Rohans. One question led to another: it was not long before Tancrède had the whole story of the events leading up to his own birth—Maman's surreptitious journey to Paris, and her secret confinement at the house of a friend, hidden away in what was little more than a garret for fear of Cardinal Richelieu and his spies. . . . Madame la Duchesse, said Ruvigny, had risen magnificently to the challenge of fate: what fortitude, what resolution, she'd shown in her hour of trial! None of her family was there to help her except her daughter Margot—not then or ever, Tancrède was made to feel, much of a comfort. "Of course I was with her, my Lord—but what could I do? A young soldier without money or influence. I've often thought since we'd have been lost without Monsieur de Candale. You've heard of him, haven't you? He was your father's best friend, who cared for him so much that he even followed the family into exile in Italy. To be sure, I went with them, too, but I was a nobody, while the Duc de

Candale was one of the greatest noblemen at court, a peer of the realm, eldest son and heir to old Epernon himself. When it became plain that your father could not go to Paris just then, Candale offered at once to make the trip in his stead, so that your mother would not be alone. He was a good man—none better—though never the equal of Monsieur le Duc as a soldier." (Ruvigny always spoke as though no-one but his former patron had a right to that title.) "I wish you had known him, my Lord. He died the year after your father did. There never was a finer gentleman, nor a truer friend. It was Candale who found the house where you were hidden, hired the nurse to suckle you, made all the arrangements just as your father would have done if he'd been there."

Tancrède hearkened attentively to everything he was told. It was all absorbingly interesting, but there were some points in Ruvigny's story he felt he did not quite understand. Why, for instance, had Maman gone to Paris *enceinte,* instead of waiting till she could travel in her usual health? Could the Sultan of Turkey have been in so great a hurry to sell Cyprus? Why, even if she and Papa were afraid of Richelieu—everyone had been, more or less, in those days—had they put their son out to nurse? Why had they not brought him back to Venice at once? Or, if that had been deemed inexpedient, at least sent him to the Rohan estates in Brittany, instead of farming him out, so to speak, where the family could not protect him? Surely all these troubles might have been avoided by clearer thinking, more forthright action, without resorting to such elaborate, unwieldy stratagems!

Although he never found the right occasion to put his

doubts into words, he could not help brooding over them. And the longer he brooded, the more plainly he saw that there was a certain constraint in Ruvigny's manner when he talked of those days. One felt, not that he said anything he didn't think, but that he knew much more he did not care, or perhaps dare, to disclose. Why was he patently anxious to make amends for the past? What had *he* to be ashamed of? How solve the mystery there?

As the weeks passed Tancrède came to feel more and more strongly that his sister must be at the bottom of it. If only he could see and talk to Margot! What harm could it do? Indeed, might it not, on the contrary, do a great deal of good? At worst, he'd be able to grasp much that now remained unclear; at best, have a chance to resolve the unhappy family drama that had them all in its clutches and was bound to bring tragedy to one of the Rohans.

This idea he did eventually broach to his friend, one afternoon when they were resting in the garden after a glorious gallop through the Bois de Vincennes. Ruvigny, who had flung himself at his master's feet, hatless and panting a little, for it was warm for October, looked up quickly with an indescribable expression on his ruddy face. (Was it pique, or surprise, or solicitude—or a mixture of all three?) Then he shook his head.

"I know Madame de Chabot better than anyone living— far better than her own mother even—and I can tell you an interview would be useless. She's a hard, haughty creature: all she cares for in life are her own comfort and happiness. And she's eaten up with pride in herself, in the race whence she's sprung. That's why she never would marry in the old days, though she'd plenty of chances. She could have been

Comtesse de Soissons, you know, or Duchesse de Longue-ville, or even Princess of Weimar. But she'd take none of the lot! She was waiting, I suppose, to find someone supple and false enough to be willing to be her husband, nothing more —to assume her name and arms and pedigree instead of t'other way round. A nonsensical notion, if ever there was one! But she's got the very fellow to suit her now—that popinjay Chabot is wax in her hands. No, my Lord, I beg of you—stay away from your sister! No good can come of your meeting—and I fear the consequences to you."

Tancrède, deeply troubled, looked away to hide the pain he felt. He decided to say no more, but to bide his time in patience, hoping that an opportunity would come to carry out his plan in secret.

VI

AT HER *lever,* one dull morning in early November, Maman turned from a boxful of new Italian leather gloves Jeanneton had unpacked for her approval to announce, with intention: "The court's come back from Fontainebleau."

As Monsieur de Vardes, to whom the remark had presumably been addressed, made no answer, Tancrède, after a pause, felt it incumbent upon him to say: "Has it, indeed? Does that mean you'll have to call on the Queen?"

"Oh, I'll go if I like, and stay away if I like," replied Maman carelessly. "There's no obligation about it, unless she gives an official reception. But I think, my dear, I ought to present you at the Palais Royal. It's no more than your duty to bow to your sovereign, and then—one never knows—it might be useful later on."

Vardes, who was seated on his accustomed stool, absorbed in a game of dice he was playing indefatigably against himself on a corner of the Duchess's dressing-table, observed without looking up, in his heavy, sulky voice: "Or again it might not. Have you asked the Queen if she'll receive you?"

· "Why should I? We've every right—"

"Just the same, if I were you, madam, I'd make inquiries first. You know how exceedingly—well, let's call it correct, Her Majesty is. And there's no doubt in this case where her sympathies lie. Madame de Chabot has always been one of her favourites and Madame la Princesse—old Condé herself —is Enghien's mother as well as her most intimate friend. She'd not likely risk offending them. Then there's the question of religion—Madame Anne's more Catholic than the Pope! Yes! If I were you . . ."

"Nonsense, Vardes, you don't know what you're talking about! Besides, even if it were true—which I don't admit for a minute—the Queen can't afford to take sides. She's got to stay neutral, officially at least, until the suit has been settled. Anyhow, I can always manage to get her ear through Orval. What's the good in having a brother who's equerry to the Regent, if he can't be made use of once in a way? I shall write a note to Orval directly."

Vardes, shrugging his shoulders, continued his game.

"Very well, madam; of course you know best."

"I should think I did!"

Maman—whom, Tancrède realized, the slightest hint of opposition never failed to spur to instant activity—was voluble with indignation. (She had finished with the gloves and was having her hands rubbed now with *eau de mille fleurs*: there was something droll in the contrast between the twittering belligerence of her words and the extreme relaxation of her attitude.) "When I need your advice about etiquette, Marquis, I'll not hesitate to ask for it, I assure you. Oh, no! Tancrède must go to the Palais Royal at once—just as soon as I'm sure of a private audience. . . . Now, my dear, what will you wear? I think you really ought to have a new suit for the occasion. How would you like white satin embroidered in seed-pearls, and a jeweled sword to go with it? Ruvigny can take you to the tailor this very afternoon. 'Twill cost a pretty penny, but no matter—after all, what else is money for? First impressions are very important, and though the Queen doesn't care about dress herself, she appreciates others who do. What say you, my son? Do my plans please you?"

"Yes, Maman," answered Tancrède dutifully, as he understood he was expected to. (In any case, though the prospect was a trifle alarming, he could not say he found it disagreeable.)

What was hard to bear was the look Vardes sent him behind his mother's back—a long, level look combining supercilious scorn with something not far from pure hatred —for he truly did not know what he had done to deserve it.

Maman, who did things at once if she did them at all, lost no time in dispatching a letter to her brother and, a day or so later, was pleased to report that she had received a favourable reply. Uncle d'Orval was apparently a prompt correspondent. . . . He and his wife were among the relatives of whom Tancrède had seen least since his arrival in Paris. The first week he had paid a ceremonial call upon them in their handsome hôtel near the Louvre, and of course they met every Sunday at Charenton; but he had got the impression, he hardly knew how, that his uncle—a lymphatic, unenterprising gentleman, markedly lacking in the more positive qualities of most of the Béthunes—disapproved of Maman. At all events, there was no intimacy between them. However, at a time like this, personal considerations were overlooked; what counted was to preserve the solidarity of the family unbroken in the face of danger. It was, therefore, a matter of only a few more days' patience: brave in festal array, the Rohans set forth, one gloomy, gusty afternoon, in their state coach for the Palais Royal.

Tancréde, uneasily conscious of his white-and-silver magnificence, envied his mother her splendid aplomb: for all the nervousness she showed, she might have been off for one of her customary drives in the Cours la Reine. But just as the carriage turned into the crowded rue Saint-Honoré she leaned towards him to give his fingers an encouraging squeeze, and in spite of her smile her hand was like ice to the touch: so, after all, Maman was frightened, too!

At the door to the palace, which was patrolled by Swiss guards in red-white-and-blue striped uniforms and feathered toques, they were met by the Duc d'Uzès, the Queen's *chevalier d'honneur*, a resigned-looking personage with a tired old face that appeared to be made of wax that had run a little. Courteously, without once relaxing his pose of decorous endurance, his air of just not saying: "I-do-this-because-I-must-but-oh-if-you-knew-how-my-feet-hurt-me!", he escorted them through a series of halls policed by more guards in uniform, then upstairs to the Grand Cabinet. To this sumptuous, heavily gilded apartment, overlooking extensive gardens, they were admitted by the Queen's usher —another old man, who carried a wand and wore a chain round his neck in token of his office. A moment later the *dame d'honneur* appeared: Tancrède thought Madame de Senecey looked rather cross, with her parrot-nose and sharp black eyes. She smiled when she saw them, though, and after exchanging polite curtsies with Maman announced that they might enter the Little Cabinet at once—Her Majesty was ready to receive them.

Tancrède had never seen a queen before. He had imagined that, just as her house was larger and finer than any other in Paris, so would its owner be more beautiful than other women. Reality was a shock: on a great golden bed—grander indeed than those of her subjects—surrounded by her ladies, reclined a stout, middle-aged woman, with a shapeless nose, a full, very red under-lip, and an indefinite number of chins. Like Maman, she was dressed in sober black, with a widow's cap on her faded auburn curls, and was wearing no jewels save a cross of pearls on a gold chain round her fat neck.

Upon entering the room Tancrède saw her pop a *dragée* into her mouth and begin to chew it with evident pleasure. As she lay there, crunching and munching, gazing up at her visitors with expressionless blue-green eyes, he thought she resembled a sheep: if she had uttered a bleat, it would hardly have surprised him! A sheep, too, one could not but feel, might really have been quite as welcoming. Her Majesty barely acknowledged Maman's punctilious curtsy before peering over the latter's shoulder at the second caller and saying, in a pinched voice: "So, madam, this is the boy we've heard about. He's very small for his age—surely a slender reed to support the House of Rohan!"

Maman flushed, but replied with spirit: "Ah, madam, the slenderest reeds are often the last to break, you know! My late husband, too, was not tall; yet I need not recall to you his valour in the field."

The Queen turned to whisper something to one of the ladies standing in the alcove by the bed; the lady whispered something back. Then Anne of Austria laughed a high, mirthless laugh, on three descending notes, and remarked: "Madame de Motteville reminds me that the Bourbons are likewise short of stature—that Caesar himself was a giant in spirit only. Well, sir, come tell me how you find our fair kingdom of France and if you are pleased with your stay in our capital city."

Her manner was not encouraging; she did not look at her interlocutor; and the hand she extended to him to kiss—

small and white and unexpectedly slender—was retracted almost more quickly than was decently polite. But Tancrède, conscious of his mother's eyes upon him, declared, in a voice he hoped held no tremor, that Paris was the finest town he had ever seen: he was delighted, moreover, to find himself once more in his native land.

As if performing a tiresome duty, the Regent embarked on a mechanical game of questions-and-answers, only half listening to what Tancrède said, and interrupting him often, in disconcerting fashion, to whisper to Madame de Motteville or Madame de Senecey. Maman, listening tensely, threw in a helpful word whenever she could; but it could not be denied that both Rohans looked relieved when the door between the cabinets opened suddenly to admit a fair-haired, brown-eyed boy, who appeared to be about seven years old. All rose: it was really unnecessary for the guard at the door to announce: "His Majesty, the King!"

Louis XIV bent over his mother's hand; then turned to stare unabashed with his big, dark, curious eyes at the younger visitor. (Tancrède decided immediately he had never seen anyone of any age so completely self-possessed.)

"Sire," said Maman magnificently, as she rose from her stateliest curtsy, "here is your faithful subject, the Duc de Rohan, who has come to pay you his humble respects and solicit the honour of your friendship."

The little King stared harder than ever.

"That's not Rohan!" he said, in his loud boy's voice. "Rohan is Monsieur de Chabot, who married our cousin Mademoiselle de Rohan. You told me so, Maman, did you not?"

The Regent, looking slightly uncomfortable, hastened to interpose: "Yes, my son; but this young man is also a member of our cousin's family. Give him your hand to kiss and take him into the Yellow Cabinet. Perhaps he would like to see the German musket Enghien brought you as a souvenir of the battle of Nördlingen."

The boys trotted off together, followed by a pair of pages. (How trying it must be always to have someone tagging after you! Weren't kings ever allowed to go anywhere alone?) After his daunting opening play young Louis seemed perfectly friendly. He chatted quite readily— Maman had warned Tancrède beforehand he must let his sovereign choose the subjects—and took apparent pleasure in showing his various possessions. There were his drum, and his fife, and his bow-and-arrows (which had been made, he said, by his father). . . . "I can shoot with them, too. I go hunting every day behind the palace." He pointed as he spoke through the window at the park, lying deserted and nearly leafless in the dull November light.

He had also a number of guns and sabres, hanging on the wall behind a heavy velvet curtain. Some of these were so old and quaint that Tancrède had never beheld their like, others as up-to-date as those in use in His Majesty's armies. "I'm not allowed to handle them yet, but I shall be soon. It's a year now since I had a governess. I'm too old to play with girls any more; I tell Maman it's time I applied myself to military science. I'm going to be a soldier when I grow up and lead my troops as my Papa did. Was *your* father a soldier?"

Tancrède nodded, proud to be able to do so. "Yes, he was. He was one of the greatest soldiers France ever had, and head of the Protestant party besides. That's what I want to be some day, if I can."

"Oh, the Protestants—they're no better than heathens,

Maman says," the King asserted airily, dropping the curtain over his collection as if it no longer interested him. "The Grand Turk says so, too. That's what I call Cardinal Mazarin, when Maman can't hear me. And if you tell her,"— he turned, dignified still in spite of his wrath, on the tittering pages—"I'll have your tongues cut out and fed to the staghounds—so there! . . . Well, cousin, if you're a heathen, I'll have to fight you and beat you and shut you up in prison, as soon as I'm a man."

"Very well, sire," said Tancrède, laughing. "But you must catch me first. Your father never could catch mine, you know."

"I don't know." Louis gave another of his strangely embarrassing stares. "I haven't read history. I'll catch you now, if you like, though!"

He opened a door at the back of the Yellow Cabinet, disclosing a hall so long that it appeared to stretch to infinity. Tancrède, nothing loath, flew along the shining parquet, his boots making a terrific clatter; young Louis after him; the pages—a poor third—several lengths behind. It was a glorious race, down passage after passage, twisting and doubling until Tancrède felt sure he was thoroughly lost. He was so much the taller and stronger of the two that he had no trouble in keeping ahead, but he was amazed none the less at the speed and stamina of the little King. Finally, upon turning a sharp corner, they found themselves without warning once more on the threshold of the Queen's reception room, where Madame de Rohan had just risen to take her leave.

"Dear me, my son!" cried Anne, raising her sandy eyebrows. "What have you been doing?"

All the ladies looked suitably shocked; Madame de Senecey made a ticking sound with her tongue; and Maman, obviously suppressing a desire to laugh, was on the point of rebuking Tancrède, when Louis intervened superbly: "Don't scold him, madam; 'twas all my own doing. Come again, cousin; we'll have another race some day soon."

"Sire, I thank you," said Maman. "Bid good-bye to His Majesty, Tancrède."

"Give your hand once more to Monsieur de Rohan, my son," admonished the Regent, who, with an aspect of complete detachment, had begun to eat another *dragée*.

"Good-bye, cousin, whatever your name is. But you aren't Monsieur de Rohan, you know—there can't be *two* Ducs de Rohan!"

"My point precisely!" Maman dropped a graceful last curtsy. "Adieu, madam; I thank you for your kindness in receiving us. Come, Tancrède!"

Backing out of the door they all but collided with the captain of the Queen's guard, Monsieur de Guitaut, a handsome, middle-aged man with a bold eye and an air of consequence about him. He bowed with slightly overdone gallantry. Maman, flurried, yielded him her hand, almost as though she had rather not, and made a rapid escape—not rapid enough, however, for her to avoid hearing the Queen's acid little laugh.

As the Rohans retreated some remarks floated along the corridor after them. Tancrède was not able to distinguish more than half the words: there was something about "ancient history" and "follies coming home to roost." Nor could he understand why all the way back in the carriage Maman remained in a shocking bad temper.

The day after their call at the Palais Royal Tancrède woke to find Paris in general—and his quarter of it in particular—in a turmoil over the impending arrival of an embassy from Poland, which had been sent to France for the proxy marriage of King Wladislas IV to Marie de Gonzague, Duchesse de Nevers. As Madame de Nevers was one of the ladies of the Regent's intimate circle, the court was naturally much concerned about arrangements for the reception of the foreigners. Rondeau reported at Maman's *lever* that they were to be lodged during the festivities at the Hôtel de Vendôme; at dinner La Mestairie had word that their solemn entry into the city through the Porte Saint Antoine would take place that very afternoon: the line of march would lead them through the Place Royale, where the young King and his mother had promised to review the procession from the Pavillon du Roi, and therefore straight past the Hôtel de Rohan.

Like most such affairs, it was late getting started. A good hour beforehand every window in the square was filled with the eager faces of the inhabitants, together with those of their friends lucky enough to have been asked to share the spectacle; but the short autumn day was well over before the heralds appeared with their trumpets. Maman had pretended to be bored by the whole business; she and her gallants took their places in the centre window of the Crimson Cabinet just as the first of the riders came into view.

Tancrède and Sidonie, greatly excited, hung over the railing as far as they dared. . . . How cold it was! Their breath rose, twin puffs of steam, in the frosty twilight. . . . It was a sight to remember: there, brave with ribbons and glittering with decorations, was the flower of the French court. (Sidonie knew most of the nobles by sight and was able to call out their names to her friend.) But they were, it had to be admitted, completely eclipsed by the barbaric magnificence of the Poles. The latter might be, as Miossens had rumoured at dinner, less than half civilized: was it really true that they subsisted on raw meat they tore to pieces with their fingers, and slept on bearskins flung wherever they happened to be on the floor? Surely they looked wild enough—greasy with dirt, their bullet-heads shaved save for one long lock depending over their shoulders—; but their flowing robes of scarlet and purple and orange and green were sewn thickly with pearls the size of pigeon eggs, and studded with precious stones—diamonds and rubies, sapphires and emeralds—which blazed like fire in the smoky light of the torches.

The crowd roared its amazement as these gorgeous savages marched along, some riding on horseback—even the steeds, painted bright red, seemed larger than life-size, imbued with the same fierce spirit as their masters—; others seated in coaches of silver and gold, also richly embossed with gems.

At the end of the cavalcade came the Bishop of Warmie, who was to perform the marriage, and the Count Palatine of Posen, the proxy bridegroom. To the accompaniment of cheers these heavily bearded worthies traversed the square in the most lavishly jewelled coach of all and disappeared in their turn in the chill November dusk.

The following day the wedding took place in splendour in the King's chapel at the Palais Royal, and, a day or two after that, the Regent gave a farewell supper and ball for the new Queen of Poland.

To this the whole court had been invited. Even Maman, who often, Tancrède observed, did not bother to attend official functions, decided that this time the show would be too fine to miss and departed, begemmed and befeathered, for the palace, escorted by the Marquis de Vardes. (It was rather surprising to find that her other very nearly as constant companion, Monsieur de Miossens, was not of the party, and that for the oddest of reasons: he had a wife, whom of course, on state occasions, it was his duty to squire.)

After Maman's departure Tancrède sat in the library mantled in thought. He was struggling with an idea as challenging as it was revolutionary. Presently, surprised at his own daring, he rang for a lackey and issued an order—almost his first since he had come to live at the Hôtel de Rohan: "I should like to speak to Mademoiselle de Montville. Please, will you ask her to come to me at once?"

Gilbert bowed and departed—how easy it was, after all! —and a few minutes later Sidonie thrust her smiling face through the door. It had been snowing a little; her red velvet cloak was dusted with silvery flakes and her cheeks were rosy from the cold.

"Good evening, my Lord. You wanted to see—"

"Sidonie," said Tancrède, "come here. . . . No, don't bother to curtsy—sit down—there, across from me—that's right. I need your advice."

"Yes, my Lord?"

"And don't call me 'my Lord'. It sounds as though we weren't really friends. Besides, there's no-one here to correct you. Do you know where my mother has gone tonight?"

"To the Palais Royal, I suppose. Everybody in Paris who can—"

"That's it: everybody who can is off to the ball. Monsieur de Vardes went with Maman. She didn't ask me if I wanted to go, too; I expect she thought I wouldn't care about it. The point is, *could* I go if I wanted to? I mean, have I the right . . . ?"

"Why, yes, I believe so," replied Sidonie thoughtfully. "You're a peer of the realm, aren't you? and you've been presented to the Queen. I think at parties like this the whole court is included. But why do you want to go, Tancrède?"

"I don't, really. As a matter of fact, it scares me to death even to think of it. I feel all trembly inside, the way I did the first time I had to ride Timoléon. But that hasn't very much to do with it, has it? I mean, if it's my duty—"

"There isn't any duty about it for persons of our age."

"You don't understand. It's like this: if all the court's invited, then my sister will be there, won't she? She's a duchess, and I heard Maman say all the duchesses are supposed to attend the Regent—that's one of the reasons she went herself. So if my sister's there and I'm there, too, I could see her and talk to her."

"Probably you could." Sidonie still looked doubtful. "Why do you want to talk to her, though?"

"Oh, don't you see?—I've *got* to! It's my only chance. I've worried and worried for weeks, wondering how I could manage to get to her. I thought at first of sending a letter . . . but I don't write French yet very well, and anyhow she might not answer it. No, this is much the best way. The only trouble is, I've never seen her—not even a picture: Maman must have thrown them all away!—so I'm not sure I'll be able to recognize her. Do you know my sister, Sidonie?"

"Of course I do—but what's that got to do with it?"

"Everything! Then you must come with me."

"Oh, I can't! How could I? What if Papa should hear—"

"Where is your father?"

"Well, he's gone to the ball himself. At least, I think he said—"

"There, you see! What did I tell you? That shows it must be all right. Rondeau has a title, too—he's the Sieur de Montville, isn't he? If anybody who's been presented at court has a right to go, then so have you, for he took you to the ballet at the Petit Bourbon last year—you told me so yourself. What are we waiting for? Please, Sidonie! This is the only thing I've ever asked of you, and it's so dreadfully important. If I can just find Margot, maybe I can settle this whole awful mess without lawsuits or anything. Do say you'll help me!"

Sidonie wavered. There was little she would have refused her friend—as she reminded him and he well knew—yet the prospect frightened her as much as it exhilarated her. Tancrède had to dispose of her scruples one by one, impelled by his own increasing conviction: the more she hung back, the more certain he grew that his plan was ideal, the one perfect solution to his problem. It took ten minutes by the clock—the gold rising sun with its curly rays that stood on the mantel under Papa's portrait—before the little girl finally relented: "Very well, my dear: if you're sure it's right, then perhaps—"

"No perhaps about it—that's splendid!" cried Tancrède jubilantly, ringing the bell again. "I'll meet you downstairs just as soon as I can. Gilbert, send word to Denis I want the carriage in half an hour. And please tell Thomas to attend me at once in my own rooms—he'd better look sharp about it!"

"Yes, my Lord; directly, my Lord," replied Gilbert, much struck by his master's triumphant pose, his new air of decision and pride; for the servants' hall was agreed that, up to now, the young Duc de Rohan had been a bit too docile and accommodating.

Having dressed in a feverish rush, the children found it easy to slip unobserved out of the house, which was dark and deserted, as always on evenings when its mistress was not at home. No-one saw their departure save the Swiss at the door, before whom Tancrède issued his command to the coachman, in a voice that shook a little (he trusted with excitement only): "To the Palais Royal!"

That, it went without saying, was the sole destination tonight; by the time they reached it the whole of the rue Saint Honoré was an all but impassable jam. It took almost an hour for their carriage to arrive at the door. Tancrède gave his hand to Sidonie and together they passed, round-eyed with admiration, into the great illuminated building.

The grand staircase was lined with lackeys and thronged with latecomers in gorgeous attire streaming up to the ballroom. Nobody paid much attention to a pair of children: they, too, were suitably dressed—Tancrède in the white-and-silver suit (he had not even forgotten to buckle on his jewelled sword)—and whenever he was accosted by a servant his murmur of "Monsieur le Duc de Rohan" seemed to serve as a passport to entry.

As everybody was headed in the same direction, it was not hard to find the Salle des Fêtes, a long vaulted and richly gilded chamber blazing with what looked like thousands of candles, at the far end of which, on a raised platform, they caught sight of the Regent and Louis XIV seated on their thrones. The sallow, rather plump woman wearing a crown and an unbecoming gown of black velvet must, Tancrède felt, be the new Queen of Poland; the dark bearded gentleman next to her, resplendent with orders, was surely the Count Palatine of Posen. Around the two queens were grouped Anne's Maids-of-Honour, distinguished by their dresses, all a fairy gold-and-silver; behind them, the Princesses of the Blood, on chairs with backs but without arms; behind these again, the Duchesses on tabourets, arranged in the order of their seniority. (Maman must be there somewhere.) The lower level of the room was filled with courtiers, the rank and file of the most brilliant court in Europe.

Plumes nodded, jewels flashed; as Tancrède and Sidonie entered an orchestra high in a gallery struck up the stately measures of the opening branle, and the couples formed for dancing. The little King, with an enviable air of grave majesty, led forth the bride; he was apparently indifferent to their awkward discrepancy in height. The second couple consisted of the Count Palatine and a scrawny young woman with high shoulders and an anxious expression on her pale, pointed features, who, Sidonie whispered, was the Duchesse d'Enghien. (Her anxiety seemed to be justified, for it was plain her partner had not much idea what he was about—they were both obviously counting out loud!) And the third couple . . . well, though they had never seen him before, they did not need to be told who this was: the huge eagle's beak and lordly swagger of Monsieur le Duc d'Enghien, heir to the First Prince of the Blood, victor at twenty-four of Rocroi and Nördlingen and countless other battles, had no counterparts in France. With interest Tancrède surveyed the intimidating presence of his chief enemy; he was so raptly absorbed in his appraisal that it took his companion's exclamation, "There she is! That's your sister, my Lord!" to make him shift his gaze to Enghien's *vis-à-vis*.

Again, as with Maman, he was not quite sure what he had expected; but Margot de Rohan-Chabot did not in the least resemble any of his tentative mental pictures. She was —he was glad to see—a pretty little woman, not even so tall as his mother, with blonde curls exquisitely dressed (were they a trifle too glossily yellow?) and an elegant carriage (was it perhaps a thought too rigidly self-contained?). At all events, her wonderful gown of blue satin sewn over with brilliants was one of the handsomest in the room: she looked what she was, a princess nobly born—and that for some reason pleased her brother even more. Whatever her disposition might be, at the moment she was smiling with bewitching amiability. . . . See, how charmingly she revealed her teeth—the traditional twin rows of pearls—as, having dropped her handkerchief, Enghien stooped to recover it and gave it back with a bow! (Who'd have thought that insolent warrior could boast such gallantry of demeanour?)

From now on Tancrède had eyes for no-one else. The whole gleaming pageant blurred into a background for one small figure in blue; his mind was entirely and agonizingly concentrated on the problem of how to accost this lovely young woman. For the time being, of course, she was out of his reach, but patience! How long had he not waited already? Surely a few minutes more and . . .

Sidonie, hitherto silent and spellbound, nervously tugged at his sleeve: "My Lord, had we not better go? I'm so afraid Papa or Madame la Duchesse may see us!"

Tancrède's eyes looked vague. "Madame la Duchesse? Oh, you mean Maman! What if she does? We've as much right to be here as she has!"

He lifted his chin haughtily as he spoke; with a sigh Sidonie relinquished her project of a strategic retreat. It was clear her friend would not consider leaving at least until the first dance was over.

When the music stopped the dancers promenaded solemnly around the room, bowing each time they passed the daïs where the thrones were. The King led the Queen of Poland back to her seat. His part in the programme appeared to be over; his mother, with an approving smile, sent him off with his tutor, the Abbé Beaumont, presumably to bed.

Suddenly Tancrède gave a great gulp: as chance would have it, Madame de Chabot, dropping a low curtsy, abandoned her partner in the middle of the floor. Evidently she had something to say to her husband, whom one had spied several minutes ago on the sidelines. (Why was he not dancing, too? With the same almost impersonal satisfaction he had felt on noting Margot's charms, Tancrède registered the fact that though seen from the front his brother-in-law was an exceedingly personable young man, his profile was disastrously less prepossessing: Chabot had the cruel mouth of a shark combined with the predatory nose of an immature falcon.) To reach him she had to pass directly by the children. There she came, with a rustle of silk, a click of her high satin heels, and the little air of assurance that became her so well. . . .

Tancrède wanted desperately to speak. In fact, he imagined for a moment he had said something; but he must have been mistaken, for Margot continued serenely on her way. He'd have to do better, and speedily, or his chance would be lost.

"Madam! Madam! One moment, please!"

Madame de Chabot turned in surprise, gathering her billowy skirts together with slim fingers, her glossy golden head a little to one side.

"Yes?"

Her manner was impatient; it seemed to declare that she could not conceive what this strange boy had to say to her, here of all places, now of all times. But her voice itself was soft and rather sweet.

Tancrède pressed forward eagerly.

"Dear madam, I am your brother. I've wanted so long to see you, so much to say . . ."

He could not get any further, faced by the glittering insolence of those topaz eyes.

Picking up her train, Margot de Rohan-Chabot swept by him. As she went she flung over her shoulder in a tone of concentrated venom, of supreme disdain—the more shocking because it was just above a whisper—: "Out of my way, Tancrède Bon!"

VII 🌿

THE CHILDREN drove home from the palace through the dark, empty streets in comparative silence, their minds busy sorting out a wealth of new impressions. At the Hôtel de Rohan the sleepy Swiss porter was waiting to admit them

"Lambert," said Tancrède, holding up his hand impressively, "mind you say nothing of this to Madame la Duchesse."

He made a gesture towards pulling a crown from his pocket, but Lambert chuckled and patted his young master's back.

"That's all right, my Lord; you can rely on me."

It appeared indeed that they could: their secret remained one.

The next day, when Tancrède came to think over his evening's adventures at leisure, he decided that, far from clarifying the situation, the encounter with his sister had only succeeded in deepening the mystery. What had Margot meant by calling him "Tancrède Bon"? Why was she manifestly unwilling to talk matters out?

These were questions he could not answer without help, and somehow he shrank from telling his troubles. It was impossible, surely, to bring up the subject with Maman; Maître Joly was far too forbidding to serve as a confidant; with Ruvigny even—faithful and devoted as he was—whenever he tried to begin, he felt his tongue stiffen and his voice die away in his throat.

The more he pondered the problem, the further it seemed

to be from a satisfactory solution. He strove not to think about it too much, but it bothered him more than he liked to admit, and he was no longer so happy as he had been during the first weeks after his arrival in Paris. From his present vantage point of bleakly superior knowledge he looked back on them as having been, in spite of callow blunders and inexperience, a golden time of very nearly unalloyed bliss. Now a thin grey veil of mistrust and uncertainty was drawn over everything, quite in keeping with the dreary weather that had set in. For winter had come at last. The cheerful, dusty, smelly summer city had long since disappeared, giving way to a place of sunless gloom, wrapped in melancholy mists or drenched by rains that fell sometimes for days without stopping, turning the dirt into nauseous slime. Then December arrived, clearer and very much colder, but still obstinately devoid of sun; the mud froze hard in the streets, so that carriages, instead of ploughing through stinking quagmires, jolted perilously over endless ruts and ridges.

The eighteenth of the month was Tancrède's birthday. He had thought about it for weeks, wondering whether his mother would remember; when she did not, he was disappointed, but not greatly surprised. The purse of gold louis she pressed on him next day, after Rondeau had belatedly recalled the date to her mind, really seemed an anticlimax.

Three days before Christmas the now famous Rohan case was heard before the Queen's council at the Palais Royal. Joubert and Pucelle departed for the meeting with Maître Joly, all three laden with sheaves of important looking papers and primed for their tussle with the lawyers of the opposition. The whole town, Tancrède knew, was in an uproar and talked of nothing else. According to etiquette, the principals could not appear: Maman and her son stayed at home, waiting with what patience they could muster till their legal representatives returned to make their report.

The news when it came was rather negative. All the lawyers, it hardly needed to be said, had delivered themselves of lengthy and florid speeches in traditional Palais style, cited Latin authors a-plenty in support of their clients' virtues, accused their rivals of unspeakable frauds and malpractices. The whole performance was merely, as Maître Joly told them, a sort of preliminary test of strength. Nothing actually was at stake except public opinion and the perplexed question as to which court was ultimately to preside over the trial.

For some reason Maman had never shown Tancrède the factums that had been prepared, nor even allowed him to discuss their content with the servants or anyone else. ("That, my dear, is what lawyers are for; it's beneath our dignity to go into details.") However, he managed to gather more or less what was in them. From the curdled mass of verbiage the opposing lines of argument emerged fairly clearly.... Madame de Rohan complained that her son, and the late Duke's, had been stolen from her in infancy by a person or persons unknown. The Chabots, on the other hand, were insisting that Tancrède was not the heir of Henri de Rohan, but an obscure foundling foisted upon the family by the Duchess purely to spite her daughter for having married against her wishes.

The Queen's councillors, the lawyers asserted, had for the most part listened to the evidence in non-committal silence. The one exception had been Monsieur le Duc, hot-headed young Enghien, who had sprung to his feet in the middle of the meeting and announced his passionate advocacy of his friend's cause.

"It was a most regrettable incident—highly irregular indeed!" remarked long, lanky Monsieur Pucelle, wagging his head mournfully till the horns on his bonnet quivered as though they, too, were aggrieved. "I've never seen His Highness in such a temper. He kept stamping his foot and shouting at the top of his voice that those who were against Chabot were against *him*—he'd know well enough, later on, how to deal with such rascals as they deserved!"

"Bourbon bluster!" said Maman contemptuously; while Tancrède felt the nerves in his temples start throbbing—with fear? with anger? or both together?

"Bluster or not, madam,"—Maître Joly's gelid tones were a rebuke in themselves—"Enghien's word carries weight with the Regent. It's extremely significant to me that neither she nor the Cardinal bade him desist. And there have been incidents in the past, you know. . . . Monsieur le Duc's Petits Maîtres are a quarrelsome crew, ready to run a man through with their swords as soon as look at him, at a word from their master."

"Pooh! I don't believe it!" exclaimed Maman.

But she looked uneasy just the same. It took all the tact and soothing phrases at plump little Monsieur Joubert's command—he was, Tancrède had already noticed, the most hopeful of the trio—to bring the scene to a harmonious conclusion. There was, for the moment, really nothing to be done; the council's decision would not be handed down for at least another fortnight. Meanwhile the lawyers intended to start to work at once unravelling a tangled skein of fresh clues. Madame la Duchesse and Monsieur le Duc would just have to resign themselves. . . .

The next two weeks seemed the longest Tancrède had ever known. He went about his daily tasks because he did not know what else to do, but he could settle comfortably to nothing. Though Paris was bubbling over, noisy and jubilant, with holiday cheer, the joys of the season were eclipsed for the Rohans by the gruelling anxiety that afflicted them. Christmas itself just meant a trip to Charenton through woods all-a-glitter with hoar frost, and a longer than usual sermon from Pastor Drélincourt. Nor was New Year's Day more inspiriting. . . . This time Maman did not forget her *étrennes,* but Tancrède took small pleasure in the string of costly trifles she gave him; and he knew that his mother was scarcely more interested in the beautiful piece of Flanders lace he had found for her in the Galérie Marchande, though she pretended to be tremendously grateful, exclaiming aloud in delight and embracing him over and over. (How had he guessed precisely what she most wanted? She'd wear the collar that very night at the Guémenées' supper-and-fireworks!)

Maman was appallingly nervous, these days; and, as always, with her nerves took the form of futile and unceasing activity. She rushed about town to innumerable fêtes and gave a great many parties of her own. In her desire to ingratiate herself with Parliament—a little late in the day, as Vardes sourly advised her—she made some strange social experiments: offering a dinner to the influential Président de Maisons (one of the six *présidents-à-mortier,* ranking just below the Premier Président himself), and attending various routs of the Noblesse de Robe, where the fame of her name and the splendour of her presence had a paralyzing effect on the ladies of Palais society.

On Candlemas Eve the judgement was slated to be delivered. Maître Joly and the lawyers went to the palace to receive it—alone: again the family were condemned to remain at home. This time, Tancrède felt, the suspense was all but unendurable. He took up his post at the window of the Green Cabinet, where he would be sure to catch the first glimpse of the returning carriage as it rounded the corner of the rue Royale. It was a very dark day—not especially cold, but raw and penetrating. Out of the slate-grey, lustreless sky snow was falling, so slowly, so lightly, that one was hardly conscious of its coming; yet so steadily that all the pointed roofs of the Place were frosted in white. So, too, were the fence-rails surrounding the square; even the statue of Louis XIII, the Well Beloved, seated proudly on his horse, was thickly powdered with flakes.

Today the Rohans were not alone, but to tell the truth they might better have been: Aunt d'Orval, who had chosen this afternoon to call on her sister-in-law, was no company at all. As languid and lymphatic as her husband, the Equerry, her wan, dissatisfied face suggested insomnia and an undependable digestion, while her dreary trick of uttering small sighs at intervals appeared to express a chronic distaste for life. She sat now on a high-backed settee by the fireplace, her pinched profile bent over a piece of tapestry-work, a bitter half-smile proclaiming the fact that she had come less out of sympathy than because she was curious to see "how Marguerite would take it."

Maman had sat with her guest as long as she could bear to; finally, unable to stand the physical inactivity any longer, she sprang to her feet and began pacing up and down—and this, oddly enough, reduced the strain in the atmosphere. Tancrède thought of his mother as always in motion: she was forever preening her curls before the glass, or adjusting her ribbons; rearranging a vaseful of flowers—"For servants have no taste, my dear!"—or simply drifting about the room with the aimless persistence of a goldfish.

Except for the rustling of her long taffeta train it was very still in the Green Cabinet. The only other sound was the gentle hiss of the logs in the fireplace; even outside the snow had deadened the usual street noises . . . muffled footfalls and the roll of carriage wheels, softened somehow the piercing note of a passing vendor's cry: *"Des couronnes, pour mettre aux Rois dessus leurs têtes!"* (That must be a man selling wreaths for the Feast of Kings.) Everyone and everything seemed to be waiting, poised breathless to hear: the glowing fire in the grate; the slow, soft snowflakes; Tancrède in the window; Aunt d'Orval at her tapestry-work. . . . Even Papa, in his gold frame high over the mantelpiece, had a questioning look, as if *he* were waiting, too . . . but patiently! It was only Maman who could not control herself. A dozen times she'd paused in her pacings to mutter: "What can be keeping that wretched Joly?", only to receive Aunt d'Orval's exasperatingly reasonable reply: "My dear Marguerite, you know very well it's a great way from the Palais Royal. And with this snow in the streets . . ."

It happened in the end as Tancrède had known it would: they had heard the wrong coach so often that when the right one came at last it was almost an anticlimax. Gilbert flung the door open and Maman stopped short in her flight, suddenly as still as the statue of Louis the Well Beloved. Aunt d'Orval arrested her needle. Tancrède braced himself for the news, which he feared, from the set of Maître Joly's firm jaw and the dejected angle of Joubert's habitually perky bonnet, couldn't be pleasant.

It appeared, said the warden—who by common consent acted as spokesman for the three—that the Queen's council had decided to hold the trial before the Chambre de l'Edit *and* the Grand Chambre united in solemn session; the court of La Tournelle, appointed to deal with criminal affairs, would be invoked also, since kidnapping was rated a crime. "Just what I expected all along, I must say, madam. 'Tis the Cardinal's old game of trying to appease everybody."

"Is that bad or good?" queried Tancrède, to be abashed by Maman's cry of despair: "Bad, of course! It's the worst thing that could possibly happen. Oh, you fools! You fools! What do you think I pay you for? Why in God's name didn't you prevent this?"

Aunt d'Orval picked up a minute pair of silver shears and snipped off her thread with an air of finality. "My dear, if you'd listened to François and me . . ."

Tancrède still didn't understand. "But *why* . . . ?"

Maître Joly shut his lips tight as if he were folding and sealing a letter, while Joubert shrugged his shoulders. It was left for Pucelle to explain, in a dry, dead voice, that the trouble was, the Protestants on the bench would find themselves now the minority party. For there were only sixteen members of the Chambre de l'Edit as against twenty-five grand councillors and twelve judges of La Tournelle. "Monsieur and Madame de Chabot are overjoyed, naturally. They feel that at least two-thirds of the assembly are, or can be made to be, on their side. In fact, they assert openly their suit's as good as won already. As the meeting was closing I heard Monsieur le Duc talk quite boldly of sweeping the opposition straight off the pavement of Paris. 'And as for young Tancrède, if he dares show his nose after this . . .'"

Tancrède, who had flushed crimson at mention of his name, lifted his head proudly. "I'd like to see him try to do it!"

Maman cried out again, but her voluble flow of emotion was cut short by Maître Joly, who unsealed his lips to remark, with asperity, that there was no time to waste in lamentation. "My colleagues and I have come upon some new evidence that puts an entirely fresh complexion on the case. What we have conjectured and claimed from the first, madam, I believe we are about to be able to prove beyond doubt. There's been word from Holland. La Cosse has been arrested at last. Better still, La Sauvetat has been found and has offered to tell us his story; if the reports that have reached us be true, all may not be lost. I would, therefore, urge Madame la Duchesse to summon her forces and be so kind as to give us her undivided attention for a few minutes, while we elucidate . . ."

"Yes, yes, of course! I am completely at your service, sirs. Jacqueline, my love, you'll forgive me? . . . Tancrède, my son, I must leave you. Stay where you are, for pity's sake, I beg you! Who knows what dangers . . . what horrible plots . . . ?"

Impetuously she rushed into her private cabinet, followed at a respectful distance by Maître Joly and the lawyers. From behind the closed doors there arose at once a feverish gabble, punctuated by an occasional loud exclamation from Madame de Rohan. Aunt d'Orval, pinched and disapproving to the last, gathered her work together portentously and rang for her *dame de compagnie* and her carriage: there was clearly nothing else for her to do. (Besides, it was equally clear that she was bursting with impatience to report what she'd already heard to Uncle d'Orval.)

Tancrède felt nonplussed. It would have seemed to him dishonourable to try to listen to a conversation he was not meant to hear. At the same time, what else could he possibly think of? He went on sitting by the fire, in the big armchair he had always supposed must once have been Papa's, a desolate small figure lost in a mist of unhappy speculations; while inside the cabinet the high, hectic clamour sank by degrees to an endless drone. . . .

It was a very long time before the door opened and Maman emerged, wearing her fur-trimmed cloak and hood. She appeared in the grip of uncontrollable excitement; her eyes were wide and staring, her voice sharp with nerves as she declared she intended to drive at once to the Cité to consult the Président de Maisons. "After all, he's the only friend I've got who can help us now—and he's told me often enough I've only to say what I want . . . ! Good-bye, my darling. Mind you stay where you are till I come back—don't venture outdoors on *any* pretext!"

She embraced her son with violence and was gone in a flash. The men must have taken their leave and departed by the front door to the Duchess's apartments, for they did not return through the library. In any case Tancrède would have scorned to question them without his mother's knowledge. But even Maître Joly's austere presence might have been welcome just now. Never had he felt so utterly alone. There was no-one, really, he could turn to. Rondeau and

Sidonie, he knew, had gone to the country to visit relatives for the Epiphany holiday; Ruvigny, too, for once had deserted his friend—there had been no word from him all day.

Slowly the light faded outside; the snow came down harder and harder; all over the city bells were tolling for the services on Candlemas Eve; while far in the distance—very faint indeed now—came the vendor's cry: *"Des couronnes, pour mettre aux Rois dessus leurs têtes! Des couronnes! Des —couronnes . . . !"*

Tancrède could not have told whether it was the big log's breaking in two in a shower of sparks that roused him, or the sudden appearance of Gilbert with a lighted candelabrum. The lackey scratched on the door and announced that His Highness the Duc de Guise had come to call. "I told him, my Lord, that Madame la Duchesse was not at home, but he replied, 'twas no matter: Monsieur le Duc," said Gilbert sententiously, "craves leave for a word with Monsieur le Duc."

The boy sat up and rubbed his eyes as his visitor made a bustling entrance. He had seen Guise several times since the day they had made one another's acquaintance at the Hôtel de Chevreuse. At each of these encounters his cousin had greeted him boisterously, uttered hearty professions of friendship, and referred in no way to the greyhound puppy he'd offered to give him at their first meeting—which only served to confirm Tancrède's increasing suspicion that Frenchmen made promises lightly, as lightly to break them.

One could not imagine what Monsieur de Guise wanted now. It was, however, distinctly cheering to be clapped enthusiastically on the shoulder and to hear a happy voice troll out: "Young friend, I have come to offer you my services.

I dare say you heard what happened in council today. They tell me Enghien used threatening words. He's all fire and bluster, that one—I doubt if he'd dare do anything, really. Bourbons are all alike—many words, but little action! It has occurred to me, nevertheless, that you and your good mother might be feeling ill at ease over the turn affairs have taken— that it might not come amiss to you to know that I, and the rest of the House of Lorraine—I speak for not a few, as you are well aware—are proud to recognize you as our cousin and our ally. My support is yours, and that of my family—my sword, should you need it, as well. I've come to fetch you now to the Hôtel de Guise, where, I can assure you, I've guards a-plenty to ward off any mischief."

Tancrède scarcely knew how to answer. He liked Guise well enough—had liked him from the beginning. There was, despite an occasional unfocussed wildness in his eyes, something peculiarly attractive in his open face and ready smile. Undependable as he might be—one had gathered from various scraps of gossip that he was considered the family scapegrace, in and out of trouble a dozen times a month —no-one bore him a grudge; it seemed impossible to resist him when he was determined to please, even though one knew that his charm and his friendliness were gifts for the moment only. "Still I gave Maman my word . . ."

It took Guise some time to convince the boy that by disregarding his mother's injunctions he would really be doing what she would approve, were she there to be consulted— for there could be no question whose house was the safest just now. From then on things happened so fast that Tancrède felt he could not have controlled them even if he had wanted to. But for the present he did not want to. It seemed much pleasanter to join the moving pageant under his masterful cousin's command. Off they bowled in the latter's coach through blowing curtains of snow to a big, black pile of buildings in the rue de Braque, with a pair of pepper-pot towers—white-capped from the storm—set at an angle on either side of the entrance.

Into the courtyard they clattered with a whoop and halloo. Through whirling snowflakes servants came running with torches; a pair of shaggy wolfhounds—almost frighteningly huge in the fading light—leaped rejoicing round their master, who turned to his guest with a genial smile: "Come, lad, you are heartily welcome to the Hôtel de Guise!"

On the way upstairs the Duke observed that one more or less could make little difference—he had really no idea how many people were living with him already. "My mother has one wing, I know, and my sister another; but I'd be hard put to it to make a tally of my pensioners. Sometimes I think more than half of the House of Lorraine have their lodgings under my roof!"

Although this might be true, Tancrède found that his cousin still possessed the whole of the central structure, a vast pavilion on an inner court, with a wide view over snow-swept gardens. His own private suite was on the first floor—the *piano nobile,* as Monsieur de Guise, who had been to Italy, called it. Here, in a row of fine, high-ceilinged rooms, he held sway in feudal splendour, surrounded by hordes of servants and an indeterminate number of hunting dogs. Tancrède had never seen such regal confusion; it was obvious that the Hôtel de Guise, or at least that portion of it occupied by its owner, lacked a mistress.

Wondering, he allowed himself to be led to the best spare chamber, a majestic apartment hung with tapestries, with an immense canopied oaken bed—made for a giant, surely—in the alcove. (How would one ever be able to sleep in it?) Supper was already laid in an adjoining saloon. Tancrède gasped as he entered it, the room was so big and so bright. His eyes were dazzled by the light of many candles; his head swam from the heat; his ears were filled with a roar of voices, for the Duke's whole troop of gentlemen-in-waiting were there to receive them.

Laughing a little, as though it were a game, Guise led his guest to his own special throne-like seat on a daïs, and insisted on serving him with the *cadenas*—that was the set of table silver kept in a jewelled casket and reserved for royalty. This rite accomplished—much to Tancrède's secret embarrassment—both dukes relaxed and fell to with a will. Tancrède discovered he was very hungry; it was hours past his supper time and that day at dinner, afflicted by nerves over the outcome of the council meeting, he had eaten almost nothing.

Guise plied him with dainties, with much the same careless benevolence that he displayed in flinging scraps off his plate to the wolfhounds, which prowled unchidden round the room—and, disconcertingly, underneath the table—seeking what they might devour. There was also a great deal to drink. Flagons of ruby Beaune—the Duke's favourite vintage—were followed by hippocras, a sweet spiced dessert wine served at banquets. Finally a towering cake was brought in—the *Gâteau des Rois,* named in honour of the Three Kings of the East, whose feast they were celebrating.

The cake was cut by Guise himself; then passed to Tancrède and each of the gentlemen-in-waiting, who'd been invited to join in the sport. According to tradition, he who received the slice containing a bean was to be King for the night. Tancrède was so sure it would not be in his that he started to eat his share of the plummy confection at once, and nearly cracked a tooth on something hard at his very first bite.

"Why—it's the bean!"

The gentlemen roared at his expression of blank surprise, while Guise affirmed that it was a good augury for the future—one could see the Duc de Rohan was born lucky.

Afterwards, when he came to think it over, Tancrède strongly suspected his cousin of having manoeuvred matters. At the time it seemed merely an agreeable coincidence. Indeed, he greatly enjoyed the whole performance, wearing his crown—a wreath of flowers and gilt leaves—and presiding over the series of romping forfeit games with grave delight.

Tancrède long remembered his evening at the Hôtel de Guise for more than one reason. It was late when the party broke up. By that time his head was spinning and he had just one wish, which was to get to the oaken bed—gigantic or not—as soon as possible. But after dismissing his suite Guise called for one final glass of wine by the hearth—the two of them together. He lay at his ease in an armchair, his long legs stretched out in front of him, one hand holding his pipe, the other idly caressing the head of his favourite hound, Mandane, who slept on the rushes in front of the fire. Mandane, it was plain, was soon to have a family: Monsieur de Guise began the conversation by offering his cousin his choice of the litter—which offer Tancrède accepted solemnly, feeling rather inclined to laugh.

Then the young man talked—as young men will—of women. It was astonishing to learn—for one had taken him for a bachelor—that he had been twice married. "I don't know how it is, though—women are all very well—in fact, I don't see how we could do without 'em—but there's something about matrimony I don't take to, and never did. So . . . "—he blew a beautifully round smoke ring into the air —"I decided I'd had enough, and that was that!"

Tancrède wondered whether it had also been enough for the two Mesdames de Guise, but before he could make inquiries Guise went on to confide that, at the moment, he was head-over-heels in love with Mademoiselle de Pons, one of the Regent's Maids-of-Honour. "As lovely as a rose she is, my boy, but as stupid as an owl: God knows how it will end! Meanwhile, all that matters is to be as merry as possible and never worry over what may come tomorrow."

This easy philosophy, which would hardly have commended itself to Tancrède in a sober mood, seemed, in his present state of dizzy cheerfulness, as logical as it was wise. He laughed unrestrainedly, rather hoping his host might continue in a similar vein. But the Duke, recalling perhaps that his *vis-à-vis* was little more than a child, switched the subject to the events of the afternoon's council meeting. What a pity it was they'd decided to try the Rohans' case before all three courts instead of in the Chambre de l'Edit alone, where they'd have been sure to get justice. "That must have been Enghien's doing, the dog! They're all afraid of him since he won those few paltry battles in Germany. Zounds! The way Madame Anne and her precious minister act you'd think there wasn't another general in France fit to hold a sword and issue orders to the troops. But never fear, it will come right in the end. That was a nasty one for the

Chabots—wasn't it?—having it all come out about the kid-napping!"

Tancrède looked bewildered, and Guise stared at him. "Do you mean to say they haven't told you?"

The boy shook his head, only wishing it felt clearer.

"My dear fellow, perhaps I shouldn't have mentioned it. After all, though, you're bound to find out sooner or later. Indeed, I'm surprised your mother hasn't given you the facts already. Your lawyers have been on the trail of your abductors for months; now at last they've got hold of the men who stole you and have forced them to confess; they can *prove* what Madame de Rohan has claimed from the first, that the whole job was planned by one person alone. The men who did it were friends of hers—*she* put them up to it—*she* had you kidnapped from the Château de Préfontaines—*she* paid your board money for years without anyone's suspecting. My God! No wonder they've got La Tournelle involved in the business! If ever there were a clear case of criminal re-sponsibility . . ."

"But," faltered Tancrède, a horrible sick sensation—that had nothing to do with the wine he'd drunk—invading his stomach, "I don't understand, cousin; I thought 'twas all Richelieu's doing. 'She,' you say. Whom do you mean? You don't—you *can't*—"

"Poor lad, but I do, though!" Guise glanced at his young guest with compassion, a look gentler than usual in his blaz-ing blue eyes. "Who else in the world but your fair and duti-ful sister, Margot de Rohan herself!"

VIII 🌿

Tᴀɴᴄʀᴇ̀ᴅᴇ had supposed, after his talk with Monsieur de Guise, that he would not be able to sleep at all; but he did, very heavily, waking late next morning with a headache and feeling just as tired as when he'd gone to bed. It was only then he realized how drunk he'd been the night before. With returning consciousness a mood of intolerable oppression seized him. He lay for some time where he was, unable to summon the will to rise, while he remembered all that Guise had told him. Again and again he asked himself, in pain and bewilderment, why Margot had done such a cruel thing. Why . . . *why* . . . ? Surely it could not have been only for money, to assure herself sole possession of the family fortune! There appeared to be no plausible answer to this most agonizing of riddles. . . .

Now at last he understood the reason for Ruvigny's air of constraint in speaking of the past; for Maman's elisions and evasions; for the fact that he himself, ever since his arrival in Paris, had been sealed up in a vacuum, carefully kept from all save the most formal contacts with his fellows. *They'd been afraid he'd find out too much.* But why had he been denied the truth, since—as Guise had said—he was sure to hear it sooner or later anyhow? Were his family fearful of wounding his feelings? Or—which, alas! seemed far more likely—was it simply because they looked upon him as a child—a mere pawn in the game—of no conceivable account in himself, and therefore best left out of his elders' councils? Either way they'd been wrong; either way, he felt now, the hurt was much worse than if he'd been confided in from the first.

Shortly after breakfast his mother arrived in her carriage to fetch him home in response to a tardy message from Guise. It came to Tancrède suddenly, when he beheld her white face and the haggard anxiety in her eyes, that he had forgotten, in his excitement over his hurried departure, to leave word where he was going. Maman embraced him with passion, crying out: "Thank God, my son, you are safe!" She had, it seemed, spent a night of terror, imagining all sorts of enormities: unluckily Lambert, the one servant who knew where his master was, had gone off duty for the Candlemas holiday.

Madame de Rohan expressed proper gratitude to Monsieur de Guise for his kindly meant intervention, but announced that no further measures would be necessary: she had succeeded in getting the Regent to offer them guards for the Hôtel de Rohan—henceforth the house and its inmates would be under the special protection of the King. Tancrède bade good-bye to his cousin, who looked sleepy-eyed and was distinctly vague in his manner—apparently the rôle of Good Samaritan had already begun to bore him —and drove away from the big black house with the pepper-pot towers, far heavier of heart than he had come to it.

There now began for both Rohans the most trying period of uncertainty they had yet known. As if in harmony with their depression, the weather continued inexpressibly damp and gloomy. The lawyers, busier than ever with new researches, seldom came to report on their progress. Tancrède, deeply distressed by what he had learned, and fearing worse discoveries still to be made, hardly knew what to do with himself. From Maman he was divided by the barrier her lack of trust in him had erected. He would not speak to her of Margot, and of the misery his new knowledge had brought him (if his mother meant him not to know, how could he force her confidence?); yet it seemed hardly possible to speak, or even think, of anything else. . . . By tacit consent his studies with Maître Joly had been temporarily suspended—the warden had little leisure these days to devote to his pupil—and the inclement weather had interrupted his daily rides with Ruvigny. Moreover neither they nor his small expeditions with Rondeau and Sidonie—which had likewise ceased—could have been a source of pleasure any longer, since wherever he went the guards had to go, too—a pair of husky policemen who rarely spoke, but acted effectually as a curb on the spirits, perpetual grim reminders of his personal plight. There were, of course, no further overtures of friendship from Monsieur de Guise, but that was scarcely to be wondered at: Tancrède would have been amazed if he had heard anything more from his volatile cousin. Endlessly lonely were his days, and lonelier still the long winter nights; even his dreams seemed tinged by dismal fancies and he rose from his bed unrefreshed, in a stupor compounded of fatigue and dismay.

As for Madame de Rohan, though she went on asserting, with shrill optimism, that she was certain everything would turn out for the best in the end, her actions rather belied her words, for she embarked on a search for amusement more frantic than ever—as if anything were better than staying home to think! Feverishly gay, she entered pell-mell into the rackety diversions of the carnival season, abetted by Vardes and Miossens, her constant companions. The two young men all but slept at the Hôtel de Rohan. Indeed, Tancrède was not perfectly sure but that . . . but there was one door in his mind he steadfastly refused to open.

The sole difference to be discerned in the Duchess's programme was that a new friend was included in it: the Président de Maisons, with whom her relations grew rapidly warmer, had developed the habit of calling upon her daily at the early morning hour when she was at home to her intimates only.

Miossens and Vardes, Tancrède saw, were rather disposed at first to resent the intrusion. Decidedly, Monsieur de Maisons was the sort of person it was impossible to ignore. Whether one liked him or not—and most people found it politic to pretend at least that they did—he gave the tone to any company in which he found himself. A big, strong, handsome, very masculine looking fellow of fifty, with a massive profile and a bold eye, he appeared to be exactly what he was—a self-made man accustomed to paying for what he wanted, and to getting it with a minimum of delay.

What he wanted from Madame de Rohan, it developed by degrees, was less her private favour than her public social support—still more, her assistance in another affair that touched him nearly. It took Tancrède some time to grasp the situation. At first all he could see was that Maman's young men, who had been restively jealous, were suddenly jealous no longer. The comedy of nods and hints and sidelong smiles, which Vardes and Miossens watched with cynical enjoyment, though it affected him unpleasantly, passed over his head. Even Maisons' not too subtle "It's all arranged, then, madam? I can count on you?" spoken out loud as he quitted the Duchess's *lever* one cold February day, and her final "I tell you, sir, the matter's as good as settled—all we need is the opportunity—the little Présidente asks nothing better!" did not provide him with the clue to the mystery.

However, he knew well enough who the "little Présidente" was, and when he found the next afternoon that his mother was giving a party for Madame Tambonneau, he could not help feeling that something very odd must be in the wind.

Madame Tambonneau was another of Maman's newest friends. Perhaps "friend" was not the right word: in her recent exploring of bizarre social by-ways Madame de Rohan had struck up an acquaintance with the wife of a president of the Chambre des Comptes and had attended one of the latter's receptions at her big, smart, new house in the Pré-aux-Clercs. Both Vardes and Miossens had accompanied the Duchess on her excursion into this hitherto uncharted region, since when all three had made merry at their hostess's expense. They had gone into fits of acidulous laughter—Tancrède had heard them often enough—over the Tambonneau's extravagant toilettes, absurd pretensions to be taken for a leader of fashion, and unsubtle attempts to abandon the solid bourgeois background that was hers by birth and marriage for the more exalted climate of court society.

Up to now Maman had shown no sign of desiring to return the hospitality she'd received and had even remarked, rather cruelly, that slumming expeditions were all very well, but it didn't do to bring riff-raff into one's own house, in which scathing judgement both young men had heartily concurred. What could have induced her to change her mind and not only invite the lady to a collation, but actually to build the whole party around her?

The gathering, from the guest of honour's point of view, could hardly have been more alluringly aristocratic or more thrillingly intimate in character. Into the crimson-hung drawing-room of the Hôtel de Rohan she was ushered at the appointed hour to find the Duchess and Tancrède with their cousins, Mesdames de Montbazon and de Guémenée. Fancy!—a duke, two duchesses, and a princess! . . .

The Tambonneau paused in the doorway, breathless with delight, sniffing the rarefied air with her sharp little nose and darting her bright lizard's eyes in every direction to be sure of missing nothing. She was a thin, eager scrap of a woman, with only a glaze of determined elegance to redeem her from total insignificance. Not that she wasn't pretty—she was, rather—; yet one could not avoid feeling that nature had done less for her than her tailor and her coiffeur, and that if she were undressed she might easily come apart like a doll, leaving nothing behind but a handful of sawdust and a few joints and strings. Her gown of crackling scarlet brocade was obviously new; the long, lace-trimmed bodice was nipped in so severely as to make one wonder how she managed to breathe; and her diamond parure was too dazzling for the occasion—the stones were so big and so brilliant that it was a temptation to count them.

Maman rose with a graceful rustle and extended her hand as Madame Tambonneau exploded into greetings and curtsies: "My dear madam! . . . My dear madam! . . . My dear madam! My Lord! This is indeed an honour. Feel myself all too unworthy . . . such a distinguished assembly . . . inner circle indeed . . . must say I never expected . . ."

"Madam, you must take us as you find us," said Maman, negligently gracious. "It's as you see just a family party. I've asked one or two friends to join us later, but for the present I fear you must put up with nothing but Rohans."

The Tambonneau could scarcely have smiled more broadly than she was smiling already. She murmured something politely incoherent about "Surely-a-host-in-yourselves!" as, with coy reluctance, she allowed herself to be manoeuvred across the room and into the place of honour next Maman on one of the benches next the fire, while on the opposite bench the other two ladies composed themselves in genteelly receptive attitudes.

Tancrède, between them, felt distinctly unhappy. He had never been able to make up his mind which of his two kinsmen's wives alarmed him the most; they were both in quite different ways uncomfortable companions. On the whole, perhaps, he preferred Madame de Montbazon—who at least was frankly what she was—to her daughter-in-law. Everything about the former seemed wildly exaggerated—her height, her embonpoint, the blackness of her eyes, the whiteness of her skin; the loudness of her laugh when she clapped her young cousin on the back and asked him how he did, letting out an oath like a guardsman meanwhile. Somehow she was less intimidating than Madame de Guémenée, who combined the languid affectations of a Précieuse with an omniscient eye and an exceedingly sharp tongue, and had a trick of fluttering her lids and crooking her rather long neck to one side as she parried Tancrède's modest efforts to entertain her with a faint "How amusing!" —looking, unfortunately, the reverse of amused.

Today, however, both ladies appeared to be in excellent tempers and to be ready, even eager, to second Maman in her amiable resolve to make Madame Tambonneau feel at home. Indeed, it looked to Tancrède as though they were acting in concert according to a pre-arranged plan; their pretty, complaisant speeches tripped out almost too patly. With honeyed insistence they complimented the guest on her gown, her ribbons, her jewels, her elegant air. The Princess declared she had heard the last *soirée* in the Pré-aux-Clercs was a triumph, eclipsing in refinement and luxury the Queen's carnival ball. "Is it not true, madam, that you had the King's Twenty-four Violins and the Italian comedians, besides fifteen services at supper? It must have been a matchlessly gallant occasion. My cousin de Rohan's been raving about it ever since. I protest I feel quite jealous not to have been included!"—to which Madame Tambonneau responded with a whistling sigh of "Oh, madam, if I dared think you'd *come* . . . !"

"Come?" exclaimed Maman. "Why should she not, I'd like to know? There's no-one nowadays entertains in such style at court, since Bassompierre's old and the Condés have grown too mean to put on a really good show. We should all be tremendously grateful to find at least one house where things are done as they ought to be. Ah, the social gift—how rare it is!"

Madame de Montbazon, true to her rôle of unfettered candour, then ventured to rally the Tambonneau on more personal successes. "Ha! Madam, they tell me we've all got to look to our laurels—that to embark on the conquest of the 'little Présidente' has become all the rage this season. I don't know whom you've *not* got dangling—Roquelaure, Châtillon—can't begin to remember 'em all! What's this I hear, though, about your latest flame? Monsieur de Maisons is said to be as hot in love as a youth of twenty, and to have vowed to win you if it cost him the rest of the winter and half his fortune!"

Madame Tambonneau gave a squeak of acute rapture, and Maman shook a reproving finger at Madame de Montbazon. "Fie, Marie—for shame, my dear! I forbid you to continue. Had I known the rumour, I should never have made so bold as to ask Monsieur le Président to sup with us this evening."

The Tambonneau looked startled, colouring up to her eyebrows—very noticeable even under her heavily daubed on rouge. "Madam, I hadn't the least idea. Madam, I don't know whether I *ought* . . . My husband . . . Jesus! If he should hear . . . Jealous is not the name for it, my dear!"

Before she could gather her forces together to make a pretence of excusing herself her retreat was cut off by the entrance of the men—Ruvigny, Miossens, Vardes, and the Président de Maisons.

It was Tancrède's turn now to look startled, for even to a boy of fifteen the meaning of what happened next was crudely obvious. Monsieur de Maisons made it plain at once that he was no man to waste breath or even an unnecessary minute: after bowing over his hostess's hand he at once approached the object of his quest. Madame Tambonneau, her cheeks still flaming, tossed her head at his opening remark and burst into shrill giggles. It did not take the pair long to find an alcove at the far end of the room, whither they retired to ensconce themselves, their heads very close together, deep in private conversation. A few minutes later, glancing that way, Tancrède saw that they had disappeared altogether.

What shocked him even more was his mother's behaviour

—the resolution and resourcefulness with which she kept her guests sufficiently amused so that the withdrawal of one couple should not be too apparent. She told a number of stories he did not quite understand, which were received with delighted applause; and induced Miossens and Ruvigny to tell stories, too. Presently the whole company managed to work themselves up into a mood of spanking high spirits, their spasms of merriment topped by the peals of Madame de Montbazon's brazen soprano. Everybody seemed to have forgotten about Tancrède; he was beginning to wonder whether he might not ask Maman for permission to go, when Gilbert came in to announce, not, as one had supposed, that supper was ready, but that Maître Joly had arrived and begged for a word with Monsieur le Duc de Rohan and Madame la Duchesse Douairière on a matter of the utmost importance.

Maman sprang to her feet in a pet. "Tiresome creature—at this hour! I'll dispose of him in short order. Tancrède, my son, do you stop here and attend to our guests till I return."

The warden's face, gravely disapproving, appeared beside the lackey's in the door-way—he must have been standing just behind him in the hall—and the moment he saw it Tancrède realized that something dire must have happened. It needed no words to convince one: unlike the lawyers, Maître Joly never used more of them than he needed. He merely observed, in his calm, toneless voice, that he deemed it expedient for Monsieur le Duc to confer with them also. "In my opinion, madam, my Lord should have been taken into our confidence from the very beginning."

Tancrède jumped up, relieved—however bad the news might be—to have an excuse to escape from the atmosphere

of intrigue and innuendo. He saw Maman and Ruvigny exchange a quick glance; then the former, suddenly serious,
bowed her head and, taking her son's hand in hers, followed
Maître Joly out of the room.

The scene that followed in the library was certainly unpleasant. Maître Joly began without preamble: "Madam,
it is my duty to inform you that our case is to come to trial
within a week."

Maman started almost out of her seat. "I don't believe
you!"

"Unhappily, madam, it is only too true. My colleagues
at the Palais have suspected it for some time; only this evening they received word from the ushers in charge of the
court that we must be ready to appear by next Monday, the
twenty-sixth of February—that is, the day after tomorrow.
We are to hear in the morning whether the date be definite
or not."

"I don't believe you!" cried Maman again. "Impossible!
This must be that wretched Enghien's doing."

"There can be no doubt of it, madam. When Monsieur
Joubert and Monsieur Pucelle objected—strenuously, as you
can imagine—they were told that the date had been advanced at the special request of His Highness—it's easy
enough to see why. The Chabots are naturally anxious to
rush things through on purpose to keep us from using all
our vital new evidence. It would be fatal to them if the
facts came to light, and they know it. On the other hand, it
will be equally fatal to us to be forced to plead prematurely."

Maman shrugged her shoulders. "So much the worse,
then. My dear man, you've simply got to face 'em—that's
all there is to it!"

"Out of the question, madam. You must see for your-self that it is. With all there is still to be done, both here and in Holland—so many witnesses to be tracked down and interrogated—it will be weeks, if not months, before your lawyers are ready. The Chabots know that, too. Moreover, I have another piece of unwelcome news for you. The de-fendants have discovered—very unluckily for us—on the parish register of the church of Saint Paul the baptismal record of one 'Tancrède Bon', dated all too appropriately for their purpose. They have bribed or bullied the curate into handing it over and intend to produce it in court—it's not go-ing to be easy to explain it away. I can't help wishing, madam, you'd seen fit to be perfectly frank with us before this. You must have known the record was there—that it was liable to turn up precisely where it would do us most harm. I must entreat you, if you can shed any light on this perplexing subject—even at so late a date—pray do so."

Maman, who during the warden's recital had sat pale and downcast, playing idly with her fan—which fluttered in her hands more than ever like a butterfly striving to escape —now looked up, though without meeting her interlocu-tor's eye, and began to speak, in a low, breathless tone. . . . She recalled, of course—now that Maître Joly mentioned it —having Tancrède baptized. " 'Twas done in a hurry—the week after he was born, if I remember correctly—the poor lamb was so sickly the doctor was afraid he might not live. I was so ill myself it's hard for me to say . . . I am almost sure, though, Monsieur de Candale arranged the whole thing. He must have done so: who else could have helped us? Dur-ing the whole of that terrible time he was always my saviour as Rohan's best friend. Naturally, I'd have chosen to go to

Charenton, but there wasn't time for that—the child was in too great danger. Besides, how then could we have kept our secret? . . . In any case, 'twas Candale, I know, took my son to Saint Paul in the middle of the night. 'Tancrède' was my choice—I've always loved unusual names—my two little daughters who died were Olympe and Sophronie. Tancrède out of Tasso, you know; for I'd been reading *Jerusalem Delivered* only the week before and the poem was fresh in my mind. . . . As for 'Bon,' dear me! after all these years, how can you expect me to be sure. . . ? It goes without saying, a child must have a last name as well as a first name. I suppose you'll agree with me, sir, it would hardly have been prudent in the circumstances to inscribe a 'Rohan' on the parish register! As a matter of fact, now that I come to recollect, Candale had a valet with him on our journey called Bon—Thomas Bon—if I mistake not. A good creature he was, faithfulness and devotion in one—a great comfort to us all in our trials. No doubt our friend, in the sudden emergency, bethought himself of him. Yes, of course! That must have been the way of it. . . ."

Maman went on for some minutes in this strain. Indeed, once having started to talk, she showed no disposition to leave off. No doubt she intended to be helpful; but somehow she wasn't, very. Maître Joly's unyielding sternness showed plainly that he thought her unconvincing. He said as little as possible: it was always his way, Tancrède noticed, to plant his dart firmly and then to let his victims squirm and struggle as they pleased. (One gathered, from what he did say, that Maman had never mentioned Candale before; his rôle in the drama struck a new, and at the eleventh hour wholly disturbing, note.)

At any rate, whatever their disparate views of the cause of their trouble, the Duchess and her employee were at one as to the remedy for it—both were agreed the only thing to be done was to seek a postponement, if possible. Maman was still not without hope that it might be arranged through the influence of Monsieur de Maisons. After all, a *président-à-mortier* was a personage of consequence. She undertook to see him directly—or at least the first thing in the morning—and do her best to persuade him . . .

Maître Joly, forbidding but dauntless, took his leave and, for almost the first time Tancrède could remember, the two Rohans were alone together. For once there was nobody to interrupt or interfere. Now at last, perhaps, they would be able to talk to each other as they had never talked. Now at last he might have a chance to show his mother what was in his heart for her and to learn what she felt in hers for him. Desperately he threw her a pleading look, in which were mingled love and pain, and the dawn of a cruel doubt. Oh, if only . . . !

But Maman, so nervously voluble before, had suddenly not a word left to say. Kissing her son with an air of abstraction, she sent him off to bed and returned to her guests in the Crimson Cabinet.

The next morning, which was Sunday, Tancrède awoke to find that there had been a sleet storm in the night. The trees in the Rohans' garden, and all the other gardens in the square, were silvered over with ice; on the way out to Charenton the whole of the Bois de Vincennes was silver, too, lacking only the sun to transform it into a frost-spangled fairyland—for it was again a very dark day: the wind whistled through the wood, rattling the branches like hostile spears.

Tancrède was alone. He had not even seen his mother, who had sent word after breakfast that she had a headache and was not to be disturbed. In any case it had been arranged the night before that he was to make the trip by himself for a special reason. It had originally been Ruvigny's idea: after all, though the young Duc de Rohan was presumed to be a Protestant, he had not yet formally joined the church of his father. Would it not, therefore, be a politic gesture for him to appear in solitary grandeur at the Temple to make a public profession of his faith? Maman and the lawyers had concurred enthusiastically. So had Maître Joly, although he could not help looking a trifle sour—no doubt because he had not thought of it himself. Even Cousin de Montbazon, who as the eldest member of the family had been hurriedly consulted at the last moment, admitted that it might not be a bad plan: at the present desperate juncture any demonstration of solidarity and support could not fail to prove helpful.

Tancrède himself made no protest. He did not want very much to do what he was asked to do, but it seemed easier to acquiesce than to go through the bother of opposing his guardians, who certainly had his best interests at heart. What did it matter? What did *anything* matter? The successive blows of the last few days had temporarily paralyzed his will; he felt frozen into a kind of numb despair. All his world—the world he had thought so warm and welcoming —seemed to be crumbling about him. On the long drive out to the Temple he sat forlorn in the middle of the back bench of the Rohans' great state coach, gazing unseeingly at the familiar road—unfamiliar today with the trees all-a-glitter in their icy sheathes.

Like an automaton set in motion that must continue on its mechanical way till its works run down, he took his place in the pew where he and his mother had sat together so often; rose and stepped forward to receive communion when the time came to do so; listened with apparent courteous attention to Pastor Drélincourt's pompous and flowery little oration—for the good man was elated by the privilege of welcoming such an illustrious lamb to the fold—; made the proper responses with the simplicity and dignity that never deserted him. His relatives and friends were there to do him honour. Wherever he looked, there were only proud, smiling faces about him; yet suddenly, helplessly, with his whole soul he loathed the whole business.

After the service, on the steps of the Temple—from which he had fled precipitately, hoping to avoid the importunities of the crowd—a lady in black and heavily veiled approached him.

"Tancrède Bon," she said, "I want to speak to you."

Even before she threw back her veil he recognized the soft, small voice as Margot de Rohan's.

"Will you come with me in my carriage to Paris? Or are you afraid?"

Her lip curled disdainfully as she spoke, but she smiled a little to take the sting away. Without an instant's hesitation Tancrède followed her.

IX 🌿

It took the Chabots' coach much longer to drive back to town than it had taken the Rohans' to drive out, for during the morning it had grown warm enough to begin to thaw: the roads were ankle deep in slush, and the white-carpeted Bois de Vincennes with its glittering spears had been turned into a spongy waste of half-melted snow drifts, the tree-trunks damply, depressingly black that had been silver before.

Tancrède and his sister sat side by side in the swaying carriage without speaking. Margot had again dropped her veil, which discouraged conversation, and in any case the boy's thoughts were too confused and tumultuous for words. Only now did it occur to him that he might have walked unsuspectingly into a trap—that perhaps he was being kidnapped for a second time. Stronger, however, than his fears was a feeling that at last all might be made clear between them, and the mystery that had tortured him solved by the one person who could do it. To grasp certainty would he not risk—had he not risked already—everything he had?

He was far too much excited to pay heed to the route they took once they got back to the city; when at length they stopped in front of a handsome hôtel, its monumental entrance flanked by twin stone goddesses with staring almond eyes, he had no idea where they were. Silently Margot led the way through the door—which was opened by a Swiss in the Rohans' own scarlet livery: that in itself was a shock!— and up the stairs to the tapestried salon on the first floor where Chabot was waiting for them.

Close to, the young man was even better looking than he had appeared from across the ballroom floor, his eyes wide and star-like, his dark curls tumbling in a scented and ordered cascade over his lace-collared shoulders. There was, nevertheless, something wispy and indecisive about him: the mouth Tancrède remembered as cruel as a shark's now appeared merely weak, and it could not be doubted—though that, in the circumstances, was surely understandable—that he was exceedingly nervous over the prospect of the interview. He had, one felt, been pacing the floor for hours; it seemed to take a real effort of will on his part for him to greet his brother-in-law—even to go through the motions of relieving his wife of her cloak and veil.

Margot, on the other hand, was entirely self-possessed. She settled herself on a high-backed chair by the hearth and waved Tancrède to another; remained where she was —on the very edge of her seat, it was true—while a servant fetched a bottle of wine and some goblets. "You'll drink something? No? As you like, then. . . . Crispin, leave the tray on the table. And for Heaven's sake do something about the fire—I'd really like to know why we should have to live in the only ill-heated house in Paris!"

If she were nervous, too—if her assurance implied the careful control of a cat preparing to pounce—it was evident only in the slight edge of impatience in her silken tones as she addressed the lackey. As soon as Crispin had left the room she turned to her brother and said—still in the gentle voice that seemed to have got by mistake into the wrong body—: "First let me make this plain to you, young man—I sought you out today for one reason alone, and that was to help you. I want to warn you before it's too late to stop your idiotic lawyers from pursuing their case any further. On no account, mind you, must they appear at the Palais tomorrow. To go on with the trial now would be fatal to you both—absolutely fatal!"

Tancrède looked his sister full in the face.

"Why?"

"Because, you little fool,"—the cat showed her claws for a moment—"your suit is lost already! We know much too much for your good. It's simply insensate obstinacy on my mother's part ... Chabot, I beg you, either sit down or stand still! I can't bear your prowling about like a wolf!"

"My dear, forgive me," murmured Chabot, pausing to lean his elbows on the back of his wife's chair. But it was to be noticed that he began his wanderings again as soon as he felt it was safe to do so. The simile of the wolf, though, wasn't the right one: Tancrède was reminded much more forcibly of a frightened cock pheasant he had seen once striving to find a way out of its enclosure in the King's menagerie at the Louvre.

Margot's glance grew increasingly menacing; it took all the boy's courage to return it without flinching as he said evenly: "*We* know things, too, sister, that may surprise you —for instance, who stole me . . ."

Madame de Chabot looked as though she would like to annihilate him, yet she kept perfectly still—even her pretty, slim hands lay idle in her lap: all the energy and malice in her being seemed concentrated in the baleful topaz eyes.

"Yes, you may know the facts—but not the reason for them. Why do you suppose I took such a risk—for it was a fearful risk—and did such a terrible thing?—for it was a terrible thing: I'm ready now to admit it! Answer me that, if you can!"

Tancrède shook his head, while his hands gripped the arms of his chair, carved to represent a pair of snarling griffins, as tightly as possible.

"Why, you poor simpleton,"—Margot's cold fury was the more alarming for being rigidly suppressed—"you may as well hear the story from me as from anyone else—better, in fact: I've the best right to tell it! I did what I did for the honour of the family. For the sake of my father Rohan, and his memory. I loved my father more than anyone else in the world—loved his name and his fame dearly enough to commit a crime to protect them. Do you understand what I mean, little boy? Up to now my husband and I have been lenient—too lenient, perhaps. We've been willing to let people believe that *we* believed you to be a foundling—a child of vile origin—maybe even the son of Thomas Bon, the valet whose name you bear. No doubt we've been foolishly weak. I wanted to spare my mother the shame of exposure . . . But if she persists in this ridiculous suit, Chabot and I will have no choice save to tell the truth."

"And what," said Tancrède, gathering all his forces together, "*is* the truth, my sister?"

Margot averted her eyes and blushed a little. "I hate to mention the subject, especially before a child. After all, though, you'll have to know some day anyhow. You're my mother's son, no doubt about that. But Rohan never got you. Your father was Candale; my mother could tell you that as well as I, if she'd a spark of honesty in her. Candale was her lover all along. Why else, do you suppose, was she stark mad to leave Venice just then, if not to hide the result of her guilt? The mission to France must have seemed to her like a godsend. There were half a score trusty followers Papa might have sent to Paris—but no: she coaxed him with cunning and falseness—of which she's plenty and to spare!—to entrust the whole business to her. And then, as if that weren't shocking enough, what did she do but take Candale with her? Oh, I could die of shame, even now, when I remember. . . ! I was only thirteen, but no fool for my age—I knew very well what the matter was. For the wrong she did my father, for the disgrace she brought on us all, I have never forgiven her. No—and as long as I live, as God is my witness, I never shall!"

At first Tancrède felt almost too much aghast to find words. He opened his mouth several times before he could even manage: "But Maman wouldn't . . . *couldn't* . . . How can you say such vile things about our own mother?"

"I can say vile things because she *is* vile. What kind of creature do you take her for? She was never faithful to my father from the first."

Deliberately, with venomous satisfaction, Margot de Chabot named a whole list of men who, according to her, had enjoyed her mother's favours. There were Arnauld du Fort and the Maréchal de Saint-Luc . . . Candale, of course . . . and Guitaut, captain of the Queen's bodyguard . . . each supplied with dates and circumstances so detailed that Tancrède was convinced against his will. The smooth, sweet voice unrolled its shocking catalogue, neither rising nor falling. . . . "Aumont . . . Louvigny . . . the Comte de Jarzé . . . Even now that she's old, do you fancy she's mended her ways? On the contrary, she's worse than ever! The only difference is that today she's forced to pay young men for what she wants. All Paris laughed itself sick when the news leaked out she'd bought that harpy Miossens a regiment in the Guards with the fifty thousand crowns I gave her. And why do you suppose a flibbertigibbet like Vardes squires a hag who might be his mother, if not in the hope that she'll do as much, or more, for him? Oh, no, thank you! I stood it as long as I could. Then I got out—long before I was married. Maman never told you *that,* did she? . . . No; I imagined not. It's true just the same. I went to live with Aunt de Rohan in her horrid little lodgings—do you know whom I mean? Old Anne with her books and her spectacles, her stuffed owls and her snuffy manuscripts. It wasn't in the least amusing—but better boredom with honour than luxury and dishonour at home!"

The voice stopped suddenly. Tancrède, overwhelmed, still was struggling to reply: "I won't—I *can't*—believe all these horrible things! Why, Monsieur de Ruvigny has sworn . . . and he's my best friend . . ."

Margot's laugh ripped out on a startling high note of scorn. "A fine friend you've got there! Let me tell you something about your precious Ruvigny. It was he who had you stolen away—he who laid the whole plot, who got La Sauvetat and the rest of 'em to help us."

Tancrède gasped.

"I don't believe that either!"

"It's true, though; I swear it."

"But why—*why?*"

"Because I asked him to. Because my lawyer told us that, if you were shown in public—even though everybody knew you were a bastard—you might be recognized as Papa's legal heir, since you were born while he was married to my mother. Because Ruvigny, too—with all his faults—cared for the honour of the Rohans."

The voice stopped once more. Tancrède, his face livid, got up to go. He was barely conscious of what he was doing, and certainly far beyond coherent speech. At the moment one desire possessed him, and that was to get out of the room as fast as possible—never again as long as he lived to be forced to see or to speak to the fair young woman with topaz eyes as hard as stones.

Monsieur de Chabot, who during the scene between his wife and his brother-in-law had remained discreetly in the background, now moved forward with a tentative smile. It was plain to be seen he was very uncomfortable: used to do only the graceful thing, he must be hard put to it to find the appropriate gesture now.

"My dear sir, you're not leaving? Madame de Chabot and I are just about to sit down to dinner. We'd take it very kind of you if you would join us—that is so, is it not, Margot, my love? After all, now that we understand one another, there's no reason—is there?—why we should not be friends."

"Friends? With *you*?"

"At least, then, let me order the carriage to take you home. My dear, the horses were waiting, I think. . . ?"

Tancrède shook his head, flung them one last look of horror and dismay, and rushed blindly from the room, down the stairs, out of the door between the two staring stone goddesses, and away into the gathering dusk.

X

HE RAN as fast as he could, and as far as his breath would take him, without looking where he was going. It was not until he was forced to stop for a moment that he realized that, even if he had looked, it would not have made any difference—he was hopelessly lost! For the life of him he could not have told what quarter he was in; all he could say with certainty was that, as he could not remember crossing it, it was reasonable to suppose he must still be on the right side of the river.

Panting a trifle, Tancrède glanced about in desperation, seeking in vain for some familiar landmark. It occurred to him then that he really did not know Paris very well. The streets all looked much alike, narrow, dark, and winding; there seemed to be no open space to which one might resort to gain a perspective on the surroundings. Moreover, what light there was, was failing fast—not that the day was over: it could not, he calculated, be much past two o'clock—but a gloomy fog was settling inexorably over the city. Worse, it was bitterly cold. . . . Tancrède had begun to shiver, despite his fur-lined cape. After reflecting for a little he came to the conclusion that there was nothing to do but continue walking until he either found his way or someone who could find it for him. Turning his collar higher and thrusting his hands deep into his pockets, he set out again at as brisk a pace as possible. The main thing, after all, was to keep moving and, whatever happened, to try not to think. . . .

For what seemed many hours—and might in reality have

been two or three—he wandered miserably about without coming upon anyone to whom he could apply for directions. As it was a Sunday and the weather was so bad, the streets were almost deserted; the few people he saw looked like beggars, so dirty and sinister that he shrank from approaching them. Once only a great black church loomed suddenly out of the fog. A bell in the steeple was ringing and the congregation was hurrying to Vespers, but nobody noticed him. When he tried to accost some of the prosperous looking burghers his voice failed him and the figures went on flitting past in the uncertain half-light. And in a minute it was already too late: the few last stragglers disappeared, the bell stopped ringing, and the doors shut with a clang, leaving Tancrède alone in the cold outside.

Finally, very nearly in tears, his teeth chattering uncontrollably, he stumbled by accident out of the labyrinth into the empty space he'd been seeking. Not only a square, but *his* square—the Place Royale at last! With amazement he discovered that he had been travelling round in a circle, at no time more than a few paces from home. In front of the Hôtel de Rohan a number of carriages—Cousin de Montbazon's amongst them—were drawn up. (Could Maman be giving *another* party?) And just as he was about to ring the bell for Lambert he almost collided with a man wearing riding-clothes and a heavy cloak coming out of the house— even in the dark it was easy to tell who it was.

Tancrède would have passed him with a bare salute—for there was no-one he less wanted to see just then than Ruvigny—if the latter had not caught him by the arm, crying out in a voice that sounded both hoarse and anxious: "My little Lord, where have you been?"

Through frozen lips Tancrède said stiffly: "Let me pass, please!"

But the officer only tightened his grip: "My Lord, don't go in just yet! They're all still upstairs, you know. Madame la Duchesse has called the whole family to a conference, in order to decide what to do. Joly and the lawyers are with them. Truly, I think 'twould be better . . ."

Tancrède was struggling to release himself. "I want to be there, too! It's my right. Let me go—let me go, I tell you!"

"Later, if you like. Not just now, I entreat you. This isn't the time . . . Come with me instead for a little. Have you dined? . . . I thought not."

Before he knew how it had happened the boy found himself swung up on a horse a groom had been holding in readiness; Ruvigny was in the saddle behind him; and away they clattered through the fog and the cold—whither, Heaven only knew!

Coiffier's in the rue du Pas-de-la-Mule, which Ruvigny said was one of the best restaurants in the Marais, was empty so long past the dinner hour. However, a fine fire was blazing on the hearth and the low-raftered room with its mullioned windows looked warmly reassuring. The serving wench, whom Ruvigny greeted with a clap on the back and called "Nanine," seemed reassuring, too; she was stout and comfortable and bustled about as if providing a meal out of season were a pleasure instead of a bother. After he had gulped down a glass of brandy and eaten a plate of steaming soup Tancrède felt better; he was even able to enjoy, in a vague way, the savoury smell of the plump fowl set to roast on the spit.

Ruvigny did not try to speak to him at first. He sat quite

quietly in his corner, gazing across the board at his young guest with a look that blended equal parts of anxiety and affection, and smiling at him whenever their glances met; but it was not until the latter had finished his soup that conversation began. And then it was Tancrède who began it. He lifted troubled eyes—for with the returning warmth of his body his thoughts had started to thaw out, too (and what thoughts! Good God! How would he *ever*. . . ?)—and said abruptly: "Ruvigny, I've something to tell you."

The soldier returned his regard with a frankness that Tancrède now felt must bespeak the very opposite.

"I know you have, my Lord, and I assure you I am ready to listen. But first, if you don't mind, I should like to say a few words to *you*. I'd rather you heard the news from me than from those—well, I won't say what I think of 'em! After all, they're your relatives; they've a right to be consulted, I suppose. To begin with, then: Joly and the lawyers have learned there's no hope of postponing the trial. It's to be held tomorrow before a full session of Parliament; there's nothing we can do to stop it. In the circumstances your family have decided that the only thing to do is to let the case go by default. Do you understand what that means? Our side simply won't appear in court at all. The Chabots, of course, will be able to win a temporary victory. . . . Just a moment, though! I'm not done yet. That's by no means the end of the story. As you, my Lord, are not legally of age, you cannot be bound by the judges' decision tomorrow—as soon as you are eighteen you can appeal against it and demand a new trial. It's true you'll have to wait three years, but we can use the time to our advantage. Madame la Duchesse is retaining her full legal counsel—indeed, adding to it. When the time comes to plead again we expect to have a water-tight case. All the necessary evidence will have been gathered and sifted. I'll say that much for those chaps from the Palais—they know their job and no mistake! In fact, they've already drawn up a list of documents they need and are hard at work procuring them. It seems to me they've really thought of everything: proof of your parents' conjugal relations in Venice—that'll involve a trip to Italy;—of the fact that Monsieur le Duc was aware of his wife's condition when he sent her to Paris and was privy to all that occurred there; of the circumstances relating to your abduction—they've an agent in Normandy now working on that—; lastly, of everything that happened in Holland. . . . There, of course, is where *I* come in! I'm going next week to Leyden myself, and I'll be greatly mistaken if I fail to get what I want out of that rascal La Sauvetat, his brother, and the rest of the crew. They're the principal fellows we're after now. And if all goes as we hope, I'll wager before the month is out—"

Ruvigny's confident monologue came to a premature close as Tancrède interrupted him by staring across at his friend with sick, unhappy eyes and speaking just five words: "How could you do it?"

The soldier's red face turned even redder, but he met the look full on. "Then you know?"

"Yes, I know—more, much more, than I wish I did. Oh, Ruvigny . . ."

"Who told you?" Ruvigny demanded fiercely.

"My sister."

"That devil! I might have known it. This is what I've been hoping to avoid from the first. There's no help for it now, I suppose. My Lord, I'd give my right hand gladly if I could relive the past and undo the wrong I've done. I beg you to believe me. But tell me what she said. . . ."

Bit by bit during dinner Tancrède related the story of his interview with the Chabots. It took a long time to tell everything; when at last the sorry facts were all exposed the boy could not help wailing again, out of his bitterness of heart: "How could you do it? *Why* did you? I thought you were my friend."

"Why?" repeated Ruvigny, a curious expression, part shame, part remorse, on his blunt, ruddy features. "I'll tell you why. Because I was a young fool, mad in love."

"Did you love Margot?"

The soldier bowed his head; even before he did so it flashed over Tancrède that he ought to have guessed it long ago.

"More than anyone or anything else in the world. More than duty, honour, truth itself. For years I lived only for her—wanted only her—saw things only through her eyes. My little Lord, you're too young yet to realize what such a passion can do to a man. I was blind to all but my love. Not that it made me happy—I could feel even then it meant nothing to her save a means to an end. Now I regret my fault more sorely, since I've learned to know and love *you*. Now I see and despise Margot for what she is—a cruel, heartless schemer, false to herself and to everyone who held her dear."

"But," objected Tancrède, with quivering lips, "she said she did what she did for honour's sake. I don't see . . ."

Ruvigny spat on the floor. "Zounds! What does a trollop know of honour? She did what she did to get money and power—the only things that matter to creatures like her. My Lord, I am going to tell you something I shouldn't—something that perhaps a boy of your age is too young to hear. When your sister prates of the intolerable conditions in her mother's house, and of how offended virtue obliged her to leave it, she is lying in her teeth. Yes, and I'd tell her so to her face if I saw her! Madame la Duchesse may have had her weaknesses in the past—who amongst us is without 'em? —but Madame de Chabot's no better. The difference between them is that one is frank about her sins, and the other is not. Believe me, I know what I'm saying! Mistress Margot left home for one reason alone: 'twas in order to be able to indulge her amorous fancies to the full without hindrance. She chose deliberately to go to her aunt because she knew right well the poor half-blind old woman was too simple to catch on to the game. Your sister lay with Chabot for years before she married him. And for years before that she lay with *me*. She could do things like that without suffering for them because she was sure, no matter what lengths she went to, with her beauty and wealth and exalted position she'd always find a husband in the end. There! that's the whole truth, so help me! and bitter it is to have to confess it to a lad like you."

During this recital Tancrède's face had grown pale and his eyes wide with a deepening horror. Now he gasped, in a voice that was half a sob: "Is there nothing I can have faith in? No-one left in the world who is good? Not you any more—not even my mother I've loved so much? Oh, Ruvigny . . ."

Ruvigny leaned forward suddenly and clasped the boy's unwilling hands in both of his.

"My Lord," he said earnestly, "you mustn't, whatever happens, stop loving Madame la Duchesse; for she loves you—rest assured of that. . . . Oh, perhaps at first she did not, so much; perhaps in those days she was mainly bent on revenge. Why wouldn't she have been? So was I—I admit it. 'Twas to pay your sister out for flouting me that I told your mother I knew you were living and where she could find you. But this I could swear to, my Lord: no-one on earth could know you without growing to care for you deeply. Madame la Duchesse is no monster like Margot; she has a woman's feelings, a mother's heart . . ."

"But if she knows she's lying—if she knows I'm not Rohan's son?"

"Nonsense! She knows nothing of the sort. That's just another of your sister's despicable falsehoods. Your mother is sure who got you—she *must* be, else she'd not fight for you as she has done, as she intends to go on doing, with all her strength and all her fortune. Never forget it; you've something to cling to there that cannot fail you. If the Rohans stand steadfast together, with God's help we'll manage to conquer the forces of evil. Lord! If I didn't believe that from my soul, I swear I'd rather die than go on living in a world where truth and justice are trampled under foot at last."

Tancrède still looked sick and shaken, and his voice still sounded sick and shaken, too; but for the first time there was a ray of hope on his ravaged young face (which seemed to be all eyes and beak like a fledgling bird's) as he said: "Do you really believe this? Do you really believe I'm the Duc de Rohan?"

And with a final comforting handclasp Ruvigny answered heartily: "As sure as we're sitting here now at this table!"

By the time Tancrède got home he found the row of carriages gone and the house dark and apparently deserted except for a pair of lackeys on duty. On the stairs going up he heard Sidonie's voice, fluting and merry, in the courtyard below; but for once he failed to call out to her; at the moment he felt no desire for company, however cheerful and undemanding. Shrinking even from the silently watchful presence of Thomas, he turned, instead of seeking his own rooms, into the library, where the conference had evidently been held, for there was a disorder of chairs and the remains of a fire still smouldered in the grate.

Papa's armchair seemed to be waiting for him; he sank into it with a sigh, intending to stay for a few minutes only. But fright, fatigue, the various exhausting emotions that had succeeded them, together with the warmth and relaxation induced by a late, heavy meal, combined to send him to sleep. . . .

When he woke, some hours later, the room was quite dark save for the faint expiring glow on the hearth. At first he was not sure where he was; then remembrance came with an unwelcome rush. Simultaneously he realized what had wakened him: a man and a woman had entered from the door that led to his mother's private cabinet and were standing near the window talking in hushed tones. They could not see him curled up in his chair, nor he, them; but he knew at once who they were—even without Vardes' peculiar clumping step and the soft rustle that could only be Maman's lacy dressing-gown, the voices were unmistakable.

The latter spoke first, in a whisper so low it was almost a sigh: "It's good-bye, then—and for the last time!"

"By your wish, madam, not mine," retorted the Marquis stiffly; and Tancrède could tell, without looking, exactly how the young man had drawn his black brows together in an ominous frown.

"What else, my dear, can I possibly do? You know I care for you as much as ever—it breaks my heart in two to let you go—but there's no other way out: or is there? After all, I've got to be sensible. Say what you will, my fortune is limited, especially since I made that unfortunate donation to Margot. If it hadn't been for that, I might just have managed—but what's the good in talking of it now? I simply can't go on throwing money left and right, the way I've been doing. As it is, Martin says I shall have to retrench— odious word!—the rest of the year, or else run into serious difficulties. And it's only too plain that this miserable lawsuit may drag on for years. One knows what lawyers are— how they love to delay things, how fiendishly clever they are at running up bills. God alone can tell how much it may cost me before they are done!"

"You may recall, madam,"—Vardes sounded frigidly unsympathetic—"I never advised the business from the first. 'Twas all Miossens' doing, I'll wager. Ah, well, why should *he* care, one way or t'other? He'd got what he wanted already!"

"How dare you reproach me?" cried Maman, furious despite her *sotto voce.* "Haven't I had to stand enough of that from the family today? It's easy to blame me now that things have gone wrong, but if we'd succeeded 'twould have been a different story. I'm sick to death of being called to account by those who think they've a right to accuse me. And as for you, sir, who've no right at all—who've less claim on my bounty than the least beggar in the street . . ."

Her voice died away suddenly. Tancrède heard the clank of Vardes' sword as the latter moved swiftly across the room; then, by turning his head slightly, he caught sight of his mother standing in her lover's embrace, half petulant, half mollified, uncertain what to say or do.

"What it comes down to is this: you care more for your son than you do for me."

"You know that's not it! You know too well what you've meant to me—what you still mean—or could, if you'd the patience to wait till this tiresome affair is settled and out of the way. You know, too . . . ah, but my dear, where's the use in arguing? I might talk the whole night through and not convince you. What's done can't be undone. What's to come is—well, you're at liberty to guess as well as I. Bid me good-bye like a gentleman and a cavalier. We'll wish each other all the luck in the world and part the best of friends, with a kiss to seal the bargain."

For a long moment they were blotted in each other's arms. Tancrède heard his mother's sigh, Vardes' smothered exclamation: "Ah, madam, if only. . . !" Then the young man was gone and Maman, crying softly, returned to her room.

It seemed a long time after that before the boy felt able to rise, stiff and sore from his cramped position, and started slowly for the door. On the way he was arrested by a vision in the glass; even in the twilight his own face, white and strained, the eyes solemn and staring, was a sight to startle. No wonder either! After what he'd seen and heard today

Tancrède was convinced that life could have little more to show him: had he not plumbed the utmost depths to which human nature was capable of sinking? Nothing, surely, was left to him—and no-one. The thought of Margot, of Ruvigny—of Maman now, above all—had become pure agony. Yet as he gazed unhappily at his pinched and woe-begone image the last log in the fire collapsed into ashes; sparks started up in showers; and by their brilliant, fleeting light he saw the topknot of the Rohans gleaming ghost-like like a plume of silver on his brow.

Part Two

Romorantin and Paris, January, 1649

I

THEY TOOK that afternoon the road to Selles along the sedge-grown, glass-green river, flecked with slowly moving cakes of ice. At the abandoned farm, with its collapsed and sagging roof and the round tower of the dovecote crumbling into ruins, without a word they turned their ponies up the hill to the immense open heath, always their favourite place for a gallop. Here in summer the grass was gay with purple heather; now the dark green of the pine wood on the far side of the heath lent the only note of colour to a landscape all dull greys and browns; even the occasional patches of snow in the hollows had lain there too long to look really white. Still the ground was dry enough to be safe for the horses and the weather was—for a wonder—quite pleasant, mild and misty, with an intermittent pale gleam of sunshine to cheer them.

As he rode along Tancrède thought—and the thought, like the ride, was by no means new—what a lonely place Romorantin was. It seemed not merely lost but deliberately hidden away, the one inhabited speck in the midst of the desolate marshy plains of the Sologne. Journey as one would for leagues in any direction—towards Bourges, towards Blois, towards Orléans—one found never a hamlet and scarcely a farmstead or two, most of these long deserted by owners who'd found life insupportable in the wilderness. There were even few travellers to be met with along the way, for Romorantin was not on the main route to any-where in particular. Was that—he asked himself for perhaps the hundredth time—why Maman had chosen it, out of half a dozen country estates at her disposal, as an appropriate refuge for her ruined hopes? She had said at the time that it was a matter of money: she wanted to secure for her son the *capitainerie* of the district—that was, the command of the royal hunting domain; for most of this queer, wild land belonged to the crown and was as full of game as it was empty of people. At all events, having made her decision, she stuck to it; in the last three years she'd rarely left her home; and Tancrède had stayed with her out of loyalty, and because there was really nothing else for him to do.

How dull it had been, this aimless time of waiting! (Could one actually believe that it was almost at an end?) Eating and sleeping and walking and riding, with an infrequent stag hunt or boar hunt to vary the drowsy monotony. Long summer days in the garden, playing mall or tennis or even blind-man's-buff; long winter evenings in the castle, at chess or alone with a book; no visitors to speak of; few letters, even—for who was there to write? Above all, a feeling that it didn't matter in the least when one stopped doing one thing and started another, since time had no value when time was all one had. If it had not been for Sidonie . . .

At the recollection of what her companionship had meant —of all they had been to each other, the only two youthful creatures in a household of rueful and embittered elders—he turned to smile at the blooming young woman riding at his side. Sidonie smiled back at him as they reached the edge of the wood; it was only then Tancrède remembered that they hadn't had their run, but it was too late now; they were already under the trees in the deep blue shade, where the snow lay so thick that the horses had to pick their way at a careful walk. He remembered something else, too—the news he had to break to his friend, and that he'd especially chosen this ride as the most suitable opportunity to tell her. It wasn't easy to know how to begin. Women were strange creatures —even Sidonie—; with them an oblique approach was generally best. Hence, after casting about in his mind for the right opening, he remarked in a sedulously casual tone: "I'm glad your father got back safely from Paris."

"Oh, so am I!" said Sidonie. "I was frightened to death all the time he was gone. I'm sure Madame la Duchesse never would have sent him if it hadn't been very important. It must be dreadful there, where the fighting is. What are they fighting for, Tancrède?"

"It's some sort of civil war, I think. I heard your father say last night Cardinal Mazarin was unpopular with the people and they wanted to get rid of him."

"That's a funny reason for Frenchmen to kill Frenchmen, it seems to me. Why, Mazarin's a foreigner—he's an Italian, after all! Do you understand what it's all about?"

Tancrède considered. "Not too well, I must say. All I'm sure of is that Parliament is on one side of the fence, and the King and the Regent on the other. Things have come to such a pass that the royal family have had to flee Paris and are living at Saint Germain, while their troops are besieging the city. Their general in command is the Prince de Condé —he who used to be the Duc d'Enghien before his father died. How I'd like a chance to pick a quarrel with *him!*"

Sidonie shivered. "Don't even mention it—they say he's as cruel as a Turk and cuts off his enemies' noses and ears! I heard Hubert in the kitchen . . ."

"My dear, if you listen to servants' tales. . . ! Well, this is the way of it, as far as I can see: the other party, called the Frondeurs—where the people and the Parliament are—is much the strongest, everybody says. They're commanded by Condé's brother, the young Prince de Conti. He's popular with the nobles at court and so a great many of them have come over to his side, too. It's my mother's idea that I join them. As she says, now my eighteenth birthday is past, our suit will be coming up soon. It's clear we've nothing to hope for from the King, so she thinks it would be best for me to throw my lot in with Parliament. Do you see what I mean? We can't lose anything that way, and we stand to gain a great deal. This is our last ride together, Sidonie. I'm leaving for Paris tomorrow."

Sidonie gave a cry and almost slipped from her saddle. "Why didn't you tell me before?"

"I didn't want to say anything until I was sure. Maman and I wrote to the Prince some time ago to offer my services —'twas your father took the letter for us—but we didn't know till he got back last night that they'd been accepted. I'm off tomorrow at dawn with Hubert and Olivier. We're going to do our best to break through the lines of the besiegers—that'll take some manoeuvring, I imagine, though Rondeau says men manage to get past every day—so that I can present my credentials to the general. Isn't it splendid? You must be glad for me, Sidonie. At last I have something to do!"

Sidonie was not at all sure it was splendid. "But you may be wounded—or killed, even! Wars are terrible things, I think."

Tancrède squared his shoulders, trying not to look too complacent. "War is what men are made for. How else are they to show what they are worth? If you love me, Sidonie, my dear—and I am sure you do: these last three years we've been brother and sister to each other—you must pray that I be given a chance to win glory on the battlefield and force the government to recognize my claims. After all, what on earth can I do here? I've got to get out into the world and prove myself with men. This is my one great chance. I'm sick to death of being nobody—who the devil's the Sieur Tancrède? It's as the Duc de Rohan I'll come riding back to you. And if that can never be, I'd rather die—a thousand times rather! As for that bully Condé, if he just comes my way. . . !"

Tancrède broke off a branch from one of the pine trees and gave the air a vicious switch as though his enemy were already within reach. Just then they emerged from the wood beside a reed-fringed pond, beyond which, across a spongy meadow, loomed the solitary tall pink brick tower of the castle of Romorantin. The sun was setting now, a blood-red ball suspended in the mists that were rising ever more thickly from the river and the marshy plains around it. With a warning squawk and a whir of heavy wings a brace of ducks rose from the reeds and scudded off into the sunset. Sidonie shivered again.

"Oh, my dear, I suppose you are right, but I can't help it —my heart misgives me. I know you mustn't stay in Romorantin forever. If only there were some other way!"

"I don't say there mightn't be, but this is the best one, believe me. Oh, God, if you knew how anxious I am to be off! I can hardly wait . . ."

Here he broke off as he saw that the girl was really upset. Her lips were quivering; two large tears had gathered on her lashes and were poised ready to fall. To cheer her the boy proposed a race over the last few fields that divided them from home; he knew from experience—who better?—that the best cure for unhappy thoughts was violent physical motion. Off they went, the hoofs of their twin bay Barbary ponies spattering the soft snow far and wide, and arrived at the gate abreast and laughing once more. Tancrède jumped off without waiting for the groom and helped his lady to dismount. Sidonie put her hand on his shoulder and looked at him questioningly; there was fear in her dark eyes, warm affection, and something more Tancrède could not put a name to. Gently their lips came together as they had often done before, but this time there was a difference: did Sidonie share his feeling that their childhood days were done forever?

Before returning to the house they stopped at the stables for a moment: Tancrède had had word that morning that one of the falcons had been hurt in an accident and he had promised Colin, the falconer, to look at it. When he entered the room where they were kept the birds set up a clamour, as if trying to tell him what was wrong: there were lanners from Sicily and a pair of handsome Swedish gerfalcons amongst them. Old Colin, almost in tears, brought the wounded bird to his master. The sleek young peregrine Dulcinée had been his chief pride; unluckily at her very first trial she had been set upon by an eagle and crippled; Colin had had great difficulty in beating off her assailant and now feared that the injured wing was too badly broken to mend.

" 'Tis a thousand pities, sir; I'd been saving her for Monsieur de Ruvigny's visit; the Marquis takes such pleasure in a well schooled peregrine. I doubt, though, if we can save her."

"Will she die?" asked Sidonie, gazing pitifully at the bird, who lay tense and miserable in the old man's arms, gazing back at them with bright, mutinous eyes, as if unable to accept the fact that this had happened to *her*.

"No, Mademoiselle; I hardly think so. But she'll not fly again. And a falcon who can't fly is little good to herself or anyone else. 'Twould be better to do away with her directly and spare her useless suffering. I'd have done it myself already, but I felt it my duty to wait and ask the master's permission."

Tancrède stretched out his hand and gently stroked the barred brown back. Dulcinée grew quieter under his touch; the frightened glare in her eyes slowly died away. Truth to tell, he cared neither for falcons nor falconry; his sympathies had always rested perversely with their prey. Now, however, it was impossible not to regret this cruel reversal of rôles—the attacker attacked, the predatory creature maimed and made helpless at her first venture, could not help arousing compassion.

"Let us wait till tomorrow," he said. "Perhaps she'll be better by then."

Colin nodded a grudging assent and carried his wounded charge back to her cage.

The great hall of the castle of Romorantin was a vast, draughty stone room, sparsely furnished, its high and otherwise bare walls lined with trophies of the chase—a fearsome boar's head or two and pair upon pair of spreading antlers. At the far end of it, on either side of the huge hooded mantelpiece—beneath which a sulky fire struggled in vain to overcome the prevailing chill—two old ladies wearing widows' caps and identical black gowns were sitting. Madame de Sully, who had arrived that afternoon to spend a month with her daughter, looked, Tancrède thought, very much the same as she had on that August day, more than three years ago, when he had seen his grandmother for the first time. At eighty-seven, she had long ago got to be as old as she ever would. Her back was still amazingly erect; her knotted fingers were busy as ever stitching at one of her interminable tapestries.

As for Madame de Rohan, she hadn't, of course, altered over night; there had been plenty of time in which to grow used to gradual changes; but it was only now, as he saw her next to her own mother, that he realized in some ways she seemed the elder of the two. Perhaps the greatest change of all was that one felt she no longer cared how she looked. She had always made the most of her appearance for others' sakes, not her own; and now when there was nobody left to deplore the hair gone grey, the face lined with grief and regret . . . Tancrède, stooping to kiss her, told himself no words were needed to make it quite plain that Vardes had not had a successor.

Grand-maman in her turn extended a claw and acknowledged Sidonie's demure curtsy with a shrill "How d'y do, my dear? And who may you be?"

"Oh, Maman, that's Rondeau's daughter, who's been with us ever since she was born! You surely can't have forgotten Sidonie de Montville. . . ."

"Tut, tut, of course not! I see now who it is. 'Tis my poor eyes' fault—they're not at all what they were—and it's shocking dark in here besides. Ring for candles, Marguerite! I hope you've not got mean living by yourself in the country. Sidonie de Montville ... bless me, my dear! You've grown a great deal taller since last summer, haven't you? It seems to me you're quite a young lady now."

Sidonie nodded and blushed and curtsied again as she took her leave, on the plea that her father was waiting for her. Her modest self-possession almost deserted her as her exit was audibly followed by the ancestress's malevolent squeak: "La, Marguerite, the girl's really astonishingly pretty! Aren't you afraid she and young Tancrède ... ?"

"Nonsense, Maman! She's nothing but a child still. Besides, Tancrède and Sidonie have always been like brother and sister."

But the boy could tell, from his mother's tone, that for the first time she might be beginning to doubt it. To gloss over the slight awkwardness he bent over Grand-maman once more and excused himself in his turn; it was time to dress for supper. Was there perhaps a twinkle lurking in the old blue eyes, as brightly inhuman as any falcon's?

That night, in honour of the visitor, and also because it was his last night at home, he donned his best black velvet suit with the Flanders lace collar and spent more time than usual at his dressing-table, brushing his unruly dark curls till they shone and submitting with less than his usual impatience to Thomas' ministrations and suggestions. After the valet was gone Tancrède placed a taper on either side of the glass and stared long and earnestly at the image reflected therein. At eighteen, he supposed he might consider himself a man. During the last six months, much to his regret, he had not succeeded in growing a single inch. This lack of height still worried him sometimes, and would have been an even worse affliction had he not recalled that Papa, too, had been short. It was also a trial that his boyish features obstinately refused to take on the longed for resemblance to the subtly aquiline profile in his father's portrait. Tancrède rather disliked his own looks—the brown face, wide mouth, and enormous grey-green eyes that still dominated, though they no longer diminished, his young face. He had no idea that he was handsome and would have been very much surprised if he'd been told that many people thought him so.

Supper was served, on Madame de Sully's account, in the banquet hall, another immense apartment as stone-cold and comfortless as all the *chambres de parade* at Romorantin. Maman often lamented their size to contrast them unfavourably with the lost amenities of the more modern and convenient Hôtel de Rohan. People in the last century hadn't really known how to live. . . .

The meal was rather an ordeal, as meals with Grandmaman always were. In the first place, she had to be swathed in a series of shawls, each of which had a name and a particular destination; a special stool must then be found for her feet, a special corner for her stick, in case she might want it in a hurry. Then she'd lately grown somewhat deaf, which meant that she preferred to do most of the talking herself, paying small heed to her interlocutors except to contradict, when she was able to hear them, their least contentious assertions.

Maman and Tancrède had decided privately beforehand that it would be better to say nothing about the latter's plans for the future, since they might well distress her—and anyhow, who could tell what her political views were likely to be? In fact, they had meant not to refer to the

Fronde at all. But Madame de Sully almost at once briskly embarked on a monologue concerning the rival merits of the two embattled parties: one gathered that she was of her grandson's opinion, that any war was better than none—though she had little use for Mazarin ("mealy-mouthed opportunist!") and seemed to care even less for the Parliamentarians. ("In *my* day, my dears, we didn't bother to ask 'em to dinner—we just told 'em what to do and shut them up in gaol if they didn't do it!") Her principal grievance, indeed, appeared to be that the days of the religious wars were irrevocably over. She did not quite say it, but one divined that what would have pleased her most was a good Catholic massacre, with no quarter given and a chance to settle old grudges in the thorough-going sixteenth century manner.

Fortunately, as soon as supper was over, the old lady called her *demoiselles suivantes* together and departed for bed. Maman led the way to her cabinet in the tall tower, one of the few rooms in the castle small enough to be adequately heated in winter, and motioned Tancrède to a seat. She herself seemed restless, drifting from the hearth to the door, and back again; then over to the window, where, with a sudden impatient gesture, she flung back the curtains on a view of the moonlit garden by the river. The terrace lay white and frozen under its coverlet of snow; beyond it, dark and secret, glittered the waters of the Sauldre, slipping past them on their long journey to the Cher, from the Cher to the Loire, and thence to the sea. Tancrède thought, as he watched their gentle, implacable flow, how often he'd watched them before, longing with all his heart to follow where they led: the river seemed to be the only thing in Romorantin that could get away. . . . But now his mother had begun to speak, in a tone of carefully controlled excitement:

"You understand, my dear—do you not?—what you are to do in Paris. The letters we've had from the Prince de Conti make it quite clear that your services will be gladly accepted by the Frondeurs. All that is necessary is for you to present yourself at the general's headquarters in the Hôtel de Ville, and honourable employment will be found for you at once. To tell you the truth, I rather agree with Grand-maman that the war's not very important; like as not, 'twill peter out without leading to anything. But that's beside the point; 'tis sure to last a few weeks longer anyhow; and we must hope that meanwhile you'll be able to find some occasions to distinguish yourself. I know I can trust you to do your best. What matters most is to come out boldly in favour of Parliament, which can do so much for you. We mustn't forget that, with all Condé's influence, and the court to back him up, Chabot's patent of title has never been legally registered at the Palais. That means he's a duke in name only; his position is open to challenge. And the time has come for you to challenge it. You've been of age now for a month; we've all the documents we need to prove your claim."

In response to Tancrède's eager questions his mother listed them, the hard won results of the lawyers' patient years of research: there were the depositions of the family servants in Venice, bearing witness to the conjugal relations of his parents, and of the doctor and the apothecary who'd given Madame de Rohan medicines for her journey. There was also the statement of the midwife in Paris who'd attended the birth. Ruvigny had fulfilled his promise and told the shocking story of his plot with Margot and the kidnapping; La Sauvetat, too, had testified. So had Cernolle, the schoolmaster, and Potenijk, the cloth merchant; even young Jacob had contributed his share. Not a link in the chain was missing. . . . "When Rondeau went to Paris last week he took all these papers with him to our friend the Président de Maisons, who writes me that we have every reason to hope for success. His colleagues, he says, are strongly inclined to be receptive to our suit, the more so as Chabot—poor fool!— has had no better sense than to follow his patron Condé into war on the Royalist side. So really I don't see what can go wrong for us now. . . . This is what I've lived for these last three years, to see your sister and that scoundrel she married punished as they deserve to be, and their goods and honours bestowed on their rightful possessor. Oh, Tancrède, my son, if only I were going with you tomorrow!"

Maman's eyes kindled; a wave of vitality and renewed youth seemed to sweep over her. Tancrède, taking fire from her enthusiasm, rose impetuously; for a moment they stood, hands clasped in each other's, completely united in purpose. Then Madame de Rohan drew her son with her to the settee before the fire. She still held his hand in hers; never before had she appeared so near. Tancrède wondered if the time had come when he might really speak to her as he had always longed to speak. Up to now, with all her charm and casual kindness, there'd always been a barrier in the way. For three years they'd lived side by side, to all appearances as close as it was possible for two people to be; yet there was no intimacy between them. Not once in all that time had they revealed their inmost thoughts to each other; not once, in spite of what he knew about his mother's actions in the past, and the nagging doubts that knowledge had sown in his mind, had he felt at liberty to mention them. After all, though, this was their last night together. If he failed to seize his opportunity now, there might not be another. With his eyes fixed on hers, he began haltingly:

"Maman, I hope you know I'll do my utmost not to disappoint you—to live up to all the family has a right to expect. Before I go I'd like to say . . . I mean, I want to ask you . . . You've never really told me how you feel about me."

"How I feel? Proud, of course! How else *could* I feel, my dear? You've grown into a fine young man, a credit to us all, an honour to your father's memory."

Maman's voice sounded warmly reassuring, but Tancrède was not satisfied.

"Yes, I know—that's not quite what I meant, though. In the beginning, when first I came to Paris, what did you think of me then?"

"In the beginning? Ah, my dear . . . Of course, I didn't know you. The whole situation was new to me. I was bewildered. . . . How could that little Hollander be my son? I was fond of you, naturally, because you were my child. My heart ached for all you'd missed—for the years we hadn't had each other. But there was the excitement of the lawsuit, too—so many things to do, to think of! In those days I led a very different life."

"Yes," said Tancrède; "that's it, precisely. 'A very different life.' You gave it up for me. Why did you do it? Why have you been content to live as we have done, so many leagues away from all your friends and pleasures—buried, alone, the year round, with nothing to distract you?"

"Why should I not have been content, my dear? I did as much for your father when he was fighting the King. I was gone then from Paris for years at a time; often in danger, besieged in a castle or hidden away in queer little towns in the south. That was no more than my duty. I was as glad to help him then as I've been glad to help you now. Besides, how else could we have lived, I'd like to know? I'm not a rich woman any more, and these lawyers eat our money as fast as we hand it to them. We've had to economize in order to do what we had to do. You know that as well as I."

"But was it worth while? Are you sorry? Would you do it again?"

Tancrède's eyes, enormous and pleading, were fixed on his mother's—which were so like them—with an almost morbid insistence. Life itself seemed to depend on her reply. She met the look bravely as she answered: "It has been worth while. No, I've not been sorry. Yes, I'd do it again."

"And that because . . ."

"Because I love you, my son."

Maman opened her arms; and Tancrède, crying: "Ah, *that's* what I wanted to hear!", was in them before he knew what he was about.

From then on all seemed blissfully easy. They talked as they had never talked before; said things that would have been impossible to say yesterday, or even ten minutes ago. Tancrède was breathless with happiness. Only one recurring thought troubled him, and now it appeared natural for him to let it rise to the surface.

"Maman, before I go, there's just one more thing. I don't know how to put it, exactly. I've thought about it so much . . . worried and wondered. Now that perhaps I'm going to be Duke . . . It *is* all right, isn't it? I mean, you must tell me . . . You're the only person living who can."

"Tell you what, my son?"

"Am I really Rohan?"

"Really Rohan! My dear, what can you mean? Of course you are! What else have I been working for all these years, pinching and scraping and scheming and contriving, if not to have your rights recognized? Really Rohan, indeed!"

"Yes, yes! I know. But still . . . If there were a doubt in your mind. . . ? Margot once said . . ."

"Margot? You'd not take her word against mine, I hope?"

"Not if you give me yours now . . . before I leave you. Don't you see how important it is? There's been so much said both for and against that I don't know what to think myself. Sometimes I've felt it *must* be all right; and then again . . . how can I tell? What do I know about Papa, really, or about . . . that other, except what people have told me? And they've told me—haven't they?—just what it was to their interests to tell. I've tried my best to work it out in my own mind. Lord! the books I've read—the letters I've dug up—the pictures I've stared out of countenance! I've talked to every human being I could find who knew them both, but still I'm in the dark. It's gnawed at my heart till I can stand it no longer. Because, Maman, unless I can be sure—unless you tell me *you* are—it's no good, after all."

Madame de Rohan looked away quickly, a deep blush mantling her haggard small face. But Tancrède persisted, undaunted:

"Oh, tell me the truth for once! Don't care if you hurt me! I'm a man now; I can bear it. The only thing I can't bear is this awful uncertainty. Don't you see, I want to know —I *must* know—who was my father?"

Maman, with a palpable effort, gave him her eyes once more, while the blush slowly receded.

"Tancrède, I believe that Rohan is your father. I've never let myself believe anything else. How could I? What would have been left for us if I had? Yet if you ask me to swear an oath, I cannot. And since Margot told you so much, no doubt she also told you why. It may be Candale. . . . God knows, I hope not. I think not. I pray with all my strength it be not. But who can be sure, if your own mother isn't?"

Now it was Tancrède's turn to look away. His mouth felt dry with anguish; his misery was as acute as his happiness had been before. There seemed to be nothing left to say. More to himself than to his mother he muttered: "Now it's spoilt. Everything's spoilt! What have I to live for, though I gain my dukedom?"

But Maman would not let it go at that. Even as she started to weep she was exclaiming that he was wrong—he must not take it so—couldn't he see there lay before him the greatest opportunity? "Don't you understand, my dear? This war was made on purpose just for you. You can *prove* who you are—prove your right to your heritage—show me, and France, you're Rohan's true-born son!"

Her tears began to flow faster; Tancrède had to stop to staunch them. His own tears were not very far away, but he choked them fiercely back: a man of eighteen could not break down before a woman, least of all his mother! Resolutely he applied himself to the task of soothing the poor little creature with tragic eyes and quivering lips. With gentle patience he kissed and stroked and comforted, murmuring reassuring words that did not have to mean very much: it seemed as if he were the parent; she, the child. . . .

For what felt like a long time they remained on the settee in the tower chamber, gazing together at the white garden and the calm black river beyond it. The night was very clear; the sky a deep, luminous blue above the bare trees on the other side of the water. A wind had arisen, however, driving flocks of little clouds across the face of the moon so fast that it looked as though the moon itself were flying. Now and then it would disappear altogether in a bed of silver fleece, only to emerge once more in cold, pure beauty.

As they sat hand in hand, saying very little now, Tancrède's mind reverted again and again to Maman's former words. Perhaps she was right, after all. Perhaps this *was* his big chance. Blood would have to tell on the battlefield, wouldn't it? If he could only win his spurs in his first engagement, for all the world to see. . .

When at last they separated, late that night, their final kiss, grave and lingering, was—on his side at least—a promise for the future.

II ❧

"Paris,
"This Twenty-seventh of January, 1649

"My dearest Maman:
    "I take my pen in hand at the earliest possible moment
to announce to you our safe arrival in Paris. The journey
hither was disappointingly dull. We travelled quite peace-
fully over the snow-covered fields of the Orléanais and the
Ile de France, spending our first night at Orléans and our
second at Fontainebleau. Hubert and Olivier are excellent
squires, as you know; I have been glad, too, of Rondeau's
company, though I still cannot fathom why he felt he had
to come with me, not forty-eight hours after returning
from his own mission. He said 'twas because he was afraid
to let me go alone, but that is nonsense: we have met no
enemies on the way and have been in no discernible danger.
It is true that as we approached our goal we came upon more
than one village that had been sacked and burned by the
Royalists to prevent the Frondeurs from getting supplies;
'twas sad to see the houses all in ruins, and the poor country
folk digging in the blackened rubble to see what they might
salvage. War, as Rondeau pointed out to me, is, alas! not
all glory and honour; there are also those who must suffer
without recompense.
    "At Juvisy, on the third day, we fell in with a troop of
militia sent out by the Prince de Conti to escort a herd of
cattle into the city. As soon as Rondeau made our purpose

known to the captain he offered to take our party under his protection: I must admit I had to laugh aloud to find myself making a triumphal entry through the Porte Saint Jacques surrounded by a score of lively, bawling steers!

"We were able to reach home without difficulty. Paris by day seems tranquil enough, although the Place Royale is full of troops marching through or occasionally being reviewed by their officers. There is a sound of perpetual drumming in the streets; at night the principal thoroughfares are barred with chains and guarded by the militia, who are instructed to let no-one pass without orders from the Hôtel de Ville. I imagine one might run the risk of getting a clout on the head, or of having a bone or two broken, if one tried to defy their authority. On the whole, the citizens aren't too badly off. They are supposed to be in a state of siege, but as far as I can make out supplies trickle in pretty constantly. The price of bread has tripled, however, and there are frequent riots in the markets whenever it is rumoured there won't be enough of it. In spite of the steady patrolling the city seems lacking in order; 'tis like nothing so much as a beehive that has lost its queen! There is no-one really to run things—or, rather, there are but too many petty officials, no one of whom has prestige sufficient to establish proper discipline.

"The people are violent against Cardinal Mazarin without exactly knowing why. Since Parliament issued its decree of banishment he is generally blamed for all the troubles of the state; anyone who is suspected of being in his favour is liable to be persecuted. Houses are pillaged every day on the merest hint that money or jewels belonging to members of the court party are concealed on the premises. Do not, however, I beg of you, worry unduly about our affairs; all is well at the Hôtel de Rohan; the servants gave me a monstrous hearty welcome; and good Lejeune has managed with his usual forethought to stock the larder with provisions enough to last for months.

"All is well with me, too. I will make a further report tomorrow after paying my respects to His Highness de Conti; it has been a long day and my head is dropping with sleep. I send my love and duty to you and my grandmother. Dear Maman, I embrace you tenderly and am ever

"Your obedient servant and affectionate son,
"Tancrède.

"P.S. My warmest greetings to Sidonie, too. Tell Colin I grieve still for Dulcinée; 'twas my own fault for not giving orders to have her destroyed at once. God preserve me from such a lingering death!"

"Paris,
"This Twenty-eighth of January, 1649

"My dearest Maman:

"I am writing again to inform you that I have this day presented my credentials at the Hôtel de Ville. As you know, since the flight of the King and his mother from Paris it has become the centre of the government: the Frondeurs have made it the seat of their councils of war and the place is swarming with troops and members of Parliament and simple curiosity-seekers. With Rondeau and my squires in attendance I was taken to the great hall where I was led up to His Highness. I am sorry to be obliged to confess—though no doubt 'tis no news to you—that the Generalissimo of the armies of rebellion is a small, sickly youth scarce older than myself. His head is not uncomely—his eyes are fine and he has a wealth of scented curls of which he's plainly over-proud—but his figure is puny, and his back so crooked that he comes within an ace of being reckoned a cripple.

"I found this weazened princeling surrounded by a number of his henchmen. There was the Duc de Bouillon, a square-faced, pugnacious looking fellow, who is said to be a fine soldier, but is unluckily so disabled by the gout that he can move only when supported by two of his sons. There was also the Duc d'Elbeuf, of the House of Lorraine, a clever, insinuating courtier who appears very jealous of Conti's authority. (When I asked Rondeau afterwards why, he explained to me that before the latter's coming Elbeuf had played the chief rôle in the party.) I must not forget the Duc de Beaufort—very blond, very handsome, and by way of being a popular hero. 'Tis said the people adore him and that the market women line the streets to cheer him whenever he clatters by on horseback, his long yellow hair streaming in the wind. He is, alas! as stupid as he's handsome—can't open his mouth without making some witless remark—and is anything but adroit at concealing his annoyance over having to defer to his elders. Last, but I conceive not least, there was present another person, not a duke and peer, Paul de Gondi, Coadjutor of the Arch-bishop of Paris—a little, ugly, squinting mole of a man, who whispered continually to Conti and appeared to be prompting our none too forward leader as to how to de-mean himself.

"These four gentlemen, whatever their private disagreements—and I heard enough this morning to make sure there were plenty—received me agreeably. They all seemed to know all about me and to be pleased to welcome a Rohan to their ranks. Conti declared 'twas an excellent sign that the Huguenots were willing to align themselves with the defenders of the people's rights—surely they stood to gain something solid by doing so. 'We are all patriots here, sir,' quoth he. 'Our lives and our swords are dedicated to our country; to the last drop of blood we belong to France!' I could but applaud his sentiments, though their vigour was somewhat impaired by the shrillness of his voice, his air of daring me to deny them.

"Monsieur d'Elbeuf—who, by the way, said he'd known Papa well and sent you his duty—then offered at once, in his capacity as active chief of the army (which, to be sure, is still nine-tenths on paper!), to find me a post. 'You're a good horseman, boy, I take it?' said he; and when I assented—as I think, thanks to Ruvigny, I had a right to do—he suggested that I go to see his Lieutenant-General, the Marquis de Vitry, who had recently escaped from Saint Germain with his whole regiment, the Queen's own: they ought, said the Duke, of a certainty to make room for a likely young volunteer there.

"I thanked him, as it was my place to do, and was about to take my leave of the company when Vitry himself entered the room. Directly he learned who I was he announced that he'd be delighted to use my services. 'Come to me, sir,' said he, 'whenever you like, and we'll see what we can do. We're neighbours, you know—or perhaps you don't? The Hôtel de Vitry's just round the corner from the Place. I shall be sadly mistaken if you don't prove a valuable addition to the

Queen's regiment. My boys will be proud to ride under a Rohan; that's a great name and a great fame in the annals of France.'

"Maman, was that not splendid of him? Truly I knew not where to look; Rondeau said later I blushed like a girl, which I'm loath to believe. You may be sure I promised to wait on my new friend at the first opportunity; he has asked me to sup with him tomorrow. Even before he made his offer I felt an instant sympathy for Vitry. I cannot tell why it is so; 'tis not alone on account of his looks, though they are well enough; he's tall and sturdy, with pale blue eyes and an aquiline nose. His manners are affable without being effusive, and he gave me the impression of meaning every word he said—which was more than I felt of some of the others. With such a man I'll gladly serve: why aren't *all* peers of the realm worthy of the name?

"The rest of the day has been spent, as you can readily conjecture, in various interviews. Upon quitting the Prince de Conti I drove straight to the Palais to pay my respects to the Président de Maisons, who greeted me cordially and seemed monstrous pleased to see me. He introduced me to several of the councillors, including Mathieu Molé, the venerable First President himself. When I disclosed to these worthies that I had joined the Frondeurs they were loud in my praise; Monsieur de Maisons asserted that my action would make everything easier. But in truth, if I may rely on our friend's veracity, our case is as good as won. As you are aware, he has examined the papers Rondeau brought him; there can be no doubt, all is in order. Parliament will give us a very different reception this time, now that that cursed Condé is no longer at hand to bully and threaten. The suit, they tell me, is to be rushed through with all possible dispatch. Old Molé and the rest salute me already as 'Monsieur le Duc.'

"Tonight, my mother, I have just come from the last of my interviews—one that surprised me greatly. As I was preparing to retire Gilbert scratched on my door to announce that an emissary from Brittany desired to see me—a certain Berrien—do you know whom I mean? He sent word to say he was one of the bailiffs in the Pays de Léon and had been in the family's service for nigh on sixty years. That I could well believe when I saw him, for he was gnarled and hoary as one of the great forest oaks Ursule was fain to describe in the old days. His errand in Paris, it seemed, was to swear allegiance in secret to the 'real Duc de Rohan.' He told me that our good Bretons had never been willing to accept Chabot as their liege lord, in spite of my brother-in-law's clever diplomacy and the perennial tricks and tantrums of Margot, my sister. 'For us, my Lord,' quoth Berrien, 'there can be only one true leader. Say the word: your men will rise behind every rock and covert to rally to your defence. But indeed there'll be none to combat us; not a soul in the province but prays for the day when you'll return!'

"Then he knelt and kissed my hand under Papa's portrait in the Green Cabinet. There were tears in his eyes; I, too, felt a tenderness swelling within me, and pride such as I had never yet known. These are my own people, whom it is my duty to succour and protect. Oh, Maman, could I feel as I do if I were not Breton born?

"It is very late now; I must to bed. I hope this may find you and Grand-maman well as it leaves me. I send you my tenderest love and remain ever

"Your obedient servant and affectionate son,
"Tancrède."

"Paris,
"This Twenty-ninth of January, 1649

"My dearest Maman:
"This afternoon I performed a duty little to my liking, and that was to attend a reception at the house of our cousins the Montbazons in the rue de Béthisy. The Duke was not at home; he's now in his eighty-third year and spends most of his time, his wife says, at Rochefort or one of his other country estates. Madame de Montbazon, however, seems not in the least abashed by her liberty. She has lately become one of the leaders of the Fronde—Lord knows why! for I need not tell you she cares nothing for politics and is the same bold, noisy creature I remember so well in the old days here. She's stouter than ever and paints her cheeks as white as chalk; still I think she'd be accounted a handsome woman. Perhaps her new celebrity is mainly due to her friendship with the Duc de Beaufort, who's her acknowledged slave—though not the only one! He spends, they tell me, all his evenings at the Hôtel de Montbazon; makes his appointments there; and transacts most of his business in our cousin's cabinet, quite as if it were his own.

"Today the Grand Saloon was full of people—rag-tag-and-bobtail of all sorts—the usual loud-mouthed mob. Most of my relatives were there, too: the Guémenées, the Chevreuses, and *tutti quanti*. Directly I appeared on the threshold they seized upon me with enthusiasm; set me in the place of honour in the Duchess's alcove; I was kissed and petted by the ladies, embraced and made much of by the men. It put me in mind of the way they behaved in the first days after my arrival from Holland and made it quite clear to me now what they think of our chances of success. Apparently nothing's too good for the man who's going to be Duc de Rohan! . . . My dear mother, I must confess their flattery fell on sterile ground. You know as well as I do how the family have treated us since the Chabots won their suit: in the three years we've lived at Romorantin who among them has gone to the trouble of paying us a visit, or even of writing to inquire how it fared with us in our exile?

"I was—never fear!—perfectly polite to everybody, receiving their compliments with an amiable smile and promising to be the bearer of a thousand empty compliments to my 'sweet mother, our beloved Marguerite.' But I felt sick at heart; when at parting Madame de Montbazon embraced me and begged me to consider her house my second home, herself a deputy parent, 'twas all I could do to reply with common courtesy. I vow it will be long before I go again to the rue de Béthisy.

"After this unwelcome experience I hastened to keep my engagement at the Hôtel de Vitry. There I was entertained royally at supper by the master of the house and his brother, the Marquis de Noirmoûtier, who is older than Vitry and graver in manner, but no less agreeable. Both gentlemen treated me as though I had already won the right to my title, deferring to me in door-ways and giving me the honours at table, in no wise with fawning servility, but sensibly, seriously, as a matter of course. In Vitry I see precisely the sort of man I hope one day to become: gently born and gently bred, his pride of race tempered by a kind of innate balance and sobriety. I'm sure Papa must have been like that— wasn't he?

" 'Twas only when my new friend spoke of his reason for

joining the Frondeurs that I suffered a slight pang of misgiving. As far as I can see, he's frankly less interested in the
people's cause and in ridding the country of a dangerous for-
eign intriguer than he is in his own advancement; it seems
he's at odds with the court for refusing him the patent of
duke that had been his late father's. But indeed, to hear
Vitry tell it, none of the nobles has an honest patriotic mo-
tive. All that high-flown talk about giving their last drop
of blood for France is, he declares, just empty oratory. Beaufort is wroth because he was in prison six years; Bouillon,
because he's been deprived of his principality of Sedan without receiving proper compensation. Noirmoûtier is moved
by personal hostility to the Prince de Condé (I can sympa-
thize with him there!). Elbeuf lacks a reason as good as any
of these—he is simply seeking to make himself important by
any available means—; while puny young Conti's a tool in
the hands of his sister, the scheming Duchesse de Longue-
ville, and the Coadjutor enjoys plotting for its own sake—
though they say his secret ambition is a cardinal's hat. A
precious crew of malcontents! Even Parliament, according
to Vitry, cares not so much for the public welfare as for
maintaining its civil authority.

"My good mother, I own when I heard all these things
I felt crestfallen. A man had rather fight in a truly great
cause than engage in a petty, undignified squabble mas-
querading as one. Still I could not forget your telling me all
that counted was for me to distinguish myself, whatever the
occasion, before the war ends. And when I came to reflect on
the matter I was obliged to admit that my own motives were
open to question. What, after all, am I doing here? Would
I have joined the army if I hadn't a dukedom to win?

"We sat long at table over our wine. Before I took leave of my host he bade me prepare for a sortie next day; Elbeuf has ordered him and Noirmoûtier to ride to Brie-Comte-Robert, which is said to be threatened by the Royalists; the place is important to us, as it guards the main supply route to the east. We shall be starting at dawn. . . . When I heard this my heart began to beat faster. Will this be the opportunity I have been waiting for? Let us pray that the battle be long and bloody!

"After quitting the Hôtel de Vitry I strolled home across the Place Royale. It was very dark—clouds obscured the moon—and very quiet; only the sound of faraway drumming broke the stillness, and the bell of the Minims striking one o'clock. ('Twas only then I realized how late it was.) I am in my own room now, having just come upstairs after issuing the necessary orders for the morrow. As soon as I've sealed this I must go quickly to bed, in order to get what rest I can. It is strange, but somehow I feel that I shall win my spurs at Brie-Comte-Robert. Dear Maman, be comforted; all will yet be well. I embrace you tenderly and am ever

"Your obedient servant and affectionate son,

"Tancrède, Duc de Rohan."

III ❧

THE RENDEZVOUS with Vitry had been made at the Porte
Saint Antoine, only a step from the Hôtel de Rohan. Punc-
tually at seven o'clock Tancrède and his squires arrived on
horseback to find the men already assembled with the Duc
d'Elbeuf at their head; the brothers Vitry and Noirmoûtier
were to serve as his lieutenants. At a curt word from their
leader the regiment formed in order and clattered out
through the gate into the Faubourg. Dawn was just breaking on a day of black frost, dark and overcast; the ground,
Tancrède noticed, was frozen so hard that the hoofs of the
horses clicked as they moved. The soldiers for the most part
rode without speaking; the cold was cruel; and it was still
too early in the morning to feel cheerful. Elbeuf himself
was silent, grim and withdrawn, under his stately plumed
helmet. . . . Tancrède regarded the general with awe as a
figure out of the fabled past, who had played his part on the
same brilliant, crowded stage as Papa. It seemed to make
him in some sort an historical personage to recall that his
wife was a daughter—albeit a bastard—of the old King Henri
IV. And he soon guessed that Vitry and Noirmoûtier were
disposed to share his feeling. The two younger men, on a
pair of prancing grey chargers, were silent and withdrawn,
too.

Tancrède, between them, was principally preoccupied at
first by his mount, a fine black stallion, Renaud, whom he
had ridden only a few times before. He could not help re-
gretting, for sentiment's sake, that Timoléon had grown too

old to be used on campaign. It had been reluctantly decided, at the last moment before leaving Romorantin, that the veteran was now too uncertain of wind to be trusted: the magnificent old chestnut had made his last battle charge. But Renaud was handsome and spirited, too. Tancrède glanced at him complacently; then over his shoulder at the squires, on matched bays, to make sure that his equipage did him credit. The boys—for they weren't much more than that—were almost as much excited as he, particularly Olivier, the younger of the two, whose face was so pale with emotion that his freckles stood out startlingly plain. . . .

On the whole, thought Tancrède, he had no reason to be ashamed of their showing. How he wished that his mother and Sidonie could see him now—a man among men—riding forth to war! What a pity, too, that Ruvigny was not there— Ruvigny, his first friend, to whom he owed what skill he'd gained at riding the Great Horse, and at handling sword and musket. But that, of course, was impossible; the Marquis had remained staunchly loyal to the crown; one must pray only that they might never meet on opposite sides of the battle lines.

For the first hour the boy was tense and rigid, straining every nerve for a sight of the enemy. But as time went on and nothing happened he began to relax slightly; he could tell from the sound of their voices, the way they laughed and chaffed each other, that the men were relaxing, too. The whole of the countryside east of the city, rolling brown fields interspersed with patches of woodland, appeared to be deserted. Here were not even the burnt houses, the sacked farmsteads, that had shown in the south where the Royalists had been. In the occasional villages they rode through people stared at them curiously, and told the Duke in answer to his peremptory questions that they had seen no-one, no-one at all.

Tancrède was really glad, once his initial nervousness had passed, to have some time to himself to think things over. It was the first time he'd been able to do so for days: so little had happened to him for so long that he felt slightly dizzy, now that, if anything, there was too much. . . . The long hours in the saddle were tiring, but not more so than hunting would have been, and he was used to that; at Romorantin he had risen at dawn twice or thrice a week all winter to follow the hounds through the endless forests of the Sologne. It occurred to him that this in a way was also a hunting party, in search of a quarry that obstinately refused to be flushed from its covert.

As the day wore on the sport grew boring, and the winds sweeping the empty plains colder and colder. By the time they reached Brie-Comte-Robert, towards the middle of the afternoon, the men were chilled through. Here, too, there was no trace of the Royalists; nobody had seen them or heard them; from Tancrède's point of view his first day as a soldier had proved oddly disappointing: he had had a long, cold ride, and that was all.

At Brie-Comte-Robert the Duc d'Elbeuf left them to return by coach to Paris, and the regiment settled into its quarters in the castle, a small but sturdy feudal fortress commanding the town and a wide sweep of wintry landscape for leagues in every direction. With the departure of their grave, bearded general discipline was eased a trifle: not that Vitry and Noirmoûtier were lax—quite the contrary—but they were younger and more approachable, and the men were used to them.

The two lieutenants asked their junior officers, including Tancrède, to sup with them. The latter, immensely flattered by the invitation—for, after all, he was a mere volunteer without rank—accepted with a touch of trepidation, fearing that his hosts would all too soon discover that he had never played reversi nor smoked a pipe before. Much to his secret relief, he found neither accomplishment beyond his powers. He also found, with delight, that it was much simpler to get on with his fellows than he had supposed. That had been his chief worry in joining the army; he could not help wondering what the men would think of him, who had led perforce a life so unlike that of other men—alone, or shut up with old people, deprived of companionship with youths of his own age. But it soon became clear that they thought nothing at all—or, rather, that they were ready to accept him as one of themselves, without speculating about possible differences in background or outlook. In the army, it seemed, all that mattered was to do your duty and to copy, as far as you were able, what others did. . . .

As the evening progressed the young men grew merry over their cards and wine. Toasts were drunk, songs sung; when at last they staggered off to bed Tancrède's head was reeling. (How lucky that Thomas wasn't there to look disapproving as he undressed his master!)

It still ached a little next morning when reveille roused him; he confessed to himself, as he sat on the edge of the bed while Hubert pulled on his boots, that he was really thankful there was no immediate prospect of combat. Today, leaving a suitable garrison in charge of the castle, Vitry and Noirmoûtier took a small group of picked cavalry—perhaps eighty in all—and rode smartly out of the little walled town on a scouting expedition. Tancrède was happy to have been chosen to go with them. The weather was still grey and gloomy, but the keen wind blew the mists out of his brain and sent the blood coursing strongly through his young body.

For hours they scoured the country again without finding the enemy. At the village of Lagny on the Marne, where it began to snow a little—light, small flakes that seemed able to sift through the warmest clothing—Vitry called a halt and, after discussing the matter with his brother, announced that he saw no use in prolonging their search: they might as well go back to Paris.

The decision was hailed with cheers. On the way home, riding beside his friend, Tancrède learned that they were now in the neighbourhood of the Château de Coubert, where the Marquise de Vitry was stopping with her grandmother, the Maréchale de la Châtre. Vitry remarked that he would be glad to take advantage of an armed escort to get his wife home in safety, and seemed pleased when Tancrède offered at once to ride ahead and warn the ladies to make ready to leave. Directly his chief gave him permission to go he galloped off on Renaud, spurring the beast ahead as if the errand they were bound on were of national importance.

Arrived at the castle, he found a coach harnessed in the courtyard, and the ladies—who had been prepared by letter for a possible sudden departure—already busy stowing their belongings in it. The Maréchale, a harridan with no chin and pop eyes like a frog's—very fussy, very frightened—was far too much concerned with her boxes and bundles, and in superintending the actions of her numerous maids (who looked very nearly as frightened as she) to pay much attention to any young man.

The Marquise de Vitry, on the contrary, proved to be both young and attractive. When the fragile, chestnut-haired beauty came forward, clasping her slim hands together as she raised lovely, anxious eyes to his and begged him to tell her if it were not very dangerous to risk a long carriage trip through the war-torn countryside, Tancrède felt both proud and very adult to reply: "No, indeed, madam; Monsieur de Vitry bade me say it will be quite all right. Besides, even if there were danger, we'd be there to protect you."

"Oh, thank you, sir!" cried the young Marquise, in a melting tone. "How grateful I am to you for bearing me such fortunate tidings!"

She insisted, on discovering that he had not dined, in offering him food and wine in the hall of the castle; and after making the further discovery who he was, her glances were turned on him no less kindly than before, but also with frank curiosity—doubtless she'd heard all the details of his story.

As soon as her husband appeared the little procession was organized. Vitry himself rode on the right of the carriage, and bade Tancrède take the left. It was colder than ever, although the sun had managed to break through the clouds and hung low and red in the sky, like a beacon to light them home. The men were tired but cheerful, bandying jokes and singing snatches of song to beguile the tedium of the march. They were glad enough not to have had a fight. It was only

Tancrède who was disappointed: he had not had his chance! (But how avoid a secret feeling, far below the level of conscious thought, that perhaps, after all, it was just as well? For he *might* have failed to live up to his own expectations of valour; and then what . . . ?)

About an hour after leaving Coubert, upon climbing a small wooded hill the regiment was halted suddenly by a sharp exclamation from the vanguard; a minute later one of the guards, on a fleabitten grey, came flying to the rear to announce to his leader that he'd caught sight of an enemy detachment below in the valley of Fécamp, on the outskirts of the Bois de Vincennes.

Vitry's eyebrows shot up in surprise.

"How many are they?"

"About two squadrons, I should judge, sir—not more than we've got here. They're German mercenaries, I think, part of the garrison from the Château de Vincennes."

"German mercenaries, eh? And we've the pick of the Queen's regiment with us. Just a moment, La Touche . . ."

He rode forward hurriedly to confer with his brother, while Madame de la Châtre and Madame de Vitry showed signs of swooning, in spite of all Tancrède could do to calm them. In a trice Vitry was back to tell them what they'd decided: Noirmoûtier would take half of their force and make for the village of Saint Mandé, in order to cut off the enemy's retreat; he himself, meanwhile, with the rest . . .

"Vitry, I forbid you!" cried his wife; and the old Maréchale, quaking with fright, asserted in a strangled croak that she'd known all along they should have had the good sense not to budge from Coubert.

"My dear Marie-Louise," said Vitry, drily and rapidly,

"you'll be perfectly safe up here; the enemy can't even see you, whereas you'll have an excellent view of the proceedings. The whole affair ought not to take ten minutes; I'll be back before you've had time to miss me. And I'm leaving a guard with the coach, of course."

His eye swept over Tancrède, who gave a visible gulp, but said nothing.

"No, little Rohan—I want you with me."

One could only admire the officers' dispatch, the cool efficiency with which they dealt with the crisis. Before the scene with the ladies was over Noirmoûtier and his men had vanished: with a brusque word of command Vitry led the rest in a glorious wild charge—pennants flying, trumpets shrilling—down the hill to attack.

Tancrède's heart gave a great thump: was it joy? Was it fear? (And oh, might Vitry never guess how near his newest volunteer came to turning tail and fleeing!) Suddenly he straightened in the saddle and cried: "Victory or death!" in a choked voice that was lost in the din already beginning below.

The Royalists, it was plain from the first, were by no means eager for the fray. They would have retreated at full speed at once had they not seen that Noirmoûtier had cut off the way to escape. As it was, there was nothing for them to do but fall back, fighting as they went, in the hope of taking refuge in the forest. Sensing their irresolution, and seeing their line commencing to waver, Vitry called out, in a high, sharp voice: "Kill them! Kill the stupid Dutch dogs! No quarter, I say!"

The air was full of hoarse shouts and whizzing bullets. Now that the battle had been joined Tancrède did not feel

afraid any more; he was in the grip of a coldly lucid excitement. Calmly he fired and reloaded, fired and reloaded,
choosing his targets with care. He did not even flinch when
he saw two of the men he had shot fall from their horses.

It became increasingly clear that the mercenaries were
principally bent on getting out of trouble if they possibly
could. As soon as they reached the edge of the wood they
disappeared one by one within its shelter and broke into a
run towards the rear, though the fact that they were
mounted made this awkward at best. Tancrède and his
squires—who had closely followed their master—in hot pur-
suit of a small detachment in under the trees, managed
somehow to get separated from the main body of Vitry's
troop; but they went on fighting just the same, using their
swords where guns were no longer practicable.

It was almost dark now. The sun had started to set, red
and slanting through the bare branches; the cries of the men
sounded very far away. The only noises near them were the
snorts of the horses—Renaud and the bays—unaccustomed
to manœuvring in such cramped quarters; the clash of the
swords; and an occasional groan from one of the wounded
Germans, who fought grimly and silently, realizing that
they were no match for the lightning-quick French rapiers.

Tancrède had unhorsed at least four of them and was
after a fifth, when a fresh band of mercenaries appeared
from behind a thicket—reënforcements from the castle. He
felt a sudden sharp pain in his right shoulder; the sword fell
from his hand. The officer in charge, a round-headed German, rode straight at him as though tilting in a tournament:
the great grinning face with its broken yellow teeth seemed
horribly near. Before he could get out of the way the Ger-

man took aim and fired—low, in the belly, holding his pistol against Tancrède's body. . . .

After that he knew nothing more for a long time. When he came to, he had no idea where he was. It was dark, and very cold, and he was lying on straw—that was all he could tell. His head felt weak and dizzy; when he tried to move a terrible pain shot through his vitals, so keen, so agonizing, that he soon gave up the effort. Presently he found that he could move his head, if he were careful, without his body; by doing so he perceived lying near him a man whom he recognized eventually as Hubert.

Hubert, seeing his master's action, called out in a whisper: "Thank God, my Lord, you're alive!"

Tancrède considered briefly. He was not at all sure whether he were glad or not, for he had identified the warm stickiness around him as blood. Then he asked, also in a whisper: "Where are we?"

"In the castle of Vincennes, I believe, my Lord. We've been taken prisoner."

"Are you—all right?"

"Oh, yes, my Lord. I've a broken leg—my horse fell under me—and a few small flesh wounds, but nothing to speak of."

"And—Olivier?" (It was extraordinary how hard it was to talk.)

"He got away, I think. At least I've not seen him. But you, my Lord—how are you? I truly feared at first you were dead. Those blasted Germans were so sure of it that they began to pillage you, there on the ground where you lay. I could have killed 'em!—and had to stay there helpless and watch. They gave over only when you showed faint signs of life; then they laid you on horseback and brought us both here. Of course, they've no idea who you are. If only you'll tell them, my Lord, I am sure they will treat you better."

"No," said Tancrède, shutting his eyes. (He seemed better able to think so.) "No; I don't want anyone to know me. It's—all over. I've failed, Hubert—I've failed!"

He lost consciousness again. . . .

When he opened his eyes once more Hubert was gone. Two strange men, one of them holding a lantern, were bending over him, asking his name. Tancrède blinked in the light and muttered something in Dutch: damned if he'd let them find out . . . ! The warm, sticky pool had grown larger, and the pain in his belly was worse than before—so torturing that it seemed impossible to think of anything else. Almost worse than the pain, though, was the cold in this unheated attic chamber. (Tancrède judged it must be the attic by the way the roof sloped and from the fact that the room was floored with bare boards and entirely empty, except for the pallet on which he was lying.)

After a few minutes, or an hour, or a day—or perhaps a whole year—a little round man in a big feathered hat came in, rubbing his hands together nervously.

"My Lord," he said, in a fussy, flustered way that just matched his squeaky voice, "the Marquis de Vitry has sent his bugler with a message. He wishes to arrange a ransom for Monsieur le Duc de Rohan. Why didn't you say . . . ?"

Tancrède shook his head, as if he failed to understand, and still spoke only in Dutch.

"But indeed, my Lord," continued the little round man, "we know now who you are. I beg my Lord's pardon most humbly; 'twas all a mistake. I am the Sieur de Drouet, captain of the garrison of Vincennes. Everything shall be done that is possible for my Lord's comfort and convenience. Surgeons are being sent for; you are to be moved to my own apartment. I assure you, no pains will be spared, short of releasing my Lord. In the circumstances, considering my Lord's exalted rank, an order from the court will be required. Now, if my Lord permits, my men will attempt to take him . . ."

Two guards, who had meanwhile appeared with a litter, slowly and gingerly shifted the prisoner to it from the floor. But, careful as they were, his pains increased to such a pitch that all the world seemed one excruciating agony. Then Tancrède fainted again. . . .

When he came to for the third time, he was lying on a real bed in a room hung with tapestries. His wounds—it was the first thing he noticed—had been properly dressed and bound. A fire was burning on the hearth on the other side of the room; before it stood a woman, heating something in a pot. Another woman was leaning over him, wiping the sweat from his brow with a towel. Her black eyes were wet with tears . . . why, Tancrède wondered, as he was sure he had never seen her before. She was moaning over and over, in a voice thick with anguish: "My Lord, my Lord, don't you know me?"

Tancrède shook his head; it seemed easier than trying to speak.

The woman cried even harder. "Of course, of course . . . how could I expect . . . ? Indeed, there is no reason why you should. I have not seen you since you were a baby. Your lady mother entrusted you to me then. I was your wet-nurse in Paris, and later in the country, at Préfontaines. Two years I stayed with you, my little love; and never was there a sweeter child, nor a bonnier . . . But oh, my Lord, to find you now—like this!"

She turned away, trying to strangle her sobs. The other woman exclaimed, quite crossly: "There now, Babette! I told you not to . . . !" and hurried over with the pot.

"Can you drink something, my Lord?"

Tancrède made an effort, but could not. It seemed too hard to raise his head from the pillow. His pains were certainly less acute as long as he kept perfectly still, but he felt very weak. There was a roaring in his brain; and every few minutes the room whirled around—then everything in it moved a little farther off and grew a little dimmer.

After a while he remembered Hubert and asked to see him, but Babette told him that the squire had been exchanged against a Royalist prisoner and was no longer in the castle. Corentin, the bugler, an abashed looking stripling, his eyes big with fright, came in for a moment with a message from Monsieur de Vitry, which he was allowed to deliver, as Tancrède had not the strength to read it for himself. The Marquis bade Monsieur le Duc de Rohan keep up good hope. All was being done that could be done to expedite his release. Meanwhile Vitry sent his compliments to his young friend, and best wishes for a speedy recovery.

Tancrède thanked Corentin gravely, speaking very slowly indeed—it was strange, his tongue seemed to be weighted down by lead. "Give my compliments to your master, too. And tell him—tell him—I did my best—I am sorry I failed him."

"Failed, my Lord?"

Tancrède tried to say something more, but his voice wouldn't work. Great tears were rolling down his cheeks and, as he did not want Corentin to see them, he turned his head away and pretended to sleep. . . .

The night dragged on, pain-racked, nightmarish, endless. Tancrède felt weaker and weaker; he could no longer even move his head, and his mind was not quite clear. In his intervals of comparative lucidity he stared fixedly at the tapestry on the wall across from the bed. The panel showed a hunting scene, with lords and ladies in mediaeval garb streaming out on to the steps of a castle or riding gaily away into a wood. In the foreground there was the figure of a boy with a falcon on his wrist: this he felt sure was meant to represent himself—but it was certainly a very poor likeness! The falcon, on the other hand, was undoubtedly Dulcinée. He wanted to tell Babette about Dulcinée, and explain how sorry he was he had kept old Colin from having her destroyed; but the woman with black eyes bending over him seemed now not to be Babette but pretty, young Madame de Vitry . . . or stay! was it not Sidonie? Yes, of course; that's who it was! And Sidonie knew all about Dulcinée, so it wouldn't be necessary to say anything. . . .

Towards dawn, when the doctor came in, it was not surprising to find that the solemn, dark-robed personage was really his old friend Monsieur de Ruvigny.

Tancrède was glad to see Ruvigny, glad to feel the comfort of a warm, strong hand in his. There was something he wanted to say to him, something he wanted Maman to know, waiting anxiously in Romorantin for news of her son. He would have liked to write a letter himself—just a few lines to tell her how he was, what he felt—but he was too tired for that today. "I'll write tomorrow, of course. Say that, Ruvigny, won't you? And say, too—it's all right. *Every-*

thing's all right. She'll understand. You must *all* understand. It's very important. Ruvigny, you must see how
important it is. If you don't, Sidonie will tell you. It doesn't
even matter any more whether I get to be duke or not. Of
course, it's fine if I do—but that isn't what counts. Do you
know what counts, Ruvigny?"

"No, my Lord: what?"

Tancrède's voice was very faint, and came now in gasps;
but he still held fast to his friend's hand as he whispered,
with the last breaths he was ever to breathe: "I am sure—
at last—who I am."

" 'Who you are,' my Lord?"

"You know, the family war-cry—Ursule told me—: *King
can't be, duke won't deign, Rohan's . . . my name!*"

The doctor gently unclasped the still clinging fingers and
pulled the coverlet over the poor staring eyes as he said to
the weeping Babette: "Whoever he was, that young man
died like a hero."

Epilogue

Paris and Geneva, February and June, 1655

IT WAS ONE of those days in mid-February that some-times in northern climes, unreasonably and unseasonably, bear a resemblance to early spring. The air was mild; the sun shone, palely beneficent, through a light haze; high over the pointed roofs of Paris the sky seemed all a tender blue, flecked by drifts of small, harmless clouds not too distinct in outline. . . . About three o'clock in the afternoon Henri de Massués, Marquis de Ruvigny et de Bonneval, Lieutenant-General and Field Marshal in the armies of His Most Christian Majesty Louis XIV, Deputy General of the Reformed Churches of France, stepped into his carriage outside the house of his father-in-law, Tallemant the banker, in the rue Neuve-des-Fossés-Montmartre. At fifty he looked the part, staid and portly in his plumed hat and ample fur-trimmed cloak; there was still, however, at times a fugitive gleam in his eye to recall the lawless Ruvigny of old.

His errand today must have reminded him of the past, for he ordered the coachman to take him to the Place Royale, where he intended to pay his respects to his former patron-ess, Madame la Duchesse Douairière de Rohan. On the long drive to the Marais his path momentarily crossed that of two men whom he had not often seen since his bachelor days: Miossens, now the Maréchal d'Albret, and Vardes, now colonel of the King's Swiss guard—side by side, stiff in velvet and gold lace. Their bows as they met at a crowded crossroads were frostily distant; successful courtiers hardly had time to be cordial to one another.

All looked much the same at the Hôtel de Rohan, though the Swiss at the door was a new one. And Madame de Rohan, who received her visitor in the Green Cabinet, appeared at first sight no older than she had six years ago. No older—but somehow more resigned to her rôle of dowager. She was quieter, too, prone no longer to sudden quicksilver flights round the room as she talked. Only her graceful hands still played idly with the black gauzy fan in her lap, perhaps more from habit than anything else; the captive butterfly seemed to have learned at last that it would never again be free. . . .

She greeted Ruvigny kindly, and made the conventional inquiries after his health, and the healths of his wife and two sons, in whom she took a special interest, for, as she reminded him with a smile, it was she who had made the match. For a while they discussed church affairs; the Duchess declared she needed to be brought up to date on the state of the Temple at Charenton, as she was not often in Paris these days. Ruvigny knew that was true: since her son's death she had been possessed by a spirit of restlessness and spent most of the year travelling from one of her country estates to another, persuaded that the air must be better wherever she was not.

Today, it developed, she had come to town for a particular purpose. For several weeks, she told Ruvigny, her daughter Madame de Rohan-Chabot had been suing for forgiveness. They had not seen each other to speak to since the latter's marriage, but the Duchess said she felt she was too old to keep up the feud any longer. Nothing Margot could do had the power to alter the past, but she, too, had had her troubles: Rohan-Chabot had been a very bad hus-

band and, in spite of his frantic ambitions, not too fortunate
in his career. He had tried to please everyone, with the usual
result of pleasing no-one at all. His Bretons had never really
accepted him. The less said about his military activities during the Fronde, the better. People were still laughing about
the miserable fizzle he'd made of the siege of Angers. . . .
"You mean," asked Ruvigny, "where they say he began as
Rohan and ended as Chabot?" "Precisely," replied the
Duchess, sharing his acid smile. . . . It had been stupid of
him, also, to change sides in the middle of the war, just to
curry favour with Condé; that had forced him and his wife,
later on when peace had been made, into temporary exile;
rendered it difficult for him to keep his governorship of
Anjou, and quite impossible to hope for anything better.
Moreover, he was rumoured now to be much out of health.

All in all, Madame de Rohan concluded, she thought that
her daughter had been punished enough. The rapproche-
ment had been brought about by Margot's friendly overtures—made through their cousins the Guémenées—on the
subject of Tancrède. After violently opposing her mother's
wishes for years, she had at last announced her willingness
to acknowledge her brother's legitimacy, and to permit his
being buried in Geneva beside his father.

Ruvigny remarked that he was glad to hear it. He agreed
with the Duchess that family quarrels were an absurd waste
of time, especially in this case, when the cause of the split
was no longer there. It could cost Margot nothing to make
a generous gesture now. On the other hand, it seemed to
him terrible still that so fine a young man should have had
to die with his promise unfulfilled, at the threshold of what
should have been—would have been, undoubtedly—a happy

and successful life. "I loved him, madam, as dearly as if he'd been my own son."

"I know you did, Ruvigny," said the Duchess. "That's why I wanted you to know what I'm going to do. I grieve for him, too—for all he should have had, and didn't. And for all he had to bear that other boys need not—the bitter disappointments, the awful doubts. Oh, if I could only relive the past, how differently I'd act! I'd spare him the heartache, the wretched uncertainty. . . . What hurts me most is to remember that the very last time I saw him—the night before he left Romorantin to join the army—I failed him."

"How do you mean 'failed,' madam?"

"I can confess it to you because you know the worst about me . . . ah, Ruvigny, when *haven't* you known that? Tancrède asked me, before we said good-bye, to tell him who his father was—to give him the assurance only I *could* give him —and I said I was not sure. I said I thought he was Rohan's son; that I hoped and believed with all my heart it was so— but I would not swear it. Oh, how could I have been so cruel? Why didn't I tell him I *knew* it to be true?"

"I suppose," replied Ruvigny slowly, "because you couldn't lie to him. I couldn't either, though I tried my best. Tancrède himself was all truth and honour—how could we give him less than he gave us? Don't weep, dear friend. If it helps at all, I'm sure *he* was sure before he died. I talked to the doctor who attended him, and the nurses. They said his last words were the family motto: '*Rohan's my name.*' Would they have been if he hadn't felt in his heart . . . ?"

"I know! I know!" exclaimed Madame de Rohan. "That's what I've told myself a hundred times a day. But still . . . if I could just go back and live it over again!"

She started to cry softly, helplessly, as one to whom tears had long become a familiar solace. Ruvigny pressed her hand and then stepped over to the window to allow her a little time in which to recover herself. As he did so he caught sight of the great coach of the Rohan-Chabots drawing up at the door, and excused himself hastily. He did not suppose Margot's magnanimity could extend to *him*.

Madame de Rohan was too much overcome to notice his departure, but, hearing voices in the hall, she pulled herself together, wiped her eyes, settled her flowing mourning veils, and turned to face the daughter and the son-in-law whom she had not seen for nearly ten years. Margot, handsomely dressed in turquoise velvet and an almost aggressive amount of Venetian lace, made as imposing an entrance as a small woman could. She was, one saw at once, plumper than she used to be, as was proper for the mother of four; but her hair was still golden and her eyes youthfully bright. What had happened to her was hard to define—she just wasn't pretty any more. She looked dissatisfied, suspicious, ill at ease; even her celebrated hauteur appeared to have deserted her.

As for Chabot, he was but a shadow of the foppish professional beauty of a decade ago. At barely thirty-nine he had become an old man—wrinkled, haggard, appallingly thin. His constant cough and the dark red flush on his cheekbones told the story plainly enough. . . . Madame de Rohan, who was unprepared for the change, had some trouble concealing her shock. It was a relief to her that the children were there to create a diversion. Margot presented the three little girls: Anne and Marguerite, who were pretty, and Jeanne—frankly plain—; also the boy, Louis, who was not yet three, too immature for them to tell what he would look like. But at least he was the heir they'd prayed for for years. Their grandmother called for syrups and sweetmeats, and made a great fuss over her small guests before letting their nurses and the servants remove them to an adjoining room, obviously wondering the while whether she were too old—and they too young—for them ever to mean much to one another.

Margot explained that her husband was leaving this week, on his doctor's advice, for the Château de Chanteloup; they felt that perhaps country air . . .

The Duchess agreed. There could be nothing better for the health—only, unfortunately, the country was so dull! Would Margot go with him?

Oh, yes, indeed, though it was most inconvenient just now, with the carnival beginning and half a dozen new gowns under way at Maître Thomas' establishment. But Margot always accompanied her husband everywhere. That had been her rule throughout their life together; she did not intend to relax it now, when he had more need of her than ever. The Duchess understood—though she didn't say so—that her daughter did not trust Henri, ill as he was, out of her sight. Madame de Rohan-Chabot's jealousy had grown proverbial at court. Everybody laughed at it, though for Margot it had been no laughing matter. The Duke had had a thousand affairs . . . but no man, not even her husband, had looked at Margot de Rohan with desire since her marriage. That was as clear to her mother as the rest of their sordid story.

The three chatted together for a few minutes with evident constraint. It was only at the very end of the interview, when Margot had risen to go, that she mentioned the subject that must have been uppermost in their minds the whole time. As she kissed her mother coldly she murmured: "I hope, Maman, that you were satisfied with the letter I wrote you?"

"Oh, certainly, my dear," Madame de Rohan replied, with an equal chilliness. "You understand, the lawyers said it was necessary. It had to be made quite clear on paper that you admitted Tancrède was his father's heir, just as little Louis is yours. Otherwise I'd have been on the wrong side of the law; why, Pucelle told me I might even have lost my dowry!"

"Rohan and I are perfectly agreeable to whatever you choose to do," said Margot. "We take it very kind of you that you're willing to assume the expense of finishing Papa's tomb. I'm ashamed to think how long the work's been under way. What with the war, and one thing or another . . . I don't know how it is, but we've never a penny to spare at the end of the year. I believe you mentioned you were having my brother's body moved from Charenton?"

"Yes; he's to be buried beside his father. I'm having the inscription made now. I'll send you a copy of it as soon as it's done, my dear. And perhaps in the spring, when the weather permits, you might care to make the journey there with me to see how it looks. It's charming country—and workmen nowadays are so tiresomely unreliable. I'd really like to see for myself that all was in order."

Margot half assented with a half-smile as she bowed herself out.

In the carriage she turned to her husband and observed: "Maman wasn't so difficult as I thought she might be, was she? I hope you don't think, though, my dear, that because

I'm humouring her now I've given way a jot on our legal position. The King quite understands. . . . I had it out with him only last week. As soon as she's gone—which in the nature of things can't be so many years more—we're to have the inscription removed, and everything will be as it was before. You agree with me, Henri, that it is the best way to handle a delicate situation?"

"Oh, by all means, my love; whatever you like," answered Chabot, leaning back in his seat and closing his eyes, as if the problem were too tiring to be considered at the moment. "Only—now that the poor young man is dead—does it really matter so much?"

"Matter?" cried his wife. "Of course it matters! Are these the thanks I get for the trouble I've gone to—the years of moiling and toiling and worrying and wire-pulling and hideous expenses? Oh, when I think what it's cost me . . ."

The whole of the way back to their house in the rue de L'Echelle-du-Temple she went on arguing, expostulating, complaining, and threatening by turns, the stream of her voice—that soft, pretty voice, made, it would seem, to express kinder sentiments—as continuous as a fountain. She felt strongly convinced of the justice of her cause. . . . Then was it not odd that, all the time she was talking, she could perceive, as plainly as though he were there before her, Tancrède's face, white and drawn, his deep grey-green eyes turned upon her in horror and dismay, as they were when he rushed from the room the last time she saw him?

The hallucination was so overwhelming that she almost mentioned it to Chabot, but he, poor fellow! was beyond sharing her feelings: his lids remained obstinately shut and *his* mind's eye, facing the short, hopeless future, quite plainly was capable of seeing nothing at all.

In the cathedral of Saint Pierre at Geneva a middle-aged man and a young woman, both dressed in black, were kneeling before a tomb. They were in a chapel to the left of the choir, shut off from the rest of the church by an elaborate metal screen. The tomb was monumental, made of great blocks of black jasper and white alabaster, surmounted by a white marble sarcophagus, on which were carved medallions representing the most famous military exploits of Henri, Duc de Rohan. In a niche above it stood a life-sized statue, also of marble, of the Duke himself, as dignified, as proudly aloof, as his followers remembered him. But the eyes of the man and the woman were fixed on a tablet below bearing the following legend:

Here lies
Tancrède, son of the Duc de Rohan,
True inheritor
Of the virtues and great name
Of his father,
Who died pierced by a lead bullet
Fighting bravely
For the besieged citizens of Paris
In the year 1649, the 19th of his life.
Through a misfortune less his than his family's
Heaven gave earth a brief glimpse of him only.
Marguerite de Béthune,
Duchesse de Rohan,
Desolate wife, inconsolable mother,
Had this monument built
As an eternal testimony to her grief
Which will show the centuries to come
The tenderness she will always cherish
For his beloved spirit.

Sidonie, wiping the tears from her eyes, rose and gave her father her hand. As they walked slowly down the aisle she said, with a catch in her voice: "It seems so queer for him to be here, in a land he never knew, surrounded by strangers."

"Ah, but he lies with his father, my dear," said Rondeau. "That's what he would have wished above all, and his mother knew it."

"Yes; that's true," Sidonie, after a moment, agreed with him. "Will Madame la Duchesse come to Geneva soon?"

"I think so. She said she intended to come, and I am sure she will, when she can. I have sent her a description of the tomb, and written her that everything has been carried out according to her wishes. I am certain Madame will be pleased, and that she will want to see for herself how it is. It's only . . . well, my dear, the nobility have so many things on their minds, so much to do and plan for, that they can't dwell with anything for very long at a time—not even their griefs."

"Oh, but *Tancrède!*" cried Sidonie, her tears starting to flow once more. "He was the highest . . . the best . . . I shall never forget him. I can't bear to think he's gone without leaving a trace—and that it will be as if he hadn't lived."

Rondeau shook his head.

"Not so, Sidonie. No life, however short, can be lived without affecting others. Madame is changed by what she's been through, only she can tell how much. Monsieur de Ruvigny, too—or he wouldn't be where he is today. Even that wicked woman who stole her brother's birthright, and the unworthy man she married, who calls himself Rohan— do you think they are happy? I tell you, no, my daughter.

Because, however long they enjoy their tarnished fortune, they must always remember the generous lad they defrauded. You yourself have said you will never forget him. Nor shall I; his dear memory is safe with us; we need no marble tombs or pompous inscriptions to remind us of our loss. We can none of us be the same again."

Comforted, Sidonie tucked her hand in her father's arm. Together they passed out of the gloomy old church into the square with its blossoming lime-trees, and the warm beauty of the fragrant June night.

A Note About Sources

As already stated in a preliminary note, the story of Tancrède de Rohan is true. It is fiction only in the sense that the author has tried to make living people out of historical characters, and has dared to put his own interpretation upon their actions; but the facts remain facts, and the actors in the drama all actually lived in France three hundred years ago. (The sole exception to this rule, Sidonie de Montville, Rondeau's daughter, was invented so that Tancrède might have a companion of his own age to share some of his early Paris experiences.)

The primary source of *The Silver Plume* is to be found in *Les Historiettes de Tallemant des Réaux*, whose pages are regularly pillaged by historians of French 17th century manners, often without acknowledgement. Indeed, until recently, it was the fashion—even while making full use of his work—to disparage the chronicler as a mere scandalmonger. In this case he was certainly in a position to know what he was talking about. As a practising Huguenot he must often have seen the Rohans at church at the Temple in Charenton. Moreover, his sister Marie married Ruvigny, who played such a curious part in the lives of the two Marguerites de Rohan, mother and daughter. The long and very interesting historiette devoted to "Mesdames de Rohan" is almost a book in itself; the novel might really have been constructed from that alone.

The author, however, consulted a great many other authorities, chiefly contemporary, before beginning to write his own book. He had been long familiar with the history of the period in general and had already read most of the French memoirs of the 17th century. These include the works of the Duc de Saint-Simon, who gives the genealogy of the Rohans and their family background (he hated them!); and of Madame de Motteville, the Duchesse de Nemours, the Duc de la Rochefoucauld, the Marquis de Montglas, and the Cardinal de Retz, all of whom specifically refer to Tancrède. The memoirs of Mademoiselle de Montpensier contain an account of Mademoiselle de Rohan's marriage; those of Nicolas de Goulas, a close friend of Chabot's, reflect the opposition's point of view; while Amelot de la Houssaye's rare *Mémoires Historiques, Politiques, Critiques et Littéraires* (Amsterdam, 1722) show society's reactions to the notorious lawsuit. Two contemporary journals, by Olivier d'Ormesson and Dubuisson-Aubenay, were especially useful in controlling dates. A few pertinent letters relative to Tancrède's journey from Leyden to Paris were found in the Duc d'Aumale's *Histoire des Princes de Condé. Les Courriers de la Fronde*, a contemporary epistle in verse, describes his brief exploits during the Fronde and the tragic circumstances of his death. One might also mention the pamphlet, *Lettre de Consolation envoyée à Madame la duchesse de Rohan sur la mort de Monsieur de Rohan, son fils, surnommé Tancrède* (Paris, 1649; written by a Sieur B.D.), and various poems: those of Marigny, beginning *Tancrède est mort de sa blessure,* in the manuscript collection of Conrart at the Bibliothèque de l'Arsenal in Paris; of Georges de Scudéry, *Regrets de la mort glorieuse de M. Tancrède de Rohan, à madame de Rohan, sa soeur* (Paris, 1649; reproduced several times); and his rhymed epitaph, composed by Gilbert and printed in Père Griffet's book, of which more later. Even Madame de Sévigné wrote a sixain on the subject! The reconciliation of Madame de Rohan and her daughter and the death of Rohan-Chabot are recorded in Loret's *La Muze Historique* on the appropriate dates.

The complete collection of the factums relating to the lawsuit are on file at the Bibliothèque Nationale in Paris. These comprise papers concerning the Duchess's donation to her daughter, and its later attempted revocation; the appointment of a warden for Tancrède; and the actual suit itself. They serve to establish Tallemant's veracity and unequalled knowledge of the inmost secrets of the Rohans' family history. Among them the most valuable to the author was the *Manifeste pour Madame la Duchesse douairière de Rohan pour prouver l'existence de son fils, Tancrède de Rohan* (Paris, E. Pepingue, 1646), which also exists in manuscript form in various collections at the Bibliothèque de l'Arsenal, notably as *Mémoires de Madame la Duchesse de Rohan* in the Recueil Conrart. This manifeste or memoir is a very circumstantial account of the whole affair from the Duchess's point of view, including a résumé of her husband's troubles with the government, his reasons for leaving France permanently, and the actions of both Rohans during the civil wars and afterwards up to the time of the Duke's death in 1638. In it she makes no mention of either Ruvigny or the Duc de Candale and appears uneasily conscious that her case is rather weak and needs constant bolstering in order to be convincing.

This document undoubtedly served as the main basis for the *Histoire de Tancrède de Rohan* (Liège, 1767), a rare

work by the Jesuit historian Père Griffet, of which the
author has read the copy possessed by the Bibliothèque
Mazarine in Paris. Griffet, writing in the 18th century, had
to depend on documentary evidence only. He seems to have
espoused the Duchess's cause wholeheartedly; he, too,
makes no mention of Candale's rôle or of the fact that many
people supposed him to have been Tancrède's father.
According to him, Marguerite de Rohan-Chabot is the vil-
lainess of the piece; it was, he says, owing to her machina-
tions that most of the Duchess's evidence has disappeared.
Griffet lists the missing papers, including the testimony of
the persons concerned in the kidnapping and the recovery of
Tancrède from Holland; there are seventeen separate items.
He also goes into his hero's posthumous history, narrating
the details of Madame de Rohan-Chabot's long opposition
to her mother's wish to have Tancrède share his father's
tomb in Geneva, and including a copy of the letter from
Louis XIV (written in 1650) officially forbidding the re-
moval of the body from Charenton. He tells us how the
Rohan-Chabots' eventual softening led to a reconciliation,
in 1655, with the Duchess; and of how, immediately after
her mother's death in 1660, the vindictive Margot had the
inscription effaced from the tomb.

Today the tomb of the Duc de Rohan is still to be seen
in the church of Saint Pierre at Geneva. The statue and
monument are modern, dating from 1890 only, the originals
having been destroyed at the time of the French Revolution.
The author has been unable to find a description of them as
they looked in the short five years when Tancrède's inscription was in place; the earliest account he knows is contained
in the *Voyage de France, Relation de Sebastien Locatelli,*

1664–65. But there is no doubt that the Duchess and Tancrède were both buried there, too. No word remains to recall them, though Madame de Rohan's pompous Latin eulogy of her husband has been discovered and restored to its place on the wall of the chapel.

As to the evidence, the author must confess he has weighed it all times without number and still finds himself less able to decide who was right than the men and women of the 17th century. Many of them agreed with Tallemant that Tancrède was a bastard; many others were equally sure that he was the true-born son of Henri de Rohan. Perhaps, all things considered, the sedately discreet Madame de Motteville may be allowed the last word: "On such matters it seems to me doubt is the surest and fairest conclusion; for what appears absolutely true often is not so; and likewise what appears to us a tissue of lies is often more deserving of esteem than contempt."

A NOTE ON THE TYPE

The text of this book was set on the Linotype in Fairfield, the first type-face from the hand of the distinguished American artist and engraver Rudolph Ruzicka. In its structure Fairfield displays the sober and sane qualities of a master craftsman whose talent has long been dedicated to clarity. It is this trait that accounts for the trim grace and virility, the spirited design and sensitive balance of this original typeface.

Rudolph Ruzicka was born in Bohemia in 1883 and came to America in 1894. He has designed and illustrated many books and has created a considerable list of individual prints—wood-engravings, line-engravings on copper, aquatints. W. A. Dwiggins wrote recently: "Until you see the things themselves you have no sense of the artist behind them. His outstanding quality, as artist and person, is *sanity*. Complete esthetic equipment, all managed by good sound judgment about ways and means, aims and purposes, utilities and 'functions'—and all this level-headed balance-mechanism added to the lively mental state that makes an artist an artist. Fortunate equipment in a disordered world. . . ."

The book was composed, printed and bound at
The Lakeside Press, R. R. Donnelley & Sons Company
Chicago, Illinois, and Crawfordsville, Indiana
under the supervision of Walter Howe